DEATH REINS IN

DEATH REINS IN

MICHELE SCOTT

THORNDIKE PRESS

An imprint of Thomson Gale, a part of The Thomson Corporation

Detroit • New York • San Francisco • New Haven, Conn. • Waterville, Maine • London

LIBRARY OF CONGRESS CATALOGING-IN-PUBLICATION DATA

Scott, Michele, 1969–
    Death reins in / by Michele Scott.
        p. cm. — (Horse lover's mystery) (Thorndike Press large print mystery)
    ISBN-13: 978-0-7862-9836-5 (hardcover : alk. paper)
    ISBN-10: 0-7862-9836-7 (hardcover : alk. paper)
    1. Horse trainers — Fiction. 2. Large type books. I. Title.
PS3619.C6824D43 2007
813'.6—dc22   2007022762

Published in 2007 by arrangement with The Berkley Publishing Group, a member
of Penguin Group (USA) Inc.

Printed in the United States of America on permanent paper
10 9 8 7 6 5 4 3 2 1

To my editor Samantha,
for her patience with me.

PROLOGUE

Memories raced through Bob Pratt's mind — both good and bad — as he lay gagged and bound in the trunk of the car. He hadn't seen the make or model, didn't even really know what had happened other than that he'd been ambushed from behind as he went to get into his truck at the end of the day. He'd worked late, jotting down his notes on one of Eq Tech's new supplements specifically designed for racehorses. Bob didn't even really feel it when he'd been slammed over the head — by *what* he didn't know, by whom, he could only guess at. There were a handful of enemies who'd want to see Bob in this state, and probably a few people he called *friend*. The trunk smelled like dirty socks and fast food. He could hear the faint thumpings of rap music, and he occasionally thought he might have recognized the sound of laughter coming from inside the car. Did that mean there was more than one person who'd taken him when he'd left work? Probably. At over six feet tall, he wasn't exactly a little guy. They knew he would've fought, so the sneak attack had to have been carefully planned.

His head ached as if it had been shoved into a vise, making it almost impossible to think but he wanted to try — try and play out what had happened. He needed to remember if he'd heard anyone say anything, if he'd noticed anything at all. Damn, he'd been so caught up in his findings on the new supplement that he simply had not been paying attention. He had to try though, in case he ever made it back alive. But the deep hole in his gut told him that wasn't going to happen, which led him to one continual thought streaming through his mind: his sister, Audrey, and what it would do to her if he didn't come back. Oh hell, what if his theories had been right? What if he had stumbled onto something sinister and revealed too much to her when they'd spoken the other night over dinner? He didn't think he had. As soon as she'd guessed something was wrong with him, which Audrey was so astute at, he'd tried hard to blow it off, said it was a little woman trouble, an issue at work here and there, that sort of thing. But he knew his sister well. He knew that nothing escaped her and if he'd said one wrong word, she might have picked up on it. He had to get out of this. He could feel his heart racing, beating hard against his chest, could smell the horse he'd been working with at the center on him, now mixed in with his own fear and angst.

Oh God, *what if?* What if he didn't get out of this? Poor Audrey. He'd given her problems all of their lives and now, finally, when the two of them had made amends over the past few years and grown close again, he was leaving her. All alone. He loved her. She was a good sister. She had a sweet smile, warmhearted nature, and a gentle touch with her animals that everyone who knew her admired. And she'd never given up on him. Never. She'd always believed in him and picked him up off the ground. Even when he'd turned his back on her, his sister had been right there with open arms, cheering him on. She was the reason he'd been able to not only maintain an equine veterinary practice, but also secure a position as a top researcher with Eq Tech in the very exciting fields of equine medicine and health.

The car slowed. What were they going over, an old bridge, a railroad crossing? A plume of exhaust wafted throughout the trunk, dizzying his already altered senses. Noises. More noise from outside. And the smell. It had changed, drastically. Petroleum; yes, that's what it was. And something else — food? Trash? Death? A mixture of all three. Then it hit him. They'd crossed the border. He was in Mexico. Oh Jesus, they were surely taking him there to kill him. He knew now that what he'd found out was the truth. And *they* knew he'd discovered it. A cold sweat broke out on the back of his neck.

The road wound around several curves, jostling him from side to side. Then, through the drone of the car and the grade of the trunk, he sensed they were going up a steep slope, maybe a mountain. And then he got it. He knew where they were going. Soon enough they'd be skirting the Baja coastline. He'd made this trip himself before. Would they kill him there along the highway down to Ensenada and dump his body in the ocean? Or would they take him east and leave him to rot in the desert? Either way, Bob realized he was totally screwed.

He should have lived differently. Should have made peace with the people he'd hurt. But it was too late for that, if he was right about who was behind this abduction. He

10

would not be coming back. He'd been found out and would be dead before the sun came up. He was sure of it. Bob prayed his sister would accept that and drop it. Oh God, how he prayed for that.

ONE

Michaela Bancroft smiled as she placed a hand over Genevieve Pellegrino's smaller one. Together they brushed the horse. Michaela spoke in calm hushed tones as the little girl's father, Joe, Michaela's good friend from childhood, had directed her. At first Michaela had been apprehensive about working with Gen. Until she started giving Gen riding lessons, Joe had never told her that Gen was autistic. She'd thought that maybe she was just quiet and a bit slow. Michaela hadn't been around Joe's family much after high school. Although they had always remained good friends, life seemed to get in the way. It was her uncle Lou's murder the previous year that had brought them back together.

"That's good. See how clean he's getting?" Michaela said. "What a good job you're doing, Gen. Look at how pretty you're making Booger. He likes that a lot."

Working with the little girl was as therapeutic for Michaela as it was for Gen. Maybe even more so.

Once Booger had the saddle on him and Michaela slid a headstall over his ears, she kept him on a lead line and put Gen up, leading him to the arena. Over the course of half an hour she watched as the child relaxed into the saddle and seemed to almost become one with the horse, a smile appearing on her face as she asked him to trot. Booger performed his version, which was more of a very fast walk, semijog. But Gen didn't seem to care that Booger was lazy. An easy calm came over the little girl's face and she truly looked happy on the horse.

"Okay, Gen. It's time to get off now and we'll give him a brushdown. Are you ready?"

Gen nodded. Michaela helped her dismount. With a slight movement of the hand, Michaela pushed aside the strands of curly black hair that had fallen out from under Gen's helmet and into the girl's eyes. "You did a great job today. I am so proud of you." She removed the school saddle from Booger's back and set it inside the tack room, which was in serious need of an overhaul. She'd have to get on her assistant trainer, Dwayne, about that. He knew better than to keep things in such disarray.

She brought a soft bristle horse brush back to Gen and placed it into her hands. She knew to keep the barn quiet when the girl was there. No country western on the radio blaring through the breezeway, and she'd asked Dwayne to wait to turn any of the horses out. He also knew to keep his distance when Gen was there. She figured at this time, mid-morning, he was likely making a feed run. They were getting low on grass hay.

As Gen slowly brushed Booger, Michaela stood back and watched her, knowing it gave the girl a sense of peace and accomplishment. There was a connection being forged between horse and child that could only benefit both of them. "Why don't we give him a treat?" she asked in a soothing tone.

She didn't get a response other than a slight glance from Gen. It was important though, she'd learned from Joe, that Gen be apprised of all that was going on. It helped her stay focused without overwhelming her. Gen handed her back the brush and followed her into the feed room; the smell of molasses and fresh-cut alfalfa perfumed the air. Michaela grabbed a blue bucket off one of the post nails and scooped it into a trashcan filled with oats. "Okay. I think he'll like this. What do you think?"

"Yes. I think so."

They gave the horse his oats, and after a good brushdown put him back in his stall. Taking him to the wash rack and bathing him would be too much for the child. She'd wait and let Katie, her afternoon student, wash him when she was finished riding.

After putting Booger away, Michaela was startled by the sound of a car horn. Oh no. She looked at Gen's face, which suddenly turned ashen. The car pulled to a stop outside the breezeway and Michaela heard Katie's voice. "Michaela, Michaela, my dad brought me early. I wanted to come help." The nine-year-old bounded down the breezeway.

Michaela started to bring a finger up to her lips to quiet the enthusiastic girl, but it was too late. Gen let out a horrible, almost primal scream. Her eyes widened with fear.

"What is it? What's wrong?" Katie yelled out, only exacerbating the problem.

Michaela was stuck between the two children and for a moment stood paralyzed, looking from one sobbing girl to the next. Regaining her wits, she went to Gen, wrapped her arms tightly around her, and in a low voice started reassuring the girl.

16

"It's okay. It's okay. No one can hurt you. I'm here. You're safe. You're safe."

"Michaela?" Jude Davis appeared in the doorway. Katie got behind her father and peered around him, looking terrified.

"Call her parents, please, Joe and Marianne Pellegrino. Their number is on the schedule list in my office. I'm going to take her to the house." He nodded and Michaela picked Gen up, continuing to talk to her as the child began to calm down.

"Can I help you?" Jude asked.

"No, just please call her dad and ask him to come over."

Gen was a tiny girl for her age, but not so small that Michaela didn't feel her fifty-some-odd pounds in her lower back. Going through the back door, she took the girl into her family room, where she closed all of the curtains and sat the child down on the couch. Gen had stopped twisting around and now fell quiet. Ah, better; but Michaela felt horrible.

Minutes later, Joe and Marianne came through the door. "I am sorry," Michaela said.

Joe waved a beefy hand at her. "Happens." He looked like an Italian Pillsbury Dough-boy, concern furrowing his bushy eyebrows. "I'm sorry we ran out on you like that."

Rather than stay to watch her lesson as they usually did, Joe and Marianne had instead dropped Gen off earlier because they'd had some errands to run.

Michaela felt responsible because she'd insisted they go on ahead and take care of what they needed to with their other four kids. She'd assured them she could handle Gen. What had she been thinking?

Marianne contrasted Joe, being ramrod thin and almost frail looking. She headed straight to her daughter and turned back to Michaela as she sat down next to Gen, grappling for something in her purse, finally finding a medication bottle. "It's okay, Michaela. This happens from time to time. Do you have a glass of water? I'd like her to take this." Marianne was calm and collected. The premature lines on her face told Michaela that she shoved much of her worry into the recesses of her soul and likely dealt with them late at night, so as not to worry others in her family. She couldn't imagine what she went through day to day to manage her large brood, and Joe on top of it.

"Sure. No problem. I can't tell you how sorry I am, though." She quickly went to the kitchen for the water. Gen seemed much better when Michaela returned and handed the glass to Marianne. She watched as the woman continued to calm her child. Michaela asked Joey what the medicine was.

"Some herbal treatment. Marianne is all into these supplements and herbs and things. Next thing you know, we'll be having gurus by the house or she'll be taking the poor kid to yoga or something crazy like that." Marianne shot him a dirty look. "I'm sure they're good for her, but I'd feel better if they was FDA approved."

Marianne stood and took Gen's hand. "We better get going."

Michaela nodded.

"You did the right thing, Michaela. No sorries needed. I'd like to talk with you about what Joe and I have been up to, because it concerns you, but she gets tired after these bouts," Marianne said. "Maybe Joe can tell you while I put Genevieve in the car."

"Tell me what?"

"We've gone ahead and recommended you as a therapeutic riding instructor."

Michaela's jaw dropped.

Marianne whispered a good-bye as she walked out, and Michaela turned back to Joe. "What is she talking about? I told you I'd think about it. Why would you put in a recommendation without asking me?"

"We was thinking, Marianne and me, and

we got to talking that you've been so good for Gen that we went to her therapist and the center she goes to for treatment and told them you would be perfect for the job. Therapeutic riding helps a lot of autistic kids and we don't have nothing like it out here in the desert. We think you'd be perfect for it."

"Oh no. No, I can't do that. Look what happened today. And" — She shook a finger at him — "you had no right to do that without running it by me."

"But you handled it the right way. The way you were supposed to. You love kids. You make my daughter happy. Give this a try. I see how much it does for you, too. After your divorce and then losing your uncle, I know what you've been through, and I see you smiling when you're teaching my daughter. Working with her makes you happy and you're damn good at it, and trust me, after all these years I've seen the good and the bad in this thing, and it takes quite a person to work with these kids. You got what it takes."

She shook her head vehemently. "Joe . . . Oh, man, I don't know." She knew that he was right about being happy when she worked with his little girl. But a center? A therapeutic center where she taught more kids? Granted, she now had the facilities to do it after inheriting her uncle's place, but could she do it? Really?

"Will you at least talk to the gal from the center?"

"I don't know, Joe. I don't think I'm cut out for it. I wouldn't want anyone to get hurt."

"No one's gonna get hurt." He raised an eyebrow, then wiggled the other. He knew how to work it. That always got her. For years she'd been trying to figure out how to wiggle just one eyebrow while keeping the other cocked.

Michaela had known Joey since junior high, when they'd bonded over pimiento loaf sandwiches, which everyone else thought were gross, and a mutual love for Billy Idol. Joe had been teased for his weight and Michaela had been on the shy side, so they'd formed a friendship that stuck over processed meat and eighties music. Joe was also known around town as the man with a million cousins. He came from a large Italian family whose ties were far reaching and, many suggested, of the unsavory nature. All Michaela knew was that Joe was a good guy with a lot of relatives, who knew how to find out information or get things done that other people seemed to have a problem doing. *And,* she was indebted to him. If not for him and the cousins, it was unlikely that the person who killed her uncle Lou last year would have been caught.

"Oh God, Joe, why do you do this stuff to me?"

"I think you should think about it," Jude said.

Michaela turned to see Jude and Katie standing in the doorway.

"Sorry," Jude said. "The door was cracked. You were talking. We didn't mean to interrupt."

Katie stood quietly next to her dad. Jude took her hand. The girl wiped her tears with her other hand. She was a petite thing with wavy, blond hair like her dad's and a splash of freckles across her nose that reminded Michaela of what she had looked like as a kid. Michaela had never lost the freckles across her nose and even sported a few more since childhood.

Joe went over to Katie. "It's okay, sweetie. She'll be fine."

Jude shook his hand. "She didn't mean to frighten her. She was excited and . . ."

"Hey, I got a handful of kids, and a lot of cousins." He laughed. "I know she didn't mean no harm and Michaela handled it. You talk to her, see if you can get her to

22

agree to running a center.

"Think about it," he said as he walked out.

She walked over and pulled Katie into her. "You didn't mean to upset Gen. We all know that."

"Why did she scream like that?"

"She's autistic, honey, which means she doesn't react the same way you and I do. She actually hears and sees everything going on around her. Like, listen quietly for a minute. Really listen." They fell quiet. "Did you hear the birds outside? What about the pool running from out back? Can you hear the grandfather clock ticking from the library? And, if a horse got out, I bet we'd hear all the horses go crazy calling out to him. Gen doesn't filter out the noises in the way that we do. She hears all of them together at once and it's very loud to her. So, she kind of shuts down to keep the noises out as much as possible. To you, it probably seems like she's not friendly or she's weird. But to her, it's the only way she can handle life."

"So, when I started yelling, it scared her and on top of all the regular noises she hears it made her really scared, so she started screaming out."

"Exactly. You're a smart kid. What do we say we go have that lesson now? I didn't know you'd be early, but it works out great because I'm going to the horse races tomorrow in Orange County and I need to be at my friend Audrey's house early in the morning."

"Okay, let's go!"

Katie ran up ahead of them. Jude walked back to the barn with Michaela. "You're headed to the races tomorrow, huh? Sounds like fun," he said.

She sensed a slight hesitation in his voice. Detective Jude Davis and his daughter, Katie, had come into Michaela's life while the detective investigated her uncle's murder. Since that time they'd shared coffee dates, lots of phone calls, even a lunch and a glass of wine one night while Katie scoped out the trophies Michaela had won over the years showing horses. There was *something* between Michaela and Jude. That much she knew, but what it was exactly, she wasn't sure. "I am. My friend Audrey Pratt is taking me. We go every year. She used to work with racehorses and has a lot of friends in the industry, plus she manages a young woman who is an up-and-coming country western singer and the girl will be entertaining before the races start. I thought it would be a good time."

"Sounds like it." He cleared his throat.

"Anyone else going with you?"

"Nope, just me and Audrey."

"Oh. Well, you'll be back tomorrow night, won't you?"

Michaela looked at him, her expression amused. His light blue eyes had darkened, and he palmed his hand through his hair, something he did whenever he seemed nervous. "Actually, no. I'm going on up to Malibu with Audrey to stay with the girl's mother, another friend of Audrey's. There are some horses we want to check out. I'm thinking about purchasing a few more, possibly a better lesson horse for Katie since Booger isn't much of a challenge for her. Audrey takes in animals off the track to let them retire in peace."

"Ah."

"Why do I get the feeling that you aren't too keen on me going?"

"Oh no. I think you'll have a great time."

She stopped and looked at him. "Jude? What's up?"

He sighed. "Actually . . . well, I wanted to ask you to dinner. That's all. I thought it was time we had dinner together. You and me. A real date. Candles, wine, flowers."

"Oh. A real date."

He nodded.

"That would be nice. Can you wait a few days?"

He smiled. "I think so." He squeezed her hand and then let it go.

Michaela's stomach dropped. She hadn't had a *real* date in years. Life was ever changing, though. She'd learned that for sure, and although she'd lost quite a bit in the past few years, it made her realize that maybe it was time to live again.

TWO

It was dusk when Michaela walked back out to the barn. She figured that she'd run into Dwayne and give him a ration about the tack room. As she headed into the breezeway, she heard Hawaiian music echoing off the walls. Ah, yes, Dwayne was close by. One thing she loved about having a Hawaiian around was that he listened to such beautiful music. She closed her eyes and could almost smell plumeria instead of horse manure. Okay, so maybe not, but she wanted to.

"Michaela, Michaela!"

Her roommate, Camden, hurried toward her. Not Dwayne. Camden, in all her red-headed glory, wearing a too tight T-shirt and jeans. Wait a minute. Something was wrong with this picture. First off, Camden wasn't wearing expensive high heels. No. She was wearing boots. Cowboy boots. Working cowboy boots, and furthermore, she was in

27

the barn. Michaela eyed her curiously.

"It's Rocky. Dwayne sent me to get you."

Rocky was Michaela's six-year-old stallion. "What's wrong?"

"I don't know," Camden said, a frantic edge to her tone.

Michaela didn't jump to any horrible conclusions, because she knew that Camden could be quite the drama queen. She hurried to the stallion's stall. Dwayne was inside. Rocky's sorrel coat gleamed with sweat. "What is it?" she asked.

"I don't know. He seem better now, but I work him on a lead line a bit ago. Didn't ride him because I notice yesterday when I did that he get tired too quick."

"He was worried about him last night," Camden interjected.

Michaela glanced from one to the other. "Last night?"

"I was coming back from shopping and saw Dwayne out here, so I stopped to say hi. He told me then that he was worried." Camden seemed flustered.

Michaela closed her eyes for a second, trying to wrap her mind around this. She held up a hand. "Okay, so Rocky was having problems last night?" She'd deal with the horse first, her friend's strange behavior later. "Why didn't anyone say anything to me?"

"No, it not like that, you know? I just thinking he be tired is all. I never say worry to her. He just being kinda slow for Rocky. Sluggish; but you know, they have moods and I figure he in one."

"Well, right now? What's going on?" Michaela placed a hand on Rocky's neck.

"His heart rate get up high and he seem . . . I don't know, different," Dwayne said.

"Antsy," Camden interrupted.

They both gave her a dirty look. As if the queen of Gucci and Charles David would know when a horse was *antsy.*

Camden seemed to get it. "You know, I think I'll go blend up some margaritas. Dwayne, you want to join us?"

He didn't answer. Michaela said, "We're going to take care of Rocky first. You do what you need to." She waved her off. For as much as she loved her longtime friend, she could be a royal pain in the ass.

Camden sulked away. Michaela asked Dwayne, "Did you call Ethan?"

"He be out of town."

"Oh," Michaela replied, surprised to hear that.

"The vet on call is gonna stop on by."

Michaela took the horse's pulse, which was normal. The sweat that had soaked him a few minutes earlier was beginning to dry. "He might have some kind of virus. Damn, I hate to leave him for a day."

"No. No. He be fine. I call you if there is a problem."

"No. I don't think it's a good idea. I can't leave him if he's sick. No way. I'll go crazy thinking about him. I better call Audrey and let her know that I won't make it."

"You being plain silly now, girl. You go, have fun with Audrey. Everything gonna be good. You see."

"I'll see what the vet has to say before I make a decision." She sighed and stroked the horse's neck. Looked into his eyes. "Hey, bud, what's wrong? You not feeling so good?"

The horse rubbed his face against her shoulder, wiping his wet mouth on her, smudging a mixture of dirt and hay across her navy blue T-shirt, already dirty from the day's work. She laughed. "Thanks."

"He love you. They all love you. He be fine. The vet gonna figure it out."

"Looks like the vet is here now." Michaela peered out the stall and could see a tall woman getting out of a truck.

She came over and introduced herself.

"Dr. Burton," she said, hand outstretched. Michaela shook it. "Let's see what you got here." Dr. Burton certainly didn't have much of a bedside manner. She must've been new to the clinic, because Michaela had never met her before.

Dr. Burton had short brunette hair that skimmed her ears, and looked to be somewhere between forty and fifty. Hard to tell, because she had quite a bit of sun damage and deep crow's feet framing her light green eyes. She did seem to know what she was doing as she went about examining Rocky, going through every detail and checklist, after getting Dwayne's story. "I'd like to run a blood test on him."

Michaela nodded. "What are you thinking?"

"Don't know. No fever, pulse is fine, pressure is fine. Everything I'm looking at screams healthy horse. But I like to take precautions and it sounds to me like he had some type of episode. I think the best method here is to do some lab workups. I'll take a look or have Dr. Slater look and get back with you."

"Okay. Well . . ." She looked at Dwayne, "I think my plans for the races are a bust."

Dr. Burton looked up from her clipboard

31

where she was making notes. "Los Alamitos?"

Michaela nodded.

"No, you don't need to miss the races. The horse looks great. He might have had some kind of anxiety attack. He's fine. I won't have anything back for a day or two anyway, so if you have plans, go."

Dwayne agreed. "I tol' you, he be in good hands. Go to the races with Audrey."

"I need to draw some blood," Dr. Burton said, and walked to her truck.

"Friendly lady," Dwayne whispered.

Michaela smiled. "Listen, you really don't need to handle all of this. I'll just stay home."

"Jeez, woman, you be worse than a mother hen. No. You going. I be calling if he feeling bad. And that's that. You deserve some fun. You go, have fun. Done deal. Got it?"

She frowned. "Got it."

When Dr. Burton was finished, Michaela gave Rocky a last pat and headed down to the house. Dwayne walked toward the guest house where he resided. She called back to him, "Hey, you want that margarita?"

He jogged toward her. "You think she got them made?"

"Please. You obviously don't know Camden *that* well."

They walked into the two-story, stone-type cottage. It had been built English-country style, and that essence was captured throughout the house. Too much of a house for Michaela. She'd been grateful that Camden didn't have any plans of moving in with a new boyfriend or getting married to another rich guy who treated her like crap. Okay, she did wish that she shared the place with someone she loved. Not that she didn't love Camden, but a husband would be nice — one who didn't cheat on her, like her ex. What she really craved was to fill up the house with a bunch of children. She'd always wanted kids. But it did not look to be in her future. She hadn't been able to conceive during her marriage, even after several attempts at various fertility treatments. Now, there was no husband, no man even to be a dad to any kids, and there certainly was no sex going on in her house. At least, *she* wasn't having any. She eyed Camden standing in the huge kitchen with its dark cherrywood cabinets, oversized refrigerator with matching wood panels, a stove and oven fit for a chef, and a granite slab in the center where a pitcher held Camden's famous blended margaritas.

When Camden spotted them, she clapped her hands. "Oh goody, happy hour can commence. I am so excited. Oh, sorry. How's the horse? I didn't mean to be insensitive."

"We don't know," Michaela said. "Hopefully, it's a short-lived virus of some sort or an isolated case of anxiety that he'll work through."

Camden handed Dwayne and Michaela each a drink. They toasted. "To Rocky," Camden said.

Michaela nodded and silently prayed that her gorgeous stallion would be as fine as Dwayne had assured her.

THREE

The next morning Michaela pulled into Audrey's ranch, Sampson's Corner, which was only ten minutes down the road. It was quite a bit smaller than her own place, but pristine. Audrey had worked alongside her husband, Charlie Sampson, for years, racing quarter horses. After Charlie died, Audrey ran the place on her own. Charlie had left her with a substantial insurance policy that kept her self-sufficient and able to take care of the horses. Money wasn't a problem, but time was. Audrey found herself needing to keep busy. That was when she'd gone back to her roots — music; she'd become a small-time entertainment manager and went back to using her maiden name, Pratt, for business purposes. She'd made a little here and there with new talent who usually wound up succeeding to a certain point with Audrey, then jumping ship to find someone bigger and better *and* located in

Hollywood. The little money she made from her management gig went back into her ranch and charity distributions. She took great pleasure in purchasing retired race-horses and providing them a home where they could live out their days in peace and solitude.

Michaela rapped on her door. Audrey appeared, smiling. "Hi honey," she said. "You ready?"

"You bet."

"Excellent." She picked up her overnight bag by the door. "I need to give Francisco some instructions. Come on out with me to the barn?"

"Sure."

They took a short walk outside to where Audrey housed her animals. She called out to her ranch hand. "Francisco?"

As they entered the breezeway, a thin, older Hispanic man appeared. *"Sí, Señora?"* He smiled and nodded at Michaela.

"I'm getting ready to head out. If you need anything, call my cell. Please feel free to eat anything you like, watch TV. The guest room is set up for you. The cat food is in the laundry room and you know what to do with the horses. My house is your house," she said in Spanish, which Michaela understood because she'd grown up on a

36

ranch, too, often working with Hispanic grooms and ranch hands. Audrey struggled to take a key off her key ring. "Damn. Thing won't come off," she said. "It's the house key."

"I've got one," Michaela said. "From when I took care of your place a few months ago."

The key Audrey had been trying to get off came loose. "Oh no, you hang on to that just in case I'm ever in a bind and Francisco can't help out. Besides, I got it now." She handed the key to Francisco.

"Have a nice time," he said. "*Es bueno* here, okay."

Audrey smiled. "Okay. *Adios.*" They started back toward Michaela's truck. "I don't know what I'd do without him. He's been a godsend since Charlie's been gone. He takes care of everything around here for me. Even changes my car's oil when I need it."

"It's good you have him."

"It is. Oh, and it is grand to see you, Michaela. We always wait way too long to get together. For goodness sakes, you're only a few miles up the road. Life really has to stop getting in the way. I am so pleased you could join me today."

Michaela took Audrey's bag and put it in

the back of the truck. Audrey, a pretty woman, looked to be aging well, with only fine lines around her lips and light green eyes, some freckles from the sun, and a hint of silver weaving through her light brown hair, which for as long as Michaela could remember had always been worn pulled straight back. When Audrey climbed into the truck, Michaela thought her thinner than usual. Though usually pleasant and generous, Audrey had a tendency to stress rather easily. Michaela hoped everything was okay with her friend.

They followed the circular drive in front of Audrey's ranch-style home. The early morning sun illuminated large paned windows that fronted the family room, a place where memories of hot chocolate with marshmallows warmed Michaela on crisp winter days after a riding lesson when she was a kid. The porch swing swayed as a slight breeze billowed down through the Coachella valley, only to be stalled by the rising dead heat of the Indio desert.

They headed down a dirt road. Beads of perspiration slid down Michaela's back as she leaned against the leather seat. She rolled down the window, the combined smell of hay, dirt, horse, and manure wafting in as they passed by Audrey's large pasture on the right, the springtime green grass beginning to yellow with the onslaught of the summer months. Rows of date palms lined the pasture fence, their olive-colored fronds casting shadows that one of the foals inside the pasture chased as he tossed his head and pawed at the ground, trying to make sense of the tricks his eyes were playing on him. All babies seemed to be ever curious of their shadows, human and horse alike. His mother and a few other horses spread out, enjoying their freedom and the grass, a couple of them hard at play, nipping at each other's rear ends, then whirling and racing down the side of the whitewashed fence, tails waving flaglike in the air, a look of wild instinct in their big brown eyes. God, they were beautiful to watch. Michaela couldn't help but smile.

They pulled out on to the highway, passing several ranches along the way, heading toward Orange County. The desert sky was cloudless, an azure blue that turned into a haze of light brown as they headed farther west. Ah, L.A.

"So, what's new? Catch me up," Michaela said.

"Good news. My brother, Bobby, is working for Eq Tech. He runs all of the research studies."

"That's great. I bet you're proud," Michaela said. She knew how close Audrey was to her only sibling and living relative. Bobby had been through a rough period over the last decade or so. He'd graduated with honors from the veterinarian school at UC Davis, but a broken heart combined with an accident where a horse had fallen on him, breaking both his hips, led him to pain medication and alcohol dependence. The addictions had consumed him for a time. But his sister never gave up on him, and about a year earlier, after paying for his treatment at the Betty Ford Center, saw him on his way to recovery. Hopefully, for both their sake, Bobby would stay clean and sober.

"I am. He's worked so hard, and they seem to be real happy with him there."

"I use some of Eq Tech's products. Good stuff. Seems to work well with my horses. My vet, Ethan Slater, recommends their products."

"Your vet? Honey, since when did you start calling Ethan your vet? I'm no fool. The two of you have known each other all your lives."

"Yeah, well. I don't think his new wife thinks much of our friendship." Michaela waved her hand. "I don't want to go into it.

Tell me more about this thing with Bob."

Audrey gave her a look that told her she'd drop the inquisition, *for now.* "Yes. Eq Tech . . . well, I don't use much of the supplements myself, though I have been giving some to that colt you just saw. Been awhile since I had a baby at home. Thought I might make sure he gets the best. The other horses I have are kind of pets, you know. And . . ." She smiled. "I suppose I pride myself in being budget-minded. Bob is good enough to give me Eq Tech samples from time to time. I just can't see spending that kind of money on vitamins."

Audrey had always been thrifty. But the woman was never cheap with her relationships. Once she made a connection it was a lifetime thing, as it had been between Michaela and her. Michaela had total respect and admiration for Audrey, who had taken her under her wing as a kid and introduced her to the show circuit. Michaela's dad and Uncle Lou had taught her the ways of the ranch and the ranch horse. She'd learned how to ride like a cowgirl. But it was Audrey who had recognized talent and put her through her paces in the show ring, until Michaela's family wound up having financial difficulties and could no longer pay the

41

entry fees. "Yes, they are expensive vita-mins."

"I'm just pleased Bob is working for them. I can't wait to get a look at his mug tonight. He had me a bit worried when I saw him recently."

"Really? Why?"

"I don't know. He seemed preoccupied. Edgy."

"Oh." Michaela didn't want to voice the question running through her mind, but Audrey answered it for her.

"No, I don't think he's using drugs again, or drinking. He just seemed distracted is all. He also gave me one of those large-sized envelopes to give to *your vet,* Ethan. I think there was a study in there he wanted Ethan to look at. He said that since we lived so close, it would be easier if I gave it to him this week because he knew that Ethan was going to be out of town for a few days and Bob was afraid he'd forget to get it to him. He knew he was going to be busy with the track and over at Eq Tech. Now, I've got that envelope out in my office in the barn, and I sure hope Ethan doesn't need it real bad. Anyway, Bob can be eccentric. When I pressed him on what was going on in his life, he told me it had to do with a woman, and some stuff going on at work. Jealousy in the company, that sort of thing. I tried to press him even more about it, but he insisted it was nothing. He clammed up and it bothered me, but I know my place, and I figured it was time for me to shut up, if you know what I mean. If you see *your vet* before I do, let him know that I have a file Bob thought he might want to look at. Some kind of research thing apparently."

"I'm sure Bob is fine, and it'll be great to see him. I think it's been a couple of years since I saw him last." And, Michaela recalled, it hadn't been pretty. A drunken Bob Pratt had made a scene at Audrey's Memorial Day party. She decided against bringing it up. "What do you think? Today's races going to be fun? It seems like every year, there's some type of craziness going on. If we don't hear about someone screwing someone over, or screwing someone else's wife, then it wouldn't be the races. What good dirt do you think we're in for today?"

"Oh, honey, today's races will be more than dirty. I am afraid the shit might fly. I got a feeling that today might prove to be downright . . . well, how do I put this? Different to say the least and sticky — even ugly — if I don't watch my step. I'm going to need your help to make it through."

Michaela stared at her, at first thinking

she was kidding. But the strain in Audrey's face told Michaela that she was dead serious.

FOUR

"What do you mean?" Michaela's stomach tightened. "I don't like the sound of that."

"You know, I realize that you've only met Kathleen Bowen a few times and she's even more high maintenance since the divorce." Audrey shook her head. "She's just not herself, and I need to ask a favor of you. It would be a good idea if you didn't mention that we're going over to Hugh's place tomorrow morning to look at horses."

"You mentioned to me that we were going to check out horses, but you didn't say anything about doing it at Hugh Bowen's place."

"I didn't?" Audrey asked, not convincingly.

"No. I think I'd remember that. It's not exactly every day that I visit the wealthiest and most famous racing quarter horse breeder in the country, not to mention restaurateur."

"Well, honey, it's not as if you haven't met Hugh before. We've known each other for years."

"I know, but, I haven't been to his place. It's kind of . . . I don't know, overwhelming. I understand it's the Taj Mahal of training facilities."

"True. Hugh, he's good man. Good natured. Even so, he's Kathleen's ex-husband, and she *is* my friend."

"Let me guess, she has that you-can't-talk-to-my-ex thing going on?"

"It goes a bit deeper," Audrey replied. "It has to do with Olivia."

"Their daughter is an adult; what's the deal?" Michaela asked. "Don't tell me they've pinned the kid between them. I hate when parents do that." In some ways, Michaela was happy she'd never been able to have a baby with her ex-husband. Surely she'd have figured him out at some point and wanted out of their marriage, and she'd never want to put a child through that. Her parents had been married for forty years and counting, and she was thankful they'd stayed together throughout the years, for better or worse.

"Kathleen has very high expectations for her daughter. She wants Olivia to be the next Carrie Underwood. And she could very well be on her way after tonight. Being a part of the opening entertainment is great for her. She's on right before Steve Benz."

"I've heard of him."

"He's moving his way up the charts; she's not yet. He's becoming quite the star, and Kathleen wants to see the same thing happen for her daughter. You know why I manage Olivia's career, don't you?"

"Because you're connected and you were in the business yourself for years," Michaela replied.

Audrey shook her head and frowned. "Sure, I thought I'd be the next Dolly Parton or Loretta Lynn. I started out my music career playing with Kathleen. It's how we became friends."

"I know."

"Anyway, Kathleen and I were wonderful together. We played some great gigs, then she met Hugh and got pregnant, and as Hugh's restaurant business took off, our career nose-dived. I don't know that many people in the biz anymore. As far as connections go, they're minimal at best. I've been able to get Olivia some decent gigs here and there, but nothing spectacular."

"Today's event is no small feat," Michaela said. "You should be proud of it. Olivia and her mom must be thrilled."

"I didn't land tonight's event for Olivia. Her father did it for me."

"Ah, now I'm catching on," Michaela said. "It's obvious that you and him have remained friends after the divorce. You've bought horses from him for quite some time, haven't you?"

Audrey nodded slowly. "True, but the divorce only happened a couple of years ago and . . ."

"And Kathleen doesn't know you still deal with Hugh. If she did, she wouldn't be too happy about it." Michaela knew of Audrey's long history with the Bowen family.

"Bingo. Hugh wasn't exactly graceful in his exit from Kathleen's life, but my friend was also no angel. No one was right in that mess, and I do agree with Kathleen on one thing: That new wife of Hugh's is no peach. She's a real pain and has driven quite a wedge between Olivia and her father. The only reason I'm managing Olivia's career is because Kathleen can't stand the idea of having her father involved in it. Olivia's dad can do things for her career that I can't. He's got the money and he *does* have connections. Today proves it, and Olivia has the talent to be a megastar, but I can't take her there. And honestly, I don't think the girl wants to be one. Olivia has her own dreams.

She wants to be a jockey."

"Interesting," Michaela said. She could hear the tension in Audrey's voice. Audrey's own dreams hadn't panned out, and there were regrets. She'd always encouraged Michaela to go after her dreams, just like her uncle had. What she didn't understand was that if Olivia did have this dream of racing horses, then why was Audrey involved in the singing part? "She's certainly petite enough. And, I'm sure she's grown up riding. Why doesn't she pursue her dream? I admire it."

"It is quite a dream. You know it's not easy for a woman riding in your circuit. Racing is probably even more difficult. The sexism is ridiculous. A lot of owners don't think a woman can ride as well as a man, and I've heard stories where an owner will let a woman ride the worst of his horses. There are also some sleazy trainers and owners out there who will allow a woman to ride for certain . . . favors."

"But Olivia shouldn't have to deal with that, with her dad being an owner. She could ride one of his horses. Can't she talk to him about this?" Michaela felt terrible for the girl.

"It's complicated, like I said. Olivia is angry with her father over leaving her mom

49

and remarrying. Kathleen is even more pissed at him and she'd come undone if Olivia started racing. Yes, Olivia can ride, but her mother won't hear of it. She is a complicated woman. She worries like crazy about Olivia but then pressures her into a business the girl doesn't want to be involved in. She's kind of pathetic. You'll see what I mean. I think Olivia somehow feels responsible for her mother's happiness since the divorce, so she keeps up the singing to please her."

"And you are caught in the middle." Michaela figured that, because Audrey had been friends with both Hugh and Kathleen for years and she adored Olivia, she felt totally stuck. "What are you going to do?"

"I don't know what I can do. I do love Olivia as if she were my own," Audrey replied. "But she isn't, and if I cause a rift, not only will I lose my friendships with Hugh and Kathleen, I may lose my connection with Olivia. So, you understand why when we see Kathleen this afternoon, we don't mention anything about Hugh? She would be horrified to learn we're going to his place, especially if the new wifey is around, and she very well could be. I don't think she goes too far from anything that glitters, and Hugh Bowen has plenty of glitter."

Michaela agreed that mum was the word. Audrey sighed heavily as they pulled in to the front gates at Los Alamitos, causing her to wonder if there was more on her friend's mind than what she'd revealed during the drive to the races.

FIVE

As Michaela got out of the truck with Audrey, the sights and sounds instantly made her smile. The blurs of bright color, people chatting, laughing, the clip-clop of horses' hooves as they were lead into the paddock for the preview of things to come, the drone of tractors dragging the track, all of it spoke of great history and tradition. What was there not to love about a sunny Southern California Saturday at the races?

"I need to check in with Olivia. She should be getting ready for the show," Audrey said, taking Michaela's hand and leading her like a child, which had always been her way. Michaela had only met Olivia twice, but she'd heard quite a bit about her from Audrey over the years. Olivia was getting ready in a room off to the side of the racetrack restaurant, reserved for VIPs.

Michaela was a bit surprised to see a meek young woman putting her makeup on. She knew Olivia to be shy. But this woman — girl, really, from the looks of her — was pale and thin. Dark circles under her glassy blue eyes made her look gaunt. Her long blond hair hung loose down near her hips. Still, she was beautiful, with an almost haunting presence. "Hi," she said, spotting them, an edge of sadness in her tone.

"Hi, honey. You look wonderful."

"Thank you. My mom says I need some more shimmer and glimmer." She frowned. "She doesn't think jeans and this blouse are appropriate," she said sarcastically, holding the ends of a flowing-type blouse, which was white with a pattern of small red roses throughout. It was on the hippy side of apparel. But it worked well for what Olivia was about: a slightly artsy, folksy sort, like an Alanis Morissette meets Tori Amos. Man, did Michaela want to run out and get her a cheeseburger. No, make that a double double. The kid needed to put on some weight.

Audrey waved a hand at her. "What does she know, right? You look wonderful. You remember Michaela Bancroft? You met her at one of my Halloween parties."

Olivia nodded. "Oh, hey, hi." She reached her hand out and shook Michaela's with the grip of a child.

"Olivia," Audrey implored, "that's not the way you greet a guest."

"Sorry." Olivia rolled her eyes. "Good afternoon, Ms. Bancroft."

Maybe it wasn't sadness Michaela detected in her tone, but surliness. It had to be the fact that she was malnourished that made her come off as irritable. "Please, call me Michaela. I feel so old when someone calls me Ms. Bancroft. Plus, I feel like I've known you forever. Audrey talks about you all the time. She's very proud of you."

"At least someone is." Olivia turned back to face the mirror. She glanced back through it at Michaela.

"I'm looking forward to hearing you sing."

"Whatever."

"Olivia!" Audrey said. She led Michaela a few steps away and lowered her voice. "I apologize for her. She's not herself these days. I don't know what has gotten into her."

Michaela waved a hand. "No biggie. She's a kid. They have moods. Trust me, I'm not taking it personally."

"Hey, sweet thing." A young man who Michaela thought she recognized breezed into the room past Audrey and Michaela, and strode on over to Olivia. He held a large bouquet of red roses. "I wanted to give these to you personally. They are from me and Marshall, and we want to thank you for opening for me today. I know you'll be awesome," he said, a southern twang icing his words. Audrey stepped between Olivia and the man, her arms crossed. "Hey, mama, what you doing? I am trying to talk to the little sweet thing there and why are you getting in my way? Do you know who I am?"

"Steve Benz," Audrey answered, her lips pursed.

Michaela knew she'd seen him before, maybe in some ad or on TV. She wasn't sure. He looked like someone who should be on TV, with his long brown hair, sculpted face, and pretty hazel eyes. They were pretty. Hell, *he* was pretty. That much she was sure of. But his personality sucked. What a pompous jerk.

"That's right. That is who I am." He tried to step around Audrey.

"I'm Miss Bowen's manager, and I'll accept those for her. Thank you. She is not interested in speaking with your manager, Marshall Friedman, or you, for that matter. If you cannot leave respectfully, I will call security."

Benz laughed. "Security. You are funny, Audrey Pratt." He shook a finger at her. "Ah, you didn't think that I knew who you were. I do and so does Marshall, and let me just say that your days are numbered running this young lady's career. Like *sayonara,* mama. Marshall will have her under contract in a week. You'll see."

"Steve, I think you should go," Olivia quietly said.

"No problem, sweet thing. Knock 'em dead. See you soon." He winked at her. Then he turned his attention to Michaela and eyed her up and down. "Hmm, hey sugar, aren't you fine. Wanna ride in my limo later?"

Michaela was speechless for about three seconds. She shook her head, her eyes forming into slits as she eyed him back. "You're kidding me."

"Oh, sugar, I would never kid about a thing like that. We can go for a long ride around town. Maybe wind up in some swanky Beverly Hills bar, then who knows. You'd like that, wouldn't you? I can tell by the way you're looking at me."

Michaela cleared her throat. "You know, Steve, as appealing as that sounds, I actually think I'd rather have dinner with a horse." Okay, she knew it was probably one of the lamest comebacks in history, but at that moment she was at a loss for words; the man was so repulsive.

"You're into that, huh? I'm sure we could arrange it."

"Get the hell out of here!" Audrey yelled.

He set the roses down. "You'll be sorry you talked to me like that. And you" — he pointed at Olivia — "will want to jump on board. Trust me. Money is good, the gigs are good. We'll talk later. Don't forget your roses, sweet thing. Bye, sugar." He looked at Michaela, who scowled.

She couldn't help but feel the need to shower after meeting Steve Benz.

Audrey turned to Olivia. "Have you been talking with that guy or Marshall Friedman?"

Olivia shook her head.

"Olivia," Audrey implored.

"My mom did. Once. They've been trying to get ahold of me."

Michaela watched Audrey's face turn a shade of red. Anger didn't cross her friend's features often, but right now she was sufficiently pissed off. "Olivia, those assholes will ruin you. I plan to speak to your mother."

Yep, Audrey was mad.

"You think if you go and sign with Friedman and do a record with Steve Benz, which is what I'm sure they're trying to talk to you about, it will make your mother happy?" Olivia's eyes widened. "If you do that, they will ruin you. They are all about the money. The next thing you know you won't be able to live your own damn life. You have dreams that I'm trying to protect. Still trying to make happen for you."

"That will never happen," Olivia muttered. "You know it will never happen. God, I just wish everyone would leave me alone. Everyone always wants something from me. Leave me alone!" she yelled. "Nothing good will ever happen! My dreams are shit and you know it!"

"Olivia." Audrey stood over her. Both women were petite but Audrey's presence was strong and overpowered the girl. "Those dreams will happen for you. Give me time. I am doing everything I can."

"I want to be left alone. That's all I want."

"That's not true. You can't be left alone," Audrey replied. "Look what you've gotten yourself into already, and this Benz character and his manager will only make matters worse. They see dollar signs flashing in front of them and if you — if *we* — allow your mother to dictate what you're going to do with your life, you will be miserable. I am convinced of it."

Olivia shook her head, her eyes welling up. Tears snaked down her face. Hmm, weren't the races supposed to be fun?

Michaela felt like an intruder on a conversation that had likely gone rounds before. She decided to exit while Audrey and Olivia hashed this out. Before leaving, she told Audrey she needed to go to the rest room and asked her for her ticket. Audrey pulled it from her purse. "I'll see you in Kathleen's box," she said tersely.

Michaela stepped outside the dressing room and took a deep breath. The simple earthen smells of horse, dirt, and southern California smog invaded her senses. Maybe it was time for a glass of champagne. Not a usual indulgence for her, but wow, what a scene. She'd never seen Audrey so intense or protective over someone. Maybe that was because she'd never had children of her own. Michaela knew there was a strong bond between her and Olivia. There seemed to be more to it than that, though. Oh well, it really was none of her business. If Audrey wanted to share it with her, then she would.

She headed to the bar, feeling good that she looked fairly close to the part of wealthy racehorse owner, trainer, or something to do with racehorses, like the other ritzy patrons. She didn't necessarily enjoy the dress-up-and-toot-your-horn crowd, but she also found it worse to stand out in these groups. The more you fit in, the less chance you had of actually being noticed. No, she felt like she blended in. Thanks to Camden and her wardrobe and the fact that the two of them wore the same size. Camden had insisted she wear a pretty, flowing, Anne Taylor spaghetti-strap dress. It was a chiffon-type material with an empire waist, red on top and pale yellow on the bottom with a red flower pattern. She'd also borrowed a pair of red slingback sandals from Camden, but found them difficult to maneuver in. With the Chanel No. 5 she'd sprayed on and the reapplication of the blush-colored lipstick she wore for ventures out, Michaela couldn't help feeling like she belonged, until she saw all the diamonds and pearls in the line at the bar, not to mention the hats. Should have listened to Camden for once. She'd told her to wear a hat, even showed her a simple, lovely pale yellow hat that matched the dress perfectly. But Michaela wasn't a hat person, unless it was a helmet for riding or a cowboy hat in the show arena. She saw them as pretentious and . . . well, yep, pretentious. Hmm, maybe she should have worn a hat.

"Kir Royal?"

Michaela glanced behind her as she felt a whisper tickle her ear. "Excuse me?"

"You look like a Kir Royal. I mean, like the kind of woman who would order one."

The man speaking to her was beautiful. It was that simple. He had a Robert Redfordesque thing, circa 1980, going on. He was probably in his forties. Gorgeous blue eyes that took her breath away, blond hair that dipped into his eyes, which he kept brushing back. Skin that looked as if he'd just come back from some island escape. Camden would definitely approve of his physique, and especially his attire — had to be Armani or some such designer. *Divine* was the only word that came to mind. Again she thought of Camden, who used that adjective on many occasions to describe men she met, but never had that word crossed Michaela's mind until now. Then, she caught herself, because that was not how she thought of men. No. She was not one of those women who went for looks and no substance. But, wait a minute, how did she know this man had no substance? Anyone who looked as handsome as he did couldn't have any substance. Obviously! She found herself coyly replying, "Really? And how does a woman who would order a Kir Royal look?" Now where in the world had that come from?

"I don't know. Sophisticated, educated,

intelligent, good taste but not materialistic. A good woman. A beautiful woman."

Michaela couldn't help but laugh. "How often does that line work for you?"

He smiled. "Often."

"I'm sure."

"Hudson Drake." He shook her hand with a nice, strong handshake.

"Michaela Bancroft."

"Do you have a horse running?"

She laughed again. "No. I actually train reining horses. I'm here with a friend of mine."

"A gentleman, I take it."

The man was interested in her. Michaela felt heat throughout her body. She *was* just like Camden. Put a pretty face in front of her and it was as if the brain cells suddenly all died and she went all gaga. Memories of her ex-husband, Brad, ran through her mind. Another pretty boy — bad news. "No," she said, surprising herself. Why couldn't she lie, even to a stranger? He smelled good though. Maybe that was why? Oh boy, the brain cells had definitely exited the brain. His smell. Mmm. Like cedar and vanilla, maybe some musk thrown in. "An old friend. We're in Kathleen Bowen's box."

"Really? I'm good friends with her ex, Hugh."

"Huh," was all Michaela could utter. It was her turn to order a drink.

Hudson Drake stepped in front of her. "Kir Royal and a dirty martini, strong."

"Thank you," Michaela said as the bartender handed them their drinks and Hudson paid. "You didn't have to do that."

"I wanted to."

"So, you know Hugh?"

He nodded. "And Kathleen and their daughter, Olivia. The entire crew."

"How do you know them?"

He took a sip from his drink. "I'm the CEO at Eq Tech. Hugh is one of our major investors; we've been friends for some time."

"My friend, actually the woman I came here with, her brother works for you."

"Who is that?"

"Bob Pratt."

Something in Hudson's eyes darkened.

"What? Did I say something wrong?"

He didn't answer her right away, taking a sip from his drink and looking as if he were trying to carefully select his words. "It's . . . about Bob. I probably need to speak with your friend."

"What? Why?"

"I didn't know when or how long I should wait before I called her. I keep thinking that . . ." He took another sip. Worry

63

wrinkled his forehead. "Really, I should speak with her."

Hudson Drake had her concerned now. "I've known Audrey for a long time. And, you are scaring me. I don't like your tone or what I'm reading from you. Can't you please tell me what's going on?"

He brought the drink to his lips again, taking a gulp. What in the hell was going on? After a few seconds he nodded. "Okay. Maybe I should tell you, and see what you think. I might be jumping the gun talking to his sister. At least that's what I want to believe. Bob hasn't shown up for work since Tuesday."

Six

"Three days?" Michaela said. "You haven't seen Bob in three days?"

He nodded. "Yeah. Today being Saturday means it's been four days, but it is the weekend, so it's not as if he'd be at work anyway. I've called his house, his cell phone, even stopped by his place last night. No one there."

"Have you called the police?"

He sighed. "No. I . . . listen, how much do you know about Bob's past?"

"Enough to know that you might be thinking he fell off the wagon and is out on a bender, and you're trying to maintain status quo before rushing to the worst possible conclusion," Michaela replied.

He smiled. "I knew I liked you. That's exactly what I'm thinking. I like Bob. He's a good man, and sometimes things happen. He mentioned that a woman he was seeing was really sick — I think he said that she had cancer — and she didn't want to see him any longer. When he didn't show up on Wednesday, I thought that maybe he wasn't feeling well. I was in and out of meetings all day. Maybe I missed his call. I don't know. Then, on Thursday, I started to grow concerned. But I didn't want to alert his family — his sister — right away because what if all it turned out to be was that he was holed up somewhere with some booze? Once he came out of it, he'd realize what he'd done. He's a smart guy. He knows I won't can him over this. I am all about second chances, and trust me, Bob is a good enough vet and scientist that I don't want to lose him. I've gone back and forth on calling his sister. I didn't want to upset her or cause problems."

"I hear you . . . but he needs to be found. I think you're probably right. I know he's fought this battle off and on for some time, but still, he needs help."

"You think I should tell his sister, then?" Hudson asked.

Michaela shrugged. "Audrey needs to know. It's that simple. I think I should tell her, though. She doesn't know you, and it might be better coming from me."

"I agree. Whatever she'd like me to do; I can call the police or a private investigator if we need one. However she thinks it should be handled. I was thinking maybe I could visit some of the bars he used to go to, but I'm not sure what they would be."

"She might know."

"Thank you. You've been a godsend. I can't tell you how stressed I've been over this. Bob was supposed to vet here today and I'd hoped he would show up, but so far he hasn't. Maybe he'll come through. Come to his senses."

"I hope so." Michaela dreaded having to tell Audrey this news, but she really didn't have a choice. She needed to know what was going on, and together they could find out where Bob was and what had happened. She tried to keep thoughts of the worst at bay. She'd dealt with addictions in her own family with her dad, who had a gambling problem. She knew the strain it put on a family, and she knew how all-consuming it could be for the addict. So consuming, in fact, that it could cause someone to fall off the face of the world and not return for some time. She even doubted that the police would get too involved if they were aware of Bob's past and his struggles with alcohol and pills. Still, a nagging sensation in her gut made her wonder if there was something more to Bob's disappearance. She knew from Audrey how wonderful he'd been doing, how much he enjoyed his new job. But Audrey had mentioned to her this morning that she'd been concerned about Bob's behavior recently. Poor Audrey. On top of her issues with Olivia and the rest of the Bowen family, the woman didn't need any more stress.

Hudson reached into his coat pocket and pulled out a couple of business cards, handing them to her. "Those are my numbers. Maybe one of you could give me a call?"

"Sure."

"Well, I've got a box full of people, I better get back."

"Okay. It was nice to meet you, and thanks for the drink."

"I couldn't pass up an opportunity to meet a Kir Royal girl."

She laughed.

"Hey, would you like to join me in my box?" Hudson asked.

Her stomach sank again. "I can't. I'm with Audrey and as I said, we were invited to sit in Kathleen Bowen's box."

"I understand." He paused for a minute. "You know, I have this benefit to go to next weekend. I hate those things, but would you like to go with me? That would sure make it less unbearable. It's a good cause. Some of the same people here today will be there. We're raising money for handicapped riders."

"I don't live here. I'm from Indio." Now, why hadn't she simply responded with a *No, thank you?* Them dead brain cells again. She did like the sound of what the benefit was for, especially since she was working with Gen and thinking about running her own therapeutic riding program.

"That's not a problem." He pulled a handful of keys from his jacket pocket and took one off the ring. "This is to an apartment I own in Century City. Actually, the company owns it. We let associates or reps coming in for the weekend, that kind of thing, stay there. Why don't you come and stay for the weekend, go to the benefit? You can do your own thing: shop, relax, whatever you want."

Michaela looked at the key, stunned. "I don't shop much. I don't know you. I like you fine. You seem nice and . . ." He certainly was handsome. "But, I can't do that."

"Why not?"

"I just can't." Okay, once again, a simple *No, thank you,* would have sufficed.

He frowned. "Are you seeing someone?"

A vision of Jude came to mind. "Sort of."

"In my book a sort of is not a yes or no.

All I'm asking is for you to come to the benefit with me. Not a date. Join me, stay in the company apartment. We'll have fun and that'll be that. It's for a good cause."

She looked down at the key in her hand. She couldn't do that, could she? What about Jude? It *was* a good cause . . . and Jude and her weren't dating, not yet, not technically. "Okay. I'll go."

"Good." He wrote down the address on the back of his card. "Why don't you call me this week and I'll give you directions?" He winked at her and walked away.

Talk about blurred boundaries. Now why had she gone and done that? Here she'd had thoughts of staying far away from men, after what she'd been through with Brad. But she'd allowed Jude to get close to her, and now she was accepting a date from a stranger. And, not just a date, but to stay in his apartment? Well, his company's apartment. What had she just done? One thing was for certain: Camden would be proud. Yes, indeed, she'd for sure get the "You go, girl," from her pal. Maybe there *was* something to this blurred boundary thing. Certainty was comfortable. But at that moment she felt a sense of excitement that she hadn't experienced in quite some time. Yes, maybe it was time to blur the lines.

SEVEN

When Michaela made it to the box, she was relieved to find herself alone for a moment. She scanned the crowd, noticing all the usual suspects and many not-so-usual suspects. The quarter horse races at Los Alamitos were a little different than Thoroughbred racing. More cowboy hats and less suits, more down-home Americana and less celebrity fare, but still plenty of folks with champagne tastes, and they'd get what they'd come here for — a run for their money and *much* more. June, in what could be considered muggy for the OC; the quarter horses would be running today. Quarters ran shorter, faster races compared to the Thoroughbred, and "the quarter-mile race" was how the quarter got its name. Back in the day, the original cowboys enjoyed racing their ponies for quarter miles, discovering they were sprinters and had extreme speed from the get-go, but weren't endurance runners like the Thoroughbred — thus the quarter horse breed was born.

Michaela set down her Kir Royal, now nearly finished, and smiled. She dug through her purse, locating a rubber band to hold her blond hair. Thankfully, the box was in the shade.

"Not bad, huh?" Audrey walked into the box. "The seats. It pays to have friends in high places."

"I can see that. You okay? That scene with Olivia didn't seem too pleasant."

"Nothing I can't handle. She's having a rough patch of it right now. We'll get through it. I see you've been to the bar." She walked around the back of the row of seats and over to a table where a bottle of champagne chilled. "I don't think Kathleen will mind. It appears as if she's already begun." She held the bottle up, which was half empty. Audrey poured herself a glass and refreshed Michaela's. She nodded to her. "A toast to Olivia today . . . and Kathleen's horse Halliday. He's a fine animal. Expected to win. We should definitely go and place a bet on him."

Michaela nodded. "To Olivia and Halliday it is."

"Here, here," another woman's voice from behind them rang out. Kathleen Bowen entered the box. "I will second that. To my daughter and my horse. Shall they both be winners today." She smiled brightly, her gray eyes — the same color as her pageboy-coiffed hair — lit up, emphasizing the deep lines around her eyes and mouth. Kathleen was a smoker and a sun lover, both of which had taken their toll on her face. "Nice to see you again, Michaela," Kathleen said, stubbing out her cigarette and blowing the smoke away from Audrey and Michaela. "Good of you to make it. Hope my horse wins and my daughter breaks a leg." She gave Audrey a hug. "And, how are you? You look great as always. Have you seen Olivia?" She asked, and took a sip of champagne from the flute she was holding.

"Just came from there," Audrey said. "You look great, too. Big day."

"Mmm, yes it is." Kathleen set her champagne down after taking another long sip.

"What time will Olivia go on?" Michaela asked.

"Soon." Audrey checked her watch. She glanced around.

"You sure you're okay?" Michaela asked. Poor Audrey. How was she going to tell her what Hudson Drake had related about Bob? She had to, though. It wasn't something that could wait.

"Sure. A bit nervous is all. You know, for Olivia."

"She'll be great," Kathleen said and tilted the light pink hat she wore with her matching Chanel suit. "I know it. My girl can sing. And, my horse can run. Going to kick Hugh's horse's ass. He'd better anyway. I'd love to see Hugh eat crow, along with that two-bit whore he married."

"Now Kathleen," Audrey said, "I thought you were past being bitter."

"Bitterness has nothing to do with the truth. And you know that I'm saying the truth. You know, I really don't want to be angry at Hugh or bitter about any of it. I wish I could let it all go. Wash my hands. It's crazy, but I still love him. He was the love of my life. How can you be married to someone for twenty-five years and then throw it away?"

Audrey sipped her champagne but didn't respond.

"Look ladies, I think the show is about to start. Audrey, would you mind pouring me another glass of champagne?" Kathleen handed her the glass. Michaela walked over to the champagne with Audrey, who leaned in and whispered in Michaela's ear as an announcer bellowed from the infield, "She gets tipsy easily, and then she gets on the

Hugh kick and there's no stopping her. Be prepared. I can't tell you how many nights in recent months have started out with her in a great mood, only to turn dark as soon as she's knocked back a few and started walking down memory lane."

"I think I can handle it," Michaela said. "Look, there's something I have to tell you —"

"Hurry up, ladies. Sit, sit," Kathleen ordered.

"Can it wait? I think we better take a seat and prepare for the entertainment," Audrey replied.

Could it wait? Michaela struggled with that for a minute. She could tell Audrey about her brother now and have her fretting during Olivia's performance, possibly ruining the experience for her completely, or she could at least wait until Olivia was finished. It wasn't as if Audrey could do anything about her brother at that moment anyway. "Sure, it can wait."

"Good afternoon, ladies and gentleman. It's a great day for the races, isn't it?" The crowd's applause and cheers echoed through the stands at the announcer's intro.

Michaela noticed that Audrey took another sip of champagne but did not applaud, while Kathleen on the other hand was squealing with delight.

"You should be really proud of yourself," Michaela told Audrey, hoping to ease her nerves about Olivia's performance.

Before Audrey could reply, the announcer welcomed "Up-and-coming superstar Olivia Bowen," to the stage.

The crowd went nuts again, especially Kathleen, who cried, "That's my baby! That's my girl!"

Olivia appeared on stage, her ethereal beauty causing many to pause and study her. "Hi everyone," she said, seeming uncomfortable.

"Goodness. I told her not to wear that. She is such a beautiful girl. Why does she have to cover herself up in a frock?" Kathleen turned to Audrey.

"You know that Olivia is shy. It's her nature, Kathleen. You may have to accept that. It doesn't take away the fact that she has talent."

"You think that Simpson girl has any talent? Ha! My daughter is far prettier and more talented, but you know why that blondie is always topping the charts? It's because she knows how to work it." Kathleen muttered something under her breath. Michaela couldn't hear what she said, but it likely wasn't a pleasantry.

Michaela squeezed Audrey's arm as Kathleen turned back to watch Olivia sing her first song: a beautiful rendition of "Blue Moon." "Don't listen to her. You're doing everything right for Olivia and you know it. It's the way you've always been with us kids. Well, I guess I'm not a kid anymore."

"Oh, honey, you'll always be a kid to me. But what do you mean?"

"I mean, you've always let us be exactly who we wanted to be. You allowed me to explore various aspects of riding and I wound up finding my niche in reining. I'm sure you would have liked to see me go down the path of say, maybe hunter jumping, or even racing?"

Audrey smiled at her. "Hmm. That *is* what I had in mind."

"Right. But I would have been the tallest jockey in town. Granted I'm no giant, but not many are five foot six." Michaela pointed at her. "Regardless, you still let me go where I needed and wanted to, and that is what you're doing for Olivia."

"I don't know about that."

When Olivia finished with "Blue Moon," she played an original song of hers, which was more upbeat, and she had the crowd on their feet clapping. Kathleen turned. "Amazing. She is amazing. I know she's going to be a superstar."

Once Olivia was done with her set, Steve Benz came on and rocked the crowd with his mixture of good looks, rock 'n' roll moves, and sweet southern sound. Even so, Michaela's brief encounter with him had soured her on enjoying his performance.

"I can see why he's a star," Kathleen said as he left the stage. "I think I'll go and refresh my drink, maybe see if I can spot anyone I know before the race starts, and get a look at Halliday." She held up a pair of crossed fingers. "Come with me?"

Before Audrey could respond, Michaela said, "I think we have some bets to place, don't we, Audrey?" She wanted a chance to speak with her about Bob.

"We do."

"I'm sure you're betting on my horse, aren't you? The odds are in Halliday's favor."

"Of course," Audrey replied as they left the box.

They entered the betting lines. Standing in line, Michaela turned to her. "Audrey, when was the last time you spoke with —"

"Audrey!" an older man shouted out as he approached them. Michaela recognized Hugh Bowen. She glanced at Audrey and caught a genuine smile spreading across her friend's face. That was the first time today that Audrey had *really* smiled, and it lit her up.

Hugh leaned in and kissed Audrey's cheek, then Michaela's. His thick silver hair, dark brown eyes, and navy blazer paired with khakis gave him quite the distinguished look. He definitely appeared happier than his ex-wife. "Olivia was wonderful up there. I am so proud of her and everything you've done," he said.

"I haven't really done anything," she replied.

He waved a hand at her. "Nonsense. I take it you're in Kathleen's box?"

"We are." Audrey sighed.

Hugh placed a hand on Michaela's shoulder. "So, you two are coming by tomorrow to take a look at some of my retirees, huh? Audrey mentioned your new venture into giving riding lessons."

"I've got a couple of students right now, and may be taking on some more," Michaela replied.

"Sounds great. I think I have some horses that might work for you. So, Kathleen pressuring you to bet on Halliday, I suppose? It's not a bad bet. But you may want to put some money down on my guy — Flashing Chico. I've got a good feeling about him, and I've got one of the best jockeys around up on him — Enrique Perez. The man can ride. Plus, I've been watching this horse out on the track every morning this week and he has it. It's a gut thing. His times have been phenomenal. Since your brother had me put him on Eq Tech's new supplement, I think it really is improving this horse's speed. I'm a real believer in that stuff."

"Bobby is here today, isn't he?" Audrey asked. "He's vetting the track, right?" she asked, a note of apprehension to her voice.

Michaela looked at Hugh Bowen. Did he know that Bob hadn't shown up at work? Oh no. Maybe she should have told Audrey before now. She wanted to jump in and tell her what Hudson Drake had told her, but she couldn't find the words.

"Should be. I haven't seen him. I missed the vet check earlier, but I'm sure my trainer and jockey saw him. He's probably swamped. You know what it's like. He's probably busy testing and checking every-thing. Quit worrying about him. He's doing great. I saw him the other day and he's fine. Trust me, the man is back on his feet again."

Michaela swallowed hard. Hugh had seen Bob the other day? Which day? This was getting really complicated. How would she break it to Audrey that it wasn't looking as though her brother was really back on his feet, but had taken a step backward?

"I can thank you for that, too," Audrey replied.

"Audrey, I don't know why you won't ever take any credit. You do so much for everyone." He reached out and took her hand. The touch was somehow intimate, and the way they looked at each other further cemented that thought in Michaela's mind. She noticed Hugh squeeze Audrey's hand and then let it go, the two of them smiling at each other.

Okay, *something* was going on between these two. Michaela wasn't quite sure what it was, but her friend had some explaining to do about Hugh.

"Hughie, sweetie, c'mon. They're about to run. Let's go." They all turned around to see Bridgette Bowen, Hugh's trophy wife, hollering out to him — tall, voluptuous, blue-eyed and dark-haired, and about twenty years younger than him. She walked over to them. "Hi, ladies." She stretched out her hand to Michaela. "Bridgette Bowen. You must be a friend of Audrey's. Hello, Audrey."

"Bridgette."

Michaela shook her hand. "Hi, I am. Michaela Bancroft. Nice to meet you."

"Pleasure is mine. You two should come by after the races. We're having a get-together at the house."

"Thank you, Bridgette," Audrey said coolly, "but we have plans."

"If you change your mind, you are more than welcome." Bridgette started to walk away. "Come on, hon."

"Be right there. Get those bets in, ladies, and I will see you both in the morning. Wave to me in the winner's circle." He whispered something in Audrey's ear. Michaela thought about asking her what their secret was, but knew it would be rude, so she let it go as they placed a small bet on Halliday and a bigger one on Hugh's horse, Flashing Chico.

"We better hurry." Audrey grabbed Michaela's arm and they jogged back up to the box where Kathleen was already seated.

"Olivia should be here by now," Kathleen said. "I don't know what's taking the girl so long."

"She probably wanted to change, and I'm sure people are asking her to sign autographs," Michaela said.

"She should be here. This is an important race." Kathleen crossed her arms, frowning.

Michaela looked down at the track, watching the horses being led out by their handler horse. A couple were being squirrelly, tossing their heads about and letting out shrill whinnies, ready to race — do what they were born to do. But for the most part, the horses on the track remained calm; it was another wonderful quality about the quarter horse breed — they typically had good heads about them. The one horse that noticeably was the most amped was Halliday.

"What's wrong with him?" Kathleen said. "He doesn't get the jitters."

Again the well-muscled, sorrel-colored four-year-old stallion let out another shrill whinny. Kathleen stood up watching, strain tightening her face as the crew got him into the chute. "I don't understand. I've never seen him behave this way."

"Oh, Kathleen, horses have moods just like people do. Maybe he's in a funk," Audrey said.

"You know, Audrey, I wanted to talk to you about something earlier," Michaela said.

"Yes?"

"It's about Bob."

"My brother?"

"Yes. I ran into his boss at Eq Tech and —"

The chute buzzer rang out and the horses were off. "There they go," Kathleen said.

Audrey jumped to her feet. Michaela realized that she had to find the right words to say to her in the next couple of minutes, when the race would be over. Maybe she should have just waited until the end of the day. Too late now. Besides, Audrey really did need to know about Bob not showing up for work. It was the right thing to do.

The horses came around the furlong, running at breakneck speed, jockeys vying for the best positions, a blur of browns, blacks, and grays intermingled with the bright colors of the jockeys' silks. Long tails flew in the air like flags as the pounding of hooves slammed hard against the ground, the rapid thud of their hooves kicking up soil. Halliday came around the bend and moved into the lead, Flashing Chico right on his tail. They were almost neck and neck, and then . . . It all happened so fast. A wrong cue, a bump from the other horse — the cause was not the issue. Michaela cringed as her stomach churned. The movement was so subtle, but Michaela knew what had happened immediately, and within seconds so did the crowd as Halliday's jockey pulled him up. The gorgeous animal had broken his leg.

EIGHT

"Oh my God, oh my God!" Kathleen brought her hands up to her face as the reality of what they'd all just seen registered.

Audrey's jaw dropped. Michaela leaned forward in the box. Low murmurs rose from the crowd as they began to understand what they had witnessed. The pounding of hooves in the distance continued but soon stopped as the race ended. Hugh's horse won. Mixed cries sounded throughout the throng of spectators.

Audrey raised a pair of binoculars to see what was going on. A moment later, she put them down and started to run out of the box.

"Where are you going?" Michaela asked.

"Down to the track to find my brother. I'm going to see what I can find out."

"Wait," Michaela yelled as Audrey dashed away. "Audrey!" But her friend didn't stop.

Michaela started to go after her when

Kathleen grabbed her arm. "Oh God, what are they doing? What's going on? I can't see!" She stood up on her tiptoes trying to get a better vantage point. Even though they had excellent seats, everyone else was also standing in an attempt to see what was going on.

Michaela stood a few inches taller than Kathleen. She didn't have time to look. She needed to go after Audrey and tell her about Bob — bad timing or not.

"Can you see what the hell is going on down there?" Kathleen exclaimed.

Michaela watched as several handlers tried to calm Halliday down. Soon an equine ambulance drove onto the track. Flashing Chico was being led into the winner's circle. Michaela saw Hugh and his wife entering the circle. A sense of helplessness and sadness came over her. This was not good.

She turned to see Kathleen slumped down in her seat. She needed to do her best to comfort the woman. Audrey would soon know the truth about Bob, and she was angry with herself for not telling her before. Michaela put a hand on Kathleen's shoulder. "I'm so sorry. It doesn't look good. They've got an ambulance on the track now."

Kathleen looked up at her, tears rolling

down her face. "They have to save him. They have to save him!" she sobbed. "I love that horse. Oh dear God, I love that animal. Please help me. I can't go down there. I can't see him like that."

"Audrey is on her way."

"Can you go, too? I can't do it. I don't want to know how bad . . . Just tell them, tell the vets that whatever it takes, please try and save him."

Michaela nodded. "I'll be back." She would do what Kathleen wanted not only because she'd requested it, but also because she needed to reach Audrey first before someone else told her that her brother had not shown up at the track.

"Thank you," Kathleen whispered.

Michaela made her way through crowds of people, her stomach lurching. She didn't want to see Halliday in any pain either, but she understood Kathleen's heartache, and she definitely understood her love for the animal. Olivia's face flashed through her mind. Had Olivia seen the race? Wait a minute! She squinted as she caught a glimpse of what looked to be Olivia up ahead, and . . . oh no, she was with Steve Benz, holding his hand and weaving quickly through people. Another man walked alongside them. He appeared to also be escorting

Olivia out at a rapid clip. She called to her, but Olivia didn't respond. Maybe they were also headed down to the track. She thought about following her, then realized that her obligations to Kathleen and to Audrey were more pressing.

When she reached ground level, she couldn't get past security. "I'm sorry miss, you're not allowed out there."

"You don't understand, I'm with Kathleen Bowen, the horse's owner. She asked me to speak with the vets." The guard eyed her up and down. "I'm not some gawker; I am with Mrs. Bowen and she has requested I speak with the veterinarian. Let me through or lose your job."

He asked for her name, then spoke into his walkie-talkie, muttering under his breath as if she were some kind of criminal. After about fifteen seconds of this bull, Michaela was ready to push him aside. He finally set the walkie-talkie back in its holder and motioned her on through. "You're lucky you know the vet. This isn't typical protocol, but he says you're his assistant," he snapped as she bolted past him.

She wanted to question him but didn't have time. Her heels caught on the divots of the track as she stumbled out to where the ambulance was parked. Damn, she should have worn paddock boots. Sure. To the races. This had been the last thing she expected. She rounded the ambulance, where the vets and handlers were with Halliday, and saw the reason she'd been allowed onto the track: Ethan Slater. He glanced in her direction, his blue eyes filled with an intensity she'd rarely seen in him. He was injecting something into Halliday's neck.

NINE

"No!" Michaela cried out. The group, all men, turned and looked at her. Ethan motioned her over. "You can't put him down! You're not euthanizing him, are you?"

"No, I can't. I'm waiting to hear from the owner. Word is that you're representing her?" He looked confused.

She shot him an equally curious expression, not clear as to what he was doing at the track almost two hours from home and his own veterinary practice. "I'll explain later. I didn't know you were vetting here."

He shrugged. "No time for details. Guys, let's get him into the ambulance and off the track. The Sedivet is starting to work. Manny, you and Gordon stay with him. Give me a minute and then I'll be on board. Michaela, let me help these guys first, then I've only got about thirty seconds to fill you in on the situation."

She nodded and stood back as six men

lifted the injured horse into the ambulance. The poor animal still wanted to get back on the track and run, his coat glistening from sweat and probably some pain as the initial injury was likely being felt by him right about now. Halliday tossed his head from side to side and let out a sharp whinny. Michaela's heart beat hard against her chest. She brought her hand up to her mouth to keep from crying as she watched the animal suffer.

Ethan came back out, sweat causing brown waves of hair to stick to the sides of his face. "Okay, so I've called ahead. If Mrs. Bowen wants us to try and save him we can take him to the Helen Woodward Center down in San Diego. If we can save him through surgery, then that's the best and closest facility to do it at."

"Yes, that's what she wants. Chances?"

"Right now, I'm not certain how bad the fracture is. I need to set the splint, get him on an IV for fluids, and shoot him full of some more painkillers. His head is still in the race. He's a strong animal. Once we get him down there, and get the x-rays on him, I'll have a better idea as to where things stand."

"Okay, thank you. Notify me as soon as you can."

"Mrs. Bowen needs to be aware that even if the break can be fixed, it'll be touch and go for a while, and after that a long period of rehab. There's the possibility of infection. It will be a long haul. I've already called in the best surgeon I know. I'll be in there with him, but Dr. Laube is top-notch."

Ethan started to climb in the ambulance.

"Hey, do you know where Dr. Pratt is?" She was hoping that Bob had at least communicated with the track vets.

Ethan shrugged. "Didn't show. Partly why I'm here."

"Call me?" Michaela asked.

Ethan nodded and closed the doors. The ambulance pulled away.

Michaela watched as they sped from the grounds. She felt on the verge of tears again. The poor animal . . . and Ethan. What was he really doing here? Ethan lived only miles from her in Indio. Memories of growing up with him interrupted her focus for a minute: hanging out with him as a teenager, holding his hand through his first heartbreak over Summer when she left him the day before their wedding, and then standing by as Summer worked her way back into Ethan's life. She couldn't help wondering if Ethan and Summer would wind up the way she and Brad had. But now Summer was due to have Ethan's baby soon. He wanted badly to be a father to the baby, insisting on solidifying his and Summer's relationship only days after she told him she was pregnant. That was eight months ago, and since then Summer had done her damndest — and had done it quite well — to purposely drive a wedge between Michaela and Ethan.

She shook off her thoughts, knowing she needed to find Audrey and tell her about Bob, and then they could go find Kathleen. The day at the races had turned quite horrible. She went looking for Audrey. Hadn't she headed down this way? Michaela glanced around, suddenly realizing she was still on the track. Turning to get off, she spotted Hugh and his trainer leading Flashing Chico back to the stalls. She called out to him.

"Michaela, I saw you on the track with the vet. What did he say?"

She briefly told him what she knew.

"Damn. He's a good horse. The last anniversary present I gave to Kathleen — for our twenty-fifth." He shook his head. "I know it won't mean anything to her, but when you see Kathleen, tell her how sorry I am."

"Sure. Congratulations." She nodded at the horse.

"Yes; bittersweet win, though. I would rather Chico had lost and have Halliday be okay than this."

She nodded. "By the way, have you seen Audrey? I thought she was going down to the track to check on Halliday, but I can't find her."

"No. Jeez, everyone seems to be disappearing. I hear Bobby didn't show up to vet today. I don't know what to think. The Eq Tech folks won't be happy about it. Hell, *I'm* not happy about it. I helped get him that job there as a favor to Audrey. He's a good man, but I sure in hell hope he hasn't gone off the wagon. I can't find my wife either. She was heading out to get a bottle of champagne. Took my jockey with her. And, I haven't seen my daughter since she was on stage."

Michaela remembered Olivia running out with Steve Benz and wondered if she should tell Hugh. Probably; but the girl was not a kid. She was an adult. Still, Hugh was her dad and she knew how much her own parents worried about her, and she was in her thirties. She'd already had misgivings about not telling Audrey about Bob, and knew it was a mistake not to have told her yet. "Uh, I saw Olivia."

"You did?"

"Yes. I saw her leaving with Steve Benz and another guy. Tall, bald, skinny."

"What?" both Hugh and his trainer said in unison.

Michaela caught the trainer's expression as his hazel eyes darkened. He was also tall; Michaela had noticed a slight limp in his left leg. He had shaggy brown hair, and some scars from the result of what had likely been aggravating acne during his teenage years. He brushed his hand through his hair and quickly introduced himself when he realized that Michaela was looking at him. "Josh Torrey. I train Mr. Bowen's horses."

"Right. Oh sorry, Josh," Hugh said. "What do you mean, Olivia was leaving with that Benz character? And who was the other man?"

"I have no idea."

"Marshall Friedman," Josh said. "I bet that's who it was. Benz's manager; they've been trying for weeks to track down Olivia. I told Audrey about it. They were really bothering her. They probably dragged her out of here to get her away from Audrey."

Michaela hadn't gotten the impression that Olivia was being dragged anywhere. Yes, they had seemed to be in a rush but it didn't look to be against anyone's will. Granted, she hadn't clearly seen Olivia's face.

"When did you see this?" Josh asked. Now he had Hugh's attention. "I'm only asking for you, sir."

"Yes, when did you see her leaving?"

"When I was running down to the track, I'm pretty sure it was them."

"That Benz guy is such an ass," Josh said.

"He's not exactly who I want my daughter with. Let's get this fellow back to the stall." Hugh patted Flashing Chico's neck. "Then I'll try Olivia's cell phone."

They rounded the corner to the stalls. Grooms, trainers, and owners were busy with their horses. Horses' whinnies resounded, along with the strains of Spanish music being played in some of the tack rooms.

Josh handed Flashing Chico off to one of the grooms. He went inside the tack room and returned with cell phone in hand. "You can use my phone to call her," he said, handing it to Hugh.

"Thanks." He started to dial when a shrill scream rang out. The screaming didn't stop; it grew louder. "What the hell?" He handed the phone back to Josh and along with Michaela and a few other people, hurried toward the source, out past the stalls near where the massive horse trailers and semis were parked. Approaching the scene, Michaela gasped. Was that Bridgette, Hugh's wife? Yes. What was she standing over, screaming bloody murder about?

She walked closer, and . . . Oh, no! No! *No!* She started running. Hugh got there first. He knelt down while Bridgette continued to scream. A man stood next to her, his mouth agape. Hugh yelled at her to shut the hell up. She did. The other man stepped back. This could not be happening. Michaela stared as Hugh picked up the hand of her friend — Audrey's hand. Then pulled her body in close to him. *Blood everywhere.* Somewhere behind her she heard someone calling 911. She couldn't move. Paralysis shrouded her as reality hit. A pair of reins encircled Audrey's neck; her face was ashen, eyes bulging out in shock and pain. A terrified look on her face — again not real — like a mask. *Couldn't it just be a mask?* Please God.

But as Hugh looked back up, tears on his face, she knew it was no mask. Audrey had been strangled to death and the blood . . . the blood was coming from her head. She must have fought. That was who she was — a fighter — and, whoever had done this was evil, pure evil. The killer had finished her off with a deep blow to the head. Michaela knew her friend was dead.

TEN

After Audrey's body was taken away, the police questioned the nearest group, particularly Bridgette and the man who had been standing next to her, Frederick Callahan. Michaela thought she'd recognized him, but in all the chaos had not been able to place him. The bad toupee should have tipped her off. It didn't even match the gray it was attached to: He'd chosen a golden blond. It was hard for people not to discuss his rug when talking about media mogul Callahan. Owner of *Pleasures* magazine for men, he was also an avid racehorse fan and owned several of them.

Michaela caught bits and pieces as to why he was with Bridgette Bowen and how they'd discovered Audrey. Callahan had been checking to see if his horse, which was running in the seventh race, had passed the vet check, claiming he was concerned about a leg. It had looked a bit lame to him that morning. He heard the scream first and ran to where Bridgette stood over Audrey.

"I-I was going to the limo." Bridgette glanced at Hugh.

Michaela studied her as she explained how she'd found Audrey. Still in shock, Michaela didn't know how to react. She wanted to fall apart, but knew this wasn't the place to do so with all the police around. She'd teared up a few times as reality came in waves. Focusing on the others around her helped keep the horrific reality at bay.

After the cops were done interviewing her, Bridgette continued explaining to her husband: "I really wanted some champagne. I decided to come out here and get it myself, what with you being busy with Flashing Chico and everything. I figured I'd make myself useful."

"Couldn't you have ordered champagne from your box?" Michaela asked, not able to help herself. She heard a tremor in Bridgette's voice; was the woman lying?

Bridgette glared at her. "I could have." She rubbed Hugh's arm. "But Hugh knew we would win today and I brought a special bottle for the occasion."

"Why not have it on ice in your box?" Michaela asked again, recalling the champagne that Kathleen had in hers.

"Who are you again? I know we met earlier and I know you're not the police. I've already answered these questions." Bridgette's eyes narrowed like a hawk readying for the kill.

"I'm not the police; I was Audrey's friend."

"I didn't kill her, if that's what you're insinuating. I found her is all. I think it's interesting, you being her friend that you weren't with her. If you had been, maybe she wouldn't have been killed . . . unless, of course you had a reason to see her dead."

Michaela took a step toward her. "Excuse me? What did you just say?" Rage boiled in her gut as tears stung her eyes. "How dare you! I would never harm Audrey!" Her entire body shook with gut-wrenching agony. "I loved her. She was my friend, you bitch!" Bridgette's eyes widened. "I want to know why in the hell you were standing over her . . ." Michaela put her face in her palms and sobbed.

Hugh put an arm around her. "I'm so sorry, honey. We're all shaken up. Bridgette didn't mean anything by it. We all need to cool off. This won't help bring Audrey back. Let's all settle down. I don't think the police would take kindly to a scene right now."

Michaela nodded and pulled away from

Hugh. He was right. She didn't need one of the cops arresting her for assaulting Bridgette, though she still wanted to.

He whispered something in Bridgette's ear and then smiled sadly at Michaela. Taking Bridgette's arm, he led her over to their limousine. Her anger started to fade as sadness and shock continued to weave through her. She waited for the police to question the rest of the group. When they got to her, she told them that she and Audrey had driven there from Indio that morning. She went on to relate the events as she remembered them, from Steve Benz's subtle threat to Audrey in Olivia's dressing room, to the fact that she'd learned Audrey's brother had not shown up for work for the past three days, nor at the track that day to vet the horses. The officer in charge, Detective Merrill, asked her where Ms. Bowen was at that moment.

"Do you mean Olivia, or her mother, Kathleen?"

"I'll start with Kathleen Bowen. My partner is trying to track down the daughter," he said, his paper-thin lips tightening with each word he spoke. It made him look ghoulish. He jotted something down in his notebook. Michaela noticed the yellow on his fingers, probably from nicotine. As he stepped closer, she decided that it definitely was nicotine. Merrill smelled like one big, stale cigarette. He wore his dark hair slicked straight back, and from the lines on his face, she couldn't help the odd thought that maybe the man used Grecian Formula to keep his hair coal black. He looked back up at her with ice-blue eyes, as if expecting something. "Ms. Bowen? Where is she?"

"I left her in her box. Her horse sustained a major injury in the opening race and Audrey was going down to the track to talk to the vet. I followed, but when I reached the track I didn't see her anywhere." She told the rest of the story to the detective about walking back to the stalls with Hugh and Josh, and how it wasn't long before they'd heard Bridgette screaming. When he finished taking her statement, Merrill asked her if she had the vet's number. He wanted to find out if Audrey had ever made it to the track. Michaela wanted to know, too, but also knew that Ethan was tied up with Halliday.

Michaela watched as Audrey's body, now covered, was loaded into the back of the coroner's van. Her stomach ached and a lump caught in her throat. She couldn't speak or even cry. For a moment she wondered if she was even breathing as the pain in her chest tightened. How could this have happened? Why had Audrey charged out of the box? Dammit! She should have gone with her. If she had, maybe she'd be alive.

Merrill asked Michaela to show him to Mrs. Bowen's box. She agreed. She had to get out of there anyway; she didn't think she could watch as the van with Audrey's body drove away, or see the onlookers and the investigators. All she wanted to do was escape from there. It took about ten minutes to walk back to Kathleen's box. Merrill didn't say much. Michaela tried to ask him about his initial impressions, but all he did was nod occasionally, which made no sense to her. "Do you think it was someone she knew?" she asked.

The detective grunted. She gave up.

Kathleen sat in her box, staring off into space, her face stained with mascara. She looked up at them. "I know," she muttered.

"Know what?" Michaela asked.

"You're going to tell me they had to put him down, aren't you? That's why you and Audrey have been gone for so long," she said, slurring her words.

Kathleen appeared to have been drinking — heavily.

"I waited and I waited. Audrey didn't come back, my daughter never came to see

103

me, and you didn't show up. I finally got up and had a drink. I was starting to think that maybe you all had left me here. I was going to call my driver. I didn't know what to do, who to call. I could see people on the track, people everywhere. They were running horses, even after Halliday, and then no one came to tell me what was going on. Who is that man?" She tried to stand.

Merrill stepped forward, steadied her, and helped her sit back down. "Ma'am, I'm Detective Tom Merrill and I need to ask you a few questions."

"About Halliday? Since when do they send in the police to ask about a racehorse breaking his leg?"

"It's not about your horse, ma'am. It's about Mrs. Pratt."

"Audrey? I don't understand."

Michaela looked at the detective. "Can I . . . ?"

He nodded. Ah, he had a heart after all.

She sat down next to Kathleen and took her hands. Kathleen's eyes widened and she pulled back a bit, but Michaela didn't let go. "This is very difficult." She felt her throat tighten. "Um, it's Audrey. She . . . she was killed earlier." The words came out, but it didn't feel or even sound like she was saying them. She'd had to do it quickly, or she didn't think she could do it at all.

"What?" Kathleen pulled her hands away.

Merrill sat down on the other side of Kathleen. She turned to look at him. "Is this true?"

"I am afraid so, ma'am. Mrs. Pratt was found murdered."

Kathleen began to shake violently. "I don't believe this. I don't, *I don't!*"

"I need to ask you some questions." He glanced over at Michaela.

She took it as a suggestion for her to leave, and stood. "Where are you going?" Kathleen asked. "Stay. Please stay."

"Miss Bancroft, why don't you have the car brought around for Mrs. Bowen? I'll escort her down."

"She can't stay?"

"Police procedure, ma'am."

Kathleen nodded. "Use my cell phone to call the driver. All you have to do is press the number five and enter." Kathleen handed her the phone.

Michaela did as instructed. She didn't want to get into Merrill's way. He seemed pretty uptight. She had to wonder what types of questions he was asking Kathleen. She had a few herself. She wondered if she'd really remained inside her box the entire time, other than to get drinks. She'd insisted that Michaela go down to the track with Audrey, but it didn't look as if Audrey had gone down to the track at all. Could Kathleen have followed her? *Could she have actually killed her friend?* Is that what the detective was also thinking? Audrey had mentioned that Kathleen wasn't herself lately. And, she was insistent that Michaela not mention her continued friendship with Hugh, for fear of it troubling Kathleen. What if she found out that Audrey was still good pals with Hugh? Maybe she had even seen her chatting with him when she and Michaela went to place a bet. Could that have set the woman off? She didn't come across as the most stable of people. Then, when Halliday broke his leg, the crying jag: Had it been for real? Michaela didn't know. It seemed real. Of course it was real. She wouldn't have killed Audrey. No. That was ridiculous. Michaela knew she was being paranoid. The two women had been friends for years. This was ludicrous.

As she walked away she pressed the number five on Kathleen's cell. A man answered. "Kathleen?"

Michaela could hear loud music in the background. "No. This is a friend. Can you please bring the car around?"

"Excuse me?"

"Yes, the car?" she shouted into the phone. Maybe he couldn't hear her. He obviously had the stereo cranked. "Can you turn down the music? Ms. Bowen needs the car brought around."

"I have no idea what you're talking about."

"Aren't you the chauffeur?"

He laughed. "Hardly."

Michaela apologized and got off the phone. Why would Kathleen give her the wrong number? Must be stress. She hit the number five again out of curiosity to see if a name came up. The initials *MF* did. Hmm. She decided to try number six, and found the chauffeur. He told her that he'd be around momentarily.

When he pulled up, Michaela explained that Ms. Bowen would be there soon. "No problem," he said.

Several minutes later, as she stood lost in thought, Detective Merrill escorted Kathleen to the car. He told Michaela he'd be in touch with both of them soon. She thanked him.

Kathleen slid into the backseat and instructed the driver to take her home. "Get in," she told Michaela.

"My truck is here. I really should head out."

"No," she whined. "You can't go home. I

need someone to stay with me tonight. I don't want to be alone. Please."

Michaela cringed. The last thing she wanted to do was stay with Kathleen. Granted, that had been the initial plan, but now everything had changed. After Audrey and Halliday, she couldn't help but want to return to her safe harbor. She wanted to see Rocky and her other animals, make sure they were all okay.

Kathleen poured herself a drink from the limo's bar. "Wait, please. Have a drink with me." She took something from her purse and put it in her mouth.

"What was that?" Michaela asked.

"Valium, for my nerves."

"You've been drinking. You really shouldn't take that on top of alcohol. Put the drink down, Kathleen. It's not a good idea."

She waved a hand at her. "If I die, then so be it. Look at all that's happened today. My friend, my horse, and my child. Lord only knows where she is. You know that she never came to the box to see me. I doubt anyone would miss me."

Oh no. Michaela shut her eyes for a brief moment. *Think, think.* She sighed. "Okay, I'll follow you home."

"You will?" Kathleen looked at her

through drunken eyes.

Michaela nodded.

"Thank you. You're a good person." She patted her hand. "I have to ask you first about my horse. Did he suffer?"

"He's alive. I told them to do whatever they needed to try and save him. Now, hand me the drink."

Her eyes brightened; she ignored Michaela's request. "Oh God, thank you. He's going to make it?"

"Hopefully."

She sighed. "I don't know what I was thinking, though. Trying to save him. I mean really, I can't afford to save him."

"Excuse me?" Michaela asked. How did she figure? The woman rolled in diamonds and spent cash like she'd picked it from trees.

She shook her head. "Nope. No money. I'm bankrupt."

"Bankrupt?"

"Yesiree. Broke." She leaned back and closed her eyes, her drink sliding from her hand. Michaela caught it before it hit the floorboard and set it aside. She started to ask Kathleen how that could be, but the woman had passed out.

ELEVEN

"Michaela, I can't let you do it! What are you thinking, anyway? Kathleen Bowen can pay this horse's bill. She's got more money than she knows what to do with," Ethan said to her on the other end of the phone.

Michaela stood facing the bay windows watching the tide roll in. She'd been sitting on Kathleen's balcony outside her room, which overlooked the ocean, since before the sun came up. Listening to the ocean's sounds had likely been what kept her sane that morning, after seeing Audrey's body, dead — murdered — the day before. She'd hated coming to Kathleen's house, especially without Audrey, but the serenity of the Pacific gave her some sense of peace where she'd thought there would be none. "I don't know about that," she finally answered.

"Michaela, you are talking nonsense. Do you hear me? That's nuts. You may have inherited some money from Lou, but trust me, Mick, do not pay for this horse's surgery and medical care. It'll likely be in the hundreds of thousands. I can't believe that Kathleen doesn't have any kind of medical coverage on the horse. I'm sure the insurance company would keep this animal alive no matter what the diagnosis is, anyhow. They do their damndest to wait until the last straw. Too many of these animals suffer, all in the name of money, so the insurance companies want to hang on for as long as possible, hoping that they won't have to make a million-dollar payout."

"How is he, anyway?"

"The good news is, I wouldn't — and neither would the other vets — recommend putting him down. The break was a condylar fracture above the ankle. That is fairly easy to repair. The bad news is, he also has a fracture below the ankle in the pastern. Very similar to what happened with Barbaro at the Kentucky Derby. It's not as bad, and with a lot of care, possibly more surgery, he'll likely grow old grazing in a pasture somewhere. I don't think he'll ever see a track again, though. He's been kept comfortable through the night, and now we're prepared to take him into surgery, but we need signed paperwork from Kathleen. Do you have the fax number there? She can sign it and fax it back to us."

"I don't know. Hang on. Actually, you know what, I'll see if I can find it and call you back." It was half past seven and she didn't know if she should wake Kathleen. She decided to check things out on her own first.

"Don't be too long. We'd like to get him into surgery before eight. The anesthesiologist is here and so is Dr. Laube and his team."

"I won't be long. I have to ask you though, how did you get involved in this? I mean, what were you doing vetting at the track?"

"It's a long story. I'll fill you in at the barbecue this weekend. You're still coming, aren't you? Friday night."

Oh no. She'd forgotten about the barbecue–baby shower thing that he and Summer were throwing. Summer had insisted on it being a get-together for everyone. Great. She sighed. How had Ethan wound up with someone like *her?*

"You're bringing that detective, right? Jude? Nice guy."

"Um, yeah. I mean, I'll be there. I don't know if Jude can make it,' she said, almost choking on her words and remembering Hudson Drake and the *date* she'd made

112

with him for Saturday. That would be awkward, wouldn't it? Jude at Ethan and Summer's house with her, then the next night a date with a man she really didn't know at all. She'd have to call that one off, especially after everything that had happened. She'd mail him back his key. Surely he'd understand. And, she hadn't even asked Jude to go to Ethan and Summer's. Ethan was obviously assuming they were seeing each other.

"You have to be there. My wife and I are counting on you."

My wife. "Okay, well, I'll see what I can do about finding a fax machine and getting Kathleen up." If she found a fax, then she could wake Kathleen and have her fill out the paperwork after Ethan sent it. Poor woman was sleeping off a mixture of heartache, alcohol, and God only knew what else. Bad combination. A few times throughout the sleepless night, she'd gone in to check on Kathleen to make sure she was breathing. She tried to keep the images of Audrey at bay, and focus on Halliday and what needed to be done for him, but it was difficult.

She found Kathleen's office and went in. It was decorated like rest of the beach house — in white. There was a lot of it: bleached hardwood floors, antique white, modern white, white sofas, white chairs; different shades of white, but pretty much everything in white, except for the paintings on the wall, which were mainly watercolor seascapes.

Michaela found the fax machine next to Kathleen's computer and copied the number taped on it. Good. Okay, time to wake her up. First she'd call Ethan back.

She walked over to a white chaise lounge by the window; a phone sat on the table next to it. She called Ethan and gave him the number. Hanging up the phone, she noticed that the drawer on the table was askew. She bent down to fix it and place it back on the rollers. She tugged on it and the drawer came flying out, knocking her on her butt. Pens, a box of tacks and Post-its came flying out, along with a 5×7 envelope. "Oh shit," she muttered, hoping she hadn't woken Kathleen. She started to clean up the mess. She picked up the envelope, which had a photo partially sticking out of it. She pulled out the picture: Olivia on a racehorse . . . Flashing Chico. Hugh's horse. There were other photos in the envelope, which Michaela thumbed through. More of Olivia on the horse, Olivia with Audrey next to the horse, Olivia with Hugh's trainer,

Josh, Olivia on the track running Chico in what looked like a practice session, then a lone picture of Audrey watching Olivia on Chico. All of the photos were candid. None of them looked as if Olivia, Audrey, or Josh knew they were being shot. In fact, they looked like the kind of photos a private investigator might take. Oh boy. Was Kathleen watching her daughter's every move? She turned around, thinking she heard someone in the kitchen. Shoving the photos back into the envelope, she quickly stuffed everything else back in the drawer and put the contents back together, then grabbed the faxed forms, which had just arrived, and joined Kathleen, who was pouring herself a cup of coffee.

"Good morning," she said to Michaela, her hands trembling.

She looked terrible and didn't appear to have heard the ruckus Michaela had caused back in the office. At least, she hoped that was the case. God forbid Kathleen find out she had snooped through photos of Olivia, Audrey, and the horse. She didn't know what it all meant, but she did know it wasn't good. Not at all. "Hi." Michaela tried to smile at her. "I hate to bother you with this right now, but the vets want to take Halliday in for surgery and they need your consent." She handed the forms to Kathleen. "I, uh, went into your office to see if you had a fax machine. Sorry. I didn't want to wake you."

"It's fine." She nodded. "I know what I said last night about saving him, but . . ."

"You have to try. I spoke with the vet and he said that it can be done, that he can survive this." She didn't want to go into the cost or rehabilitation time. Michaela's stomach knotted, feeling sick that Kathleen might change her mind.

"I know I told you last night about my financial situation. I said too much, I remember, and I don't have any insurance on him. I couldn't keep it up. I've been stupid with my money."

"I'll take care of the bill."

Kathleen looked at her. "What?"

"I'll loan you the money until you get back on your feet. Let me take care of the expenses for now. I can cover them."

"No. I can't let you do that."

"You have to. You can't let him go without giving this a try. I insist."

Kathleen walked over to the window. She stood, staring out at the expansive ocean in front of her. "Why would you do this for me?"

"Honestly, it's not for you. It's for the

horse. He's an amazing animal. I've followed his career, seen the heart he has, and I can't bear to have him destroyed without giving him a chance. Don't have him put down. You can still stud him out with the use of AI," Michaela said, referring to artificial insemination, which was quite popular amongst quarter horse breeders. "You'll be happy you did it. Let me do this. You'll pay me back when you can."

Kathleen slowly nodded and signed the consent form. Michaela faxed the paperwork back to Ethan, and Halliday was on his way to surgery. When Michaela returned, Kathleen was crying again. "Thank you. Thank you so much. After Audrey's death last night, the thought of destroying Hal . . . I can't; as much as I feel ashamed about letting you front the cost, I agree with you."

"Can I ask you something?"

"Yes."

Michaela wanted to ask her why she was in a financial bind, even though part of her felt like it really wasn't her business. The flip side of her told her that at this stage of the game, with her paying the medical expenses on Hal, she did have a right to know why Kathleen was broke. Then, Olivia walked in.

"Mom! Mom!" Olivia cried out. "I heard

117

about Audrey. I came right over. Oh God, how did this happen? I'm sorry I wasn't there." Olivia put her arms around her mother, who pulled away, her face drawn as she looked past Olivia. Josh Torrey stood behind her.

"Have you been with Josh at your father's place, celebrating the win? How could you? Do you even know what I've been through? What happened? I was worried about you. I didn't hear from you. I called your apartment, your cell phone. I had no idea where you were. Nothing. Dammit, Olivia. I am tired of this with you. It's time you move back home. I've let you play grown-up long enough, but it's obvious that you can't handle it." Kathleen's hands were on her hips, her face twisted in anger. Prior to Olivia's arrival, Kathleen had seemed so sad, desperate almost, but something about her daughter being with Josh set her off. Michaela remembered the photos in Kathleen's office.

"Josh picked me up and brought me home. I needed a ride. That's it. End of story." She looked at Michaela. "Hi."

"Hi," Michaela replied. Olivia looked as if she'd been through the wringer — makeup smeared across her usually flawless ivory face, long blond hair totally disheveled, and she wasn't wearing the cute blouse and jeans she'd had on for the concert the day before. She did have jeans on, and what looked to be a man's T-shirt.

"That is the truth," Josh replied. "She was not celebrating with us. In fact, we weren't exactly in a celebratory mood, Kathleen."

He didn't look as unkempt as Olivia. He looked ready to be out with the horses — breeches, paddock boots, and tucked-in T-shirt. He did, however, appear exhausted, with dark circles under his eyes and a lack of color in his face. Had he been as worried about Olivia as her mother claimed to be? He certainly seemed disturbed yesterday at the mention of Olivia sneaking off with Steve Benz and the mystery man. Benz was really the man toward whom Kathleen should be directing her anger.

"And, where did you pick her up *from?*" Kathleen squared up with Josh, who didn't answer. She stepped away from him and yelled at Olivia, "Where were you?"

"You know what, Mother? It's none of your business." She walked past Michaela and down the hall. "I'm going to have a smoke." A few seconds later a door slammed in the back of the house.

Kathleen fumed at Josh. "You had something to do with this. It's obvious, and I know — I know all about what you and Audrey have been up to with Olivia. Letting her ride those damn horses of Hugh's."

So, she *had* been spying on her daughter. What a tangled web of deceit. Who knew these people would have so much to hide. Why, *why* had Audrey gotten herself mixed up in all of this crazy business?

"I don't need this. I brought her home safely. I gave her a ride, and that's it. I don't believe you. Your horse is suffering, and now with Audrey? You're really disturbed."

"Stay away from my daughter. Do you hear me? Stay away from her!"

"You might be able to control Olivia, but you can't control me. Why don't you let her grow up and live the life she wants to live, not the life you want her to." Josh flicked back a lock of his brown hair that had fallen down over his eyes and walked out.

Kathleen stormed into the back of the house to find Olivia. Michaela heard them shouting back and forth. She couldn't make out exactly what they were saying, but she knew one thing for sure: She needed to get the hell out of there. Luckily because of last night's events, she hadn't even unpacked her overnight bag. When they'd arrived at Kathleen's place, Michaela had put the woman to bed with the help of the driver, then changed into a T-shirt and jeans and stayed awake through night.

She scribbled a note to Kathleen telling her that she'd be in touch, and then she hightailed it out of there. Before heading back to Indio, she decided to have a talk with Josh. She'd see if he was at Hugh's place. He'd been in those photos with Audrey, and they looked chummy. Audrey hadn't mentioned Josh to her, but that didn't mean anything. And, now he was closely linked to Olivia, whose unstable mother kept tabs on her as if she were five and not twenty. And, Josh had behaved oddly last night when he'd learned that Olivia was with Steve Benz. Had she really wound up with Josh? What was that all about?

Plus, what about Bob Pratt? Maybe Josh knew him. Hugh did. It was a small community within the horse-racing world and it was likely that Josh might have known him. Or maybe, just maybe, Audrey had mentioned something to Josh about Bob that, although it had seemed like nothing at the time, could lead to something. No matter what, Michaela couldn't shake the tug inside of her telling her that Bob Pratt's disappearance and his sister's murder were somehow linked. It made sense. But when she'd mentioned it to Detective Merrill last night, he didn't seem too concerned. Then again, the detective appeared to be holding his cards close. Maybe he also thought there was a link. What a mess.

Michaela knew she should just get on the freeway and head home, but someone had murdered her friend, and the ache she felt in her body every time she thought about what had happened to Audrey compelled her to find the answers. *And,* she had an inkling that the answers might lie somewhere amongst this strange crew of individuals Audrey had been associated with.

TWELVE

Michaela pulled into Hugh Bowen's estate and training facility up in the hills of Malibu. Although her ranch was not shabby in the least — her uncle had built up quite an estate — it paled in comparison to Hugh's place. After ringing the button on the security gate and responding to what she guessed had been Hugh's wife, Bridgette, on the other end, the gate opened. She wondered if Bridgette realized who she was. Doubtful.

The road up to the house, if it could be called a house — more of a mansion . . . no, a villa, actually — was cobblestone. Off to one side was a large pasture filled with grazing mares and their foals, the moms busy eating, their babies romping, some nursing. Pretty picture. Michaela sighed and rolled down her window, taking in the sweetness of the leftover marine layer wafting up from the coast only a few miles away.

Off to the other side was a racetrack. Straight ahead she could see an indoor arena, and next to it, holding what she figured was up to a hundred horses, a large barn built of light wood and trimmed in teal and yellow — Bowen's ranch colors. All of his jockeys' silks were in these colors. Amazingly artistic looking. Farther back up on a hill stood the villa, replete with that old-world Italian look: arches and large paned windows, brightly boxed flowers hanging off balconies, and on one side of the house, ivy entwined from the ground on up. The place truly looked like it should be set amid the rolling hills of Tuscany.

She spotted Hugh as she got out of her truck, seated with another man on the first-floor balcony. Her initial plan had not been to see him, but maybe this was a good thing. She could find out if Josh was on the property, and maybe she'd ask Hugh a few questions about Audrey. It had been her impression when they'd run into him at the races that they were still quite close — more than simply a business relationship. Kathleen had obviously failed to come between the friendship that Hugh and Audrey shared.

Hugh waved to her. "Come on up. The front door is open. Go to your right and then out through the doors in the kitchen."

Entering the place, she decided the kitchen area could have filled the first floor of her home. Boy, the Venetian in Vegas had nothing on this place. Once she did find her way outside, Hugh ushered her over. "Good morning. I'm pleased you decided to come by today. I wasn't sure you'd make it, considering last night."

"Me either —" Michaela stopped short. The man with Hugh was Hudson Drake, looking as spectacular as she remembered. She quickly chastised herself for being so shallow, but dammit, the man was handsome and the human side of her told her that it was okay to think that. The friend of Audrey and Jude's — uh, sort of more than a friend — told her that it definitely was *not* okay. Being human right now was not an option.

Hudson extended a hand. "Nice to see you again, Michaela."

"You've met?" Hugh asked.

She nodded.

"Yesterday, as a matter of fact, at the races. We bumped into each other at the bar and discovered we have quite a bit in common," Hudson said.

"Actually, we realized that we both knew you."

"Oh," Hugh replied. "Good. Good."

"I came by, actually," Hudson said, "to talk with Hugh about Bob." He looked at the other man. "I had already told Michaela what I just told you about Bob. It came up in our conversation and we felt it was appropriate for Michaela to tell Audrey that Bob hadn't shown up for work, considering that she knew his sister, and I didn't. It is kind of . . . sensitive."

"No, no, I agree. Of course." Hugh sat back down in one of the wicker chairs and motioned for them to do the same. "Hudson was telling me that he's quite concerned Bob has not shown up at work, and now with Audrey . . ." He shook his head. "I don't know what to think. And, take a look at this." Hugh handed her the newspaper off the table.

It wasn't a front-page story but close enough. The headline read "Police Focus on Brother's Disappearance in Murder." The story went on to say that a source from the Orange County Sheriff's Department believed that Bob Pratt might be responsible for his sister's murder.

Michaela shifted uneasily in the chair.

"Would you like coffee, juice, water, anything?" Hugh asked.

"No thank you. I don't believe this.

They're saying that they think Bob might have killed Audrey and skipped town? But you told me that you haven't seen Bob since Tuesday."

"I told the police that, too," Hudson replied. "The detective — Merrill — seemed to think that Bob not showing up for work since Tuesday was only a guise, possibly to make the police think that he'd been gone since then."

"They're thinking he planned this out, went into hiding, killed his sister, and then took off?" Michaela couldn't believe it. That didn't sound like the Bob Pratt she'd met or heard Audrey talk about.

"It's hard to say what the police think," Hugh said.

"What do you think? Michaela asked.

"I have my suspicions," Hugh said. "But I don't believe that Bob murdered Audrey."

"Hugh was thinking along the same vein as we were yesterday," Hudson added.

"That he's fallen off the wagon and hiding under a rock somewhere?" Michaela asked.

"It is a possibility," Hudson said.

"There's another one," Michaela replied. "What if Audrey's murder is connected to Bob's disappearance? Not that Bob killed Audrey, but . . ."

"You mean, whoever killed Audrey could have taken Bob? *Abducted* him?" Hugh finished her sentence.

"Yes. It does seem strange that Bob disappears, then his sister is murdered. I can understand why the police might target him, but I can't believe he would kill Audrey. What for? Why would he do it?"

Hudson sighed and crossed his arms, leaning back in the chair. "I hate to even think that the cops are right with their speculation, but what if they are? Maybe Bob did kill her for some reason, or had someone else do it."

Hugh shook his head. "No way. Bob and Audrey were close. They loved each other dearly. I can't believe that. Not for a minute. Sure, they had their problems when they were younger, but they'd worked them out, and Audrey always supported Bob. Hell, she came to me about helping him get the job with Eq Tech."

Hudson nodded. "I know. I interviewed Bob. He's great. He really is and I really don't believe that he would do something like that, but it is still difficult to ever really know people, and maybe there were underlying issues that none of us were aware of. It's only a theory and I doubt it's even close to the truth, but we all know that the cops

128

may consider it because of Bob's past addictions."

Hugh fidgeted with one of the buttons on his shirt. "Addictions can destroy you."

Michaela agreed, thinking of her dad, who'd nearly lost his family and himself to his gambling addiction more than once over the years. She also thought she detected something in Hugh's voice that made her wonder if he might have also dealt firsthand with the issue of addiction, or if he'd had a loved one with a problem. She couldn't put her finger on it; maybe it was the tone of his voice or his distant gaze when he'd made the comment. For a second Michaela thought of Olivia and her strange behavior and frazzled appearance that morning. Could Hugh's daughter have a problem with drugs or alcohol?

"Look, the police will be working on locating Bob, in connection with his sister's murder," Hudson said. "It doesn't look good. But we need to find him, to help him out and make sure that he really is all right. I'm planning on hiring a private investigator."

"I know someone. He's good, too," Michaela interjected. Both men looked at her. Hmm, maybe she shouldn't have said anything. Joe Pellegrino was not a PI . . . not technically, anyway. He just had all those cousins who seemed to have numerous ways of finding out information.

"I actually have someone in mind," Hudson said.

"Oh. Well, okay. I just thought that I could help in some way."

"Why don't you talk to your guy, then? I'll talk with this other man I've worked with in the past, and maybe we can come up with something between the two of them."

Hugh nodded. "How can I help?"

Hudson stood and clapped him on the shoulder. "I think you're doing all that you can. We just have to find him."

"Right."

"Didn't you say to Audrey yesterday that you saw him only a few days ago?" Michaela asked Hugh.

He nodded. "I did. He came by and did a vet check on a few of my horses. I talked with him for a few minutes. That was Monday. He didn't act strange or anything. Friendly as always. Pleasant. I only had a few minutes with him, though. I had a meeting to get to. Josh helped him with the horses."

"It makes no sense at all," Michaela said.

The men agreed.

"I hate to run, but it's Sunday morning

and I typically try and make it to mass. I'll be praying about this," Hudson said.

Michaela smiled. She liked the fact that Hudson had faith. She didn't attend church regularly herself, but her mother was a devout Catholic and she'd been raised Catholic, so her roots remained in the church.

"Michaela, I'll see you Saturday night," Hudson said. "I have to get to my office. I'm sorry about your loss. I know your friend meant a lot to you."

"Thank you."

"And Hugh, thank you." Hudson held up a check and waved it. "This will help us to keep up with the growth the company is experiencing."

"I believe in the product," Hugh replied.

Michaela started to bring up Saturday night and how it wasn't going to work out, but Hugh stood and walked Hudson to the door. The timing to bring up Saturday right now was awkward anyway. She'd have to call him about it. She'd also have to give Joe a call and see if he would help her find out what might have happened to Bob Pratt. She didn't like this one bit. She'd been sucked into what had happened to Bob and Audrey, and now a compulsion drove her to want to find out who had done this horrid thing to Audrey, and thus find justice for her friend.

THIRTEEN

When Hugh returned, Michaela decided to ask him some more questions. At this point she had nothing to lose. "I know it might be awkward, but I wanted to talk to you about Audrey and take a look at the horses we discussed. I know that she would have wanted me to do that anyway, and honestly I'm not sure it's sunk in for me yet that . . . she's really gone."

He nodded. "Nor me. Come on down to the barn. I've got to deliver these supplements that Hudson dropped off." He picked up a bucket of Eq Tech's all-around athlete vitamins and minerals. "Good stuff. I'm telling you; since putting my horses on it, I've seen a difference in their performances. I know I sound like a salesman, and sure, I've got plenty of cash tied up in that company, but I really do believe in the product. You using it?"

"Some," Michaela replied. "It's pretty

expensive though. I've got a few of my horses on it."

"I'm sure Hudson would cut you a deal on it." He winked at her. "Did I notice a bit of an interest there?"

Michaela knew she was blushing. "No. As he said, we met yesterday and started talking, that kind of thing. Nice man. Really . . . nice."

Hugh raised his brows. "Uh-huh. Is that why you're going to see him on Saturday night? I imagine he's asked you to the Eq Tech charity event and auction. That's great. He's a good man, and I'll be there, too. I'm offering up two weeks at my vacation home in Capri for the auction. I'm certain we'll be seated at the same table. Josh and Olivia will be there . . . and word is, so will my ex-wife." His face darkened.

"Oh, that. No. Well, yes, he did ask me. Actually, agreeing was a rash decision on my part, and now the timing couldn't be worse. I won't be going. Speaking of Josh, is he around?" She wanted to change the subject.

"No. He's out right now. But we don't need him to show the horses. Back to Saturday night. I disagree with you. I think the timing is what we all need."

"What?"

"I know what Audrey would have told you. She would have wanted you to go out and live your life. Live it up."

"I'm sure that's what she'd say, too, but I don't feel right about it."

"Bull. I say think about it. Losing Audrey makes me realize a lot about the way I've been living my life, and I plan to make changes. Big changes."

Michaela thought she heard a catch in his throat. She wanted to ask him what he meant but didn't feel all that comfortable prying.

They started to walk out the massive front door, only to run into Bridgette, Hugh's wife, sauntering down the stairs and into the entryway dressed to the nines. She froze when she spotted Michaela. "Hello," she said curtly.

"Good morning," Michaela replied and decided it best to bury the hatchet with her, even though she didn't trust the woman as far as she could throw her. "I want to apologize for yesterday. It was an awful situation and I was pretty emotional."

"I understand and accept your apology." She looked at Hugh. "Honey, I have to go into L.A. for a lunch appointment, and I thought maybe I'd do some shopping on Rodeo Drive first." She ran her hands over

135

her tight black pencil skirt — as if it needed any straightening — then fiddled with the waist of her white crepe low-cut blouse, which exposed cleavage and a very large diamond necklace matching the stones in her ears. She fluffed up her long brunette hair and smiled. "I shouldn't be too late."

"Considering what's happened, I'm not sure that going to Beverly Hills makes sense," he said.

"What? Why?"

He looked at her incredulously. "Bridgette, you found a friend of ours murdered yesterday. I would think that might affect you."

She nodded and frowned. "It was horrible. I liked Audrey."

Michaela watched her face. She was lying again. She had *not* liked Audrey. And Michaela did not like Bridgette Bowen any better today. She could even hear the lie in the woman's voice. But why lie? And why did she dislike Audrey? Because Audrey didn't care for her, or because of Audrey's relationship with Kathleen and Olivia? Or . . . was there another reason?

"I can't cancel my luncheon," Bridgette said. "It's for the charity event I'm doing with my Cedars-Sinai hospital group. We're trying to raise money for heart disease research. It's important and it will keep my mind off of yesterday's horrible events."

"I don't think it's a good idea. It feels insensitive to me," Hugh said.

"Honey, I am on the board and I can't bring Audrey back. I might as well raise money to help others."

"Fine. You go do what you need to do."

"Thank you." She nodded at Michaela. "Nice to see you again."

Oh, she was good with the lies. Actually she kind of sucked at them, but she sure dispensed plenty of them. "Nice to see you, too." Two could play that game.

"Ciao, honey. I'll be home in time for dinner. I've asked Lucita to make your favorite pork loin recipe. And her delicious crème brûlée. I thought a good meal would lift the gloom a bit."

Hugh opened the front door for Michaela. "Let's go see the horses." She followed him out and around the corner, where he climbed into a golf cart. "This driveway is a bitch to get around, and the older I get the less I want to make that trek down to the barn and back. Come on, hop in. Wanna drive it?"

"I think I'll let you do the honors." Michaela laughed as she got into the passenger seat.

"Can I ask if your ex-wife knew that you

and Audrey had remained such close friends?"

"Oh, ha. No, she didn't. Kathleen has a horrid temper. Piss her off, she's like a rattlesnake. No one wants to get in the way of her wrath. I know, because I'm always in it. She is constantly taking me back to court for more money. Don't ask me what she spends it on, but the woman can go through cash faster than anyone I've ever known. Everything has to be first class. And now I've married her younger twin. Kathleen plays up the martyr act, but it's only an act. Trust me."

Michaela recalled Kathleen's anger toward Olivia that morning. "Did you see Audrey other than when she came to buy horses?"

"Now and again. She'd come up to take a look at horses, or we'd visit over lunch. We talked every week about Olivia or . . . you know, life, things." His voice trailed off. "I'll miss her."

Michaela noticed tears in his eyes. "Me, too."

"I can't believe she's gone. Nor why anyone would do this. Everyone loved Audrey. Dearly. How could you not? She was kind, generous, loving, and beautiful. I adored her."

"Sounds like you did."

His words again made Michaela think that there had been something going on between Audrey and Hugh. This was the second time she'd wondered about it. "You knew Audrey for a long time, didn't you?"

"More than twenty-five years."

"She worked for you?"

"She did."

"Waitress, wasn't she?"

"She was more than a *waitress*. She and Kathleen were the entertainment at the original Bowen's in Malibu. That's how we all met. They worked for me, and one night I overheard them talking about how they'd like to sing. I asked them if they had any talent and they said that they did. I told them to put something together and I'd listen, maybe let them sing at the restaurant. They did, and they were great. Packed them in. Audrey had a beautiful voice and could play the guitar. And Kathleen, she could sing, too, and play the harmonica."

Michaela laughed. That one was hard to imagine.

He looked at her with amusement as they entered the impressive barn, row upon row of horses — some sticking their heads outside their stalls to see the guests, a few nickers here and there, some pawing at the ground. "I know what you're thinking —

Kathleen playing a harmonica."

"It doesn't quite fit with the picture of your ex."

He frowned. "Not today, anyway. But she wasn't always so uptight. She was a wild one. Audrey had a calming influence on her. Always the peaceful one, you know."

"I do. Audrey's nature was definitely gentle."

"I look back on those years and I know that she was the one I should have married. If I had, she might be alive today, and I know we would have lasted."

His words took her aback. She decided to take a chance: "You were in love with her, weren't you?"

Hugh didn't hold back his tears any longer. "I always was. Always."

"Did she know?"

"Yes. She knew. She definitely knew. I asked her to marry me last week."

FOURTEEN

"Wh-what?" Michaela asked, sputtering on the question.

Hugh nodded slowly, tears now streaming down his face. "I've made huge mistakes in my life, and letting Audrey slip through my fingers was the biggest. And now, she's gone."

"But you're married. I mean, I guess, um . . ." Michaela's head spun over this revelation. "Okay, I'm sorry, I know this is none of my business, but I have to ask: Were you and Audrey having an affair?"

"No. Audrey would never do that. Never. What we had was far more special than something as lurid as an affair. We had a *connection*. A real connection. We may not have ever had anything physical, but we did have an affair of the heart. In a sense, I suppose that's as bad. But I think it's worse for the two people who love each other not to figure it out than it is for the spouses. It's a travesty all the way around. I realized that last week after we had lunch, so I bought a ring and asked her to marry me."

"Did she say yes?"

"She did. And it was yesterday that I planned to tell Bridgette." He smiled, but his eyes betrayed his sadness.

Something told Michaela she'd found the reason why Bridgette didn't think highly of Audrey. Somehow, Bridgette knew about Audrey, or at least the love Hugh felt for her. How could a woman not sense that type of thing?

"And, now . . . now she's gone." He broke down.

Michaela put her arms around him. "I am so sorry."

He gently pulled away from her and wiped his face. "Please don't tell anyone. You're the only one who knows. I know what she meant to you and I had to tell someone. We were getting ready to tell everyone after I ended things between me and Bridgette. I wanted it to be as amicable as possible. I wasn't out to hurt anyone; I just didn't want to live a lie any longer. I've been doing it for years. And, even though she's gone and we won't ever be married, I have to divorce Bridgette. That's what I meant when I said that I needed to make changes. I also need to find out who murdered Audrey." The lines in his forehead creased deeply. "I'll kill whoever did this!" he exclaimed.

Michaela wanted to ask him why, if he'd loved Audrey for all these years, had this revelation not dawned on him earlier, causing him to pursue Audrey sooner than later. But he was so upset that she decided not to say anything further about their relationship for now. The man was distraught and it didn't feel right to delve into his or Audrey's personal life any more than she already had.

Hugh seemed to want to change the subject as he stopped in front of one of the horse's stalls. "Geyser. Good boy, he is. Audrey loved him. Wanted to take him to her place, but with the changes we were about to make that wouldn't have been necessary. She would have moved in here with me and sold her place in Indio." Geyser stuck his head out of the stall. Hugh patted the handsome dapple gray. "Hey, there." He looked back at Michaela. "Won a lot of races. And, he's sound."

"Rare," she replied, referring to the horse's legs. Soundness in a horse signified that they weren't lame, which was hard to come by, especially in a retired racehorse. These were animals that for a time in their life went at full speed, with all one thousand pounds or more beating down on their fine legs. "How old is he?"

"Eleven now. I've had him all his life, and he likes it here, but he's a real social guy. He'd love the attention that kids would shower on him."

"I can see that," Michaela said and laughed as the gelding nudged her hand, wanting a pat.

"But there are no kids around here, and when Audrey called me to ask if I might have a good horse for a kid, my first thought was Geyser. I have to tell you, he's not one I want to let go of. But when Audrey told me that he'd be for you, I knew he'd have a great home. Plus, she wanted you to have him."

"You know how I feel about my animals. They come to stay."

"That's a good thing. I don't know how profitable it is, but it's a good thing. You want to take him out, give him a go?"

"Yeah."

Hugh led Geyser from the stall. One of the grooms came by and offered to saddle him up. Hugh said that would be fine, and he finished showing Michaela around the barn.

When Geyser was ready, she put him first through some basic paces and then challenged him some. He still had his get up and go, but was responsive and definitely good natured. He'd be perfect for what she had in mind. "I love him. How much do you want for him?"

"He's yours."

"What?"

"Take him. My gift; but if you ever want to get rid of him, you bring him back here."

"But why? Why would you give him to me?"

"Because I know how much Audrey cared for you, and I want you to have him. And as I said, *she* wanted you to have him."

"I can't do that."

"Fine. Give me a dollar and we'll call it even." He smiled and it was warm, kind — just as Audrey had been.

God, she wished they could have been together.

"Please, Michaela. He's a good boy. He'll make the kids you're working with happy. I want you to have him."

The kids. Joe's proposition of working with his daughter and more autistic kids crossed her mind. Geyser would be perfect for the children. Was she really thinking about accepting the position? Maybe so. As Hugh had told her, Audrey would have wanted her to enjoy her life, and the joy she got out of working with Genevieve was evident.

She finally agreed. "I'll pick him up later this week, if that's okay. I need to get back home, check on things. And I don't have my trailer with me. Day after tomorrow work for you?"

"Works great."

"Good. But you have to promise me that you'll come out and visit. Watch him with the kids."

"You can count on it. Like I said, I hate to see him go, but know he'll be in a good place. I will be out to see him. He'll be great with the kids. Won't you?" Hugh rubbed Geyser's face.

Michaela hung his bridle back up in the tack room as Hugh put him back in his stall. Turning around, she bumped into a slightly built Mexican man. "Oh, excuse me. I didn't know anyone was there."

"Is okay," he replied curtly.

Hugh walked in. "Oh, I see you've met Enrique."

"Sort of," Michaela replied and laughed. Enrique didn't smile. *Jeez, lighten up.*

"Enrique Perez, this is Michaela Bancroft. Enrique is my jockey. The best around."

"Thank you, sir."

"It's true. Won the race on Chico yesterday."

"Good horse. Nice to meet you, *señorita.*" He warmed slightly.

"You, too," she replied.

"*Señor,* I need to leave a bit early. It's my brother. I have something to take care of with him."

Hugh frowned. "Is he in trouble again?"

"No, no. He promise me no more problems especially now that you give him a job. He real happy about it, and me, too. No problems at all, just need to go with him to an appointment."

Hugh slapped Enrique on the back. As the jockey left the barn, they returned to the golf cart. "Man works so hard with these animals and he's got this brother — Juan — who has had some troubles with the law, but Enrique assures me the man is turning his life around. Sure hope so. I took a chance on him because of Enrique and hired him to take care of the mechanical stuff around here. So far so good. He does do a good job, but the jury is still out, if you know what I mean."

"I know what you mean. Family can be difficult."

"Yes, they can."

"Before I head out, do you think your

trainer might be back?"

"Josh? I'm not sure. He may be with a horse on the exercise track. I know that he got a late start this morning. Why?"

"I . . . have some technical stuff to ask him." She didn't know if Hugh was aware that Josh had brought Olivia home, that the girl and her mother had already had quite an argument that morning. She decided to find out if he knew the answer to the burning question. "Hey, did you ever locate Olivia last night?"

"Yes. I sent Josh to pick her up. That idiot Steve Benz convinced her to go out with them."

"Them?"

"Him and his manager — Marshall Friedman. Don't trust either one of them as far as I can throw them. Friedman has been trying to get Olivia to sign with him and leave Audrey. Sure, the guy can boost her career, but I don't like it at all. The guy is a jerk."

"Was she here then, last night?"

"By the time I located her it was almost one in the morning. I told Josh to pick her up and take her to her mother's, who I figured would be worried sick to death about her. She's recently moved into her own apartment, but I knew with what had

148

happened yesterday that Kathleen would've expected Olivia to come home."

Michaela decided not to tell him that Olivia hadn't made it to Kathleen's until after seven that morning. Where she'd been with Josh for those six hours was a question. Her mind wandered — could the two of them have simply been comforting each other all night?

Or did they have something to hide?

FIFTEEN

After saying good-bye to Hugh, Michaela found Josh down at the exercise track, dismounting a beautiful sorrel horse. She called to him. He waved at her. She walked up and the horse turned his head, taking curious note of the newcomer. "Gorgeous animal."

"Chapman's Lightning. We call him Chappy around here. A lot of heart, but not so fast on the track. The lightning part of the name is kind of a joke. He'd rather be back in his stall finishing his breakfast. But they all need their exercise. Personally, I think Hugh should sell him and a few others. Racing is a money-making business, but Hugh has a philosophy: Horses come here to stay and if they leave, he knows where they're going. It's either on their way to heaven or to the barn of someone he knows and trusts."

"Like Audrey."

Josh nodded and looked down at the ground, digging his paddock boots in. "Like Audrey. Can't believe what happened. She was a nice woman and good with horses."

"I know."

"I thought coming out here this morning that maybe I'd be able to erase some of yesterday from my mind, but it's not possible."

"For me either," Michaela replied.

"I'm guessing you're here to look at some of Hugh's old guys. He mentioned to me that you had an interest in lesson horses."

"I already had a look. I'll be picking up Geyser later this week. I wanted to talk to you before I left, though."

"Ah. Geyser, huh? Good boy. He'll be great with kids. Look, I can figure out why you wanted to talk to me. I'm sorry about that scene this morning with Kathleen and Olivia. I wish you hadn't seen that. Kathleen is difficult to deal with." He shoved a hand into a pocket of his breeches and pulled out a can of chew.

Michaela nodded. "She does come across as high-maintenance."

"You don't know the half of it. She wasn't so bad when she was married to Hugh. But after the divorce she wigged out. I think Audrey was probably one of the last ones to stand by her. The rest of her friends disappeared. And, Olivia . . . well, this thing is going to be hard for her to deal with. I think she loved Audrey more than her own mother. Not that anyone would blame her for that." He fiddled with the can and then shoved it back into his pocket. "Trying to quit."

"Kathleen does seem to keep a tight leash on Olivia."

"You saw it for yourself. The woman is a total control freak. Olivia has no desire to sing. She wants to be a jockey."

"And you've been letting her ride, haven't you?"

Josh didn't answer her right away. Her stomach sank as his eyes narrowed at her question. "Kathleen put you up to this? Are you here to grill me about Olivia because that old bag sent you? She's sicker than I thought."

Michaela shook her head. "No. That's not why I'm here. I'm trying to make some sense out of what happened to Audrey. There probably isn't any to be made, but I feel like I have to try. Olivia, Kathleen, and I were the last people to have any interaction with her before she died, and I thought that maybe Olivia said something to you about Audrey since you were with her last night. I already know that Hugh asked you to get her from Steve Benz's place around one this morning, and I also know that by the time she got home, it was after seven. I thought maybe you two would have talked."

"I told Olivia about Audrey on the drive back from Beverly Hills. She lost it, which I expected. I took her home with me because she asked me to. Said that she didn't want to be alone and she couldn't deal with her mother yet. I comforted a distraught friend. That's it." His anger was obvious. He started to lead the horse away from her toward the barn.

"Sorry, I didn't intend to upset you."

He stopped. "What do you want? Really?"

She sighed. "I want to know why Olivia went off with Benz in the first place. I want to know if she ever said anything to you about Audrey acting strange, especially lately."

"Olivia was shanghaied last night by Steve Benz and his ass of a manager, Marshall Friedman."

"How did that happen? I was with Olivia when she was getting ready to perform and he came by, hitting on her. She didn't seem interested in him." Michaela also recalled how rude Benz was to Audrey, who had tried keeping him away from her god-daughter.

"She's not interested in him. You can probably thank Kathleen for Benz dropping by to bug Olivia."

"What?"

"Sure, she played all innocent this morning. The *ever*-concerned parent. I'll tell you what she is: She's one of those psycho stage mothers. Olivia is a grown woman and her mother wants to make a superstar out of her . . . forget what her daughter wants."

That didn't make a lot of sense. Sure the control freak–psycho mother part sort of fit, but Kathleen's anger about Olivia's disappearance seemed real to her.

Chappy stomped his foot and pawed at the ground. "I've got to get this saddle off of him."

"Sure." Michaela followed him to the barn set up next to the track. This one was smaller than the other across the track and up the hill, where Hugh had taken her. It was obviously only used for the horses just after their exercise. Josh slid the horse's bridle off him and replaced it with a halter, securing both sides of it with cross ties to finish taking off his tack and get him over to the wash rack. As he scraped Chappy with a sweat scraper, she continued to probe. "Tell me how Olivia wound up with Benz and

Friedman."

"Olivia was angry."

"About what?"

"No, angry with me."

"Why?"

"I wouldn't let her exercise Chico that morning."

"Does her dad know?"

"No. She asked me not to tell. She's afraid her mom would find out."

Michaela didn't tell him that Kathleen already knew. Those photos she'd found proved that much. She was afraid that if she revealed it to Josh, he'd go ballistic. Although he seemed like a nice guy, he'd also given her reason to believe he had a temper.

"Olivia is a good kid, but she does like to get her way. How could she not, being the only child in this clan? She doesn't like to hear the word *no*."

"From what I've heard so far, she does seem to have a problem saying it to her mother."

He agreed. "I don't get it. Kathleen has a hold on her. And she had one on Audrey. As much as I know Audrey loved Olivia, and she knew what Olivia's real dream in life is, but she'd never say a word to Kathleen about it. She'd never tell her to back off or leave her alone and let Olivia live her

155

own life. I could never get that."

"It wasn't really Audrey's responsibility, do you think? To tell Kathleen to not interfere with her daughter?"

"I do think she was responsible in some way. Audrey knew Olivia better than her mother does, and they were tight. Do I think she should have told Kathleen to back off her daughter? Yeah, I do. I also think that she shouldn't have been a partner in Olivia's career. But even Audrey, who could see how happy Olivia was when she rode on the track, came to me and asked me to try and dissuade Olivia — that her parents wouldn't be happy about our morning sessions."

"Did Olivia exercise horses a lot?"

He shrugged. "When she could get away from Mama's clutches. Audrey brought her here when she was in town. Kathleen trusted Audrey with Olivia and would have never guessed she was bringing her to the track to ride. Since Olivia moved into her own place last month after a battle with her mother, she's been showing up here more often."

"You said that Olivia was angry with you yesterday, but what does that have to do with her going with Benz, and her mom setting it up?"

He unhooked Chappy from the cross ties and walked him over to the wash rack, Michaela in tow. She turned on the hose while he led the horse onto the concrete slab, then took the hose from her, rinsing him down. Water sprayed onto Michaela. "Sorry," Josh said.

"No biggie. I do it every day."

"You train reiners, don't you?"

"Yeah. It's a great sport."

"Fun to watch, kind of like the dressage of the western discipline, but for me, there's nothing better than the track."

"I can see that. For Olivia, too, obviously." Michaela was starting to wonder if Josh was deliberately trying to change the subject. "What do you think about this thing with Olivia and Benz?"

He turned off the hose and threw it to the ground. "The dickhead got Olivia plowed, probably spiked her drink. I don't know, because she told me that she didn't have any more than two drinks before leaving the track with them. They took his limo up to Beverly Hills, where they had dinner. She says that Benz and Friedman harangued her, promising her the good life and telling her they could make her a star and she should sign on with Friedman as her manager."

"Did she?"

"Nope. It was about that time when I found her. Her dad tracked her down and sent me to get her. They even had a contract already drawn up, and like I said, I would not be surprised if Kathleen was behind the whole thing. It'd be just like her."

"What about you and Olivia?"

He stopped grooming the horse and eyed her. "What about me and Olivia? There is no *me and Olivia*."

Michaela studied him, not knowing if she should believe him about what had happened with Olivia last night. Her gut, his actions and reactions to her questions, caused her to believe that, if there was not anything more going on between Josh and Olivia than just friendship, Josh would have liked there to be. "I better get going. I've got a long drive back to Indio."

He nodded. "Hey, I am really sorry about Audrey. It's a shame."

Michaela nodded and walked to her truck. She got the feeling after talking to Josh that he had some ill feelings toward Audrey. He felt that she needed to be the one to make Kathleen loosen the noose around her daughter's neck. And, there were feelings there. Michaela could tell that Josh cared for Olivia. He was far more defensive about her than he needed to be. She could not help wondering if Josh was so infatuated with Olivia and possibly so twisted in his thinking when it came to her, that he'd do anything to see the young woman get her way.

Even kill for her?

SIXTEEN

Michaela placed a call to Ethan as she drove the 10 East back to Indio.

"Hey, you," he said, sounding more upbeat than he had early that morning.

"Hi. Well?" She sucked in a breath.

"He's out of surgery and in the recovery pool so that when he wakes up, he doesn't thrash about and reinjure himself. We were lucky this facility is so close to the track. They have an excellent team here."

"What can you tell me about the break? What are his chances?"

"I'd say they're good. As I explained, he has a condylar break. He broke it all the way through. It was clean. The break below the pastern is what could threaten him, but he didn't shatter it, so from this point on we're looking at a long haul. I'm optimistic, though. In a lot of ways, this will be up to Halliday. His attitude is going to be important, just like a human patient, and how well he reacts up in the hoist, off his feet for some time. It's vital that we keep his weight balanced and not put any undue pressure on the other three legs. We want to avoid laminitis at all costs because then we could have an entirely new problem on our hands. It'll really be his temperament that gets him through. If he can tolerate us and him babying that leg for the next several weeks, then he should come out of this."

"That's great."

"Yeah, and from everything I've seen so far, this animal has a good temperament. Sometimes in these cases, if a horse can't tolerate the treatment there's the risk of re-injuring the leg, and if that happens it can be many times worse than the initial break. So that's why we'll stay cautious, plus watch for infection. He should be coming out of the anesthesia soon and once that happens, I'm going to head back home. I'll make the commute over the next few weeks rather than stay here. With Summer only being a few weeks from delivering the baby, I'm trying to stay close to home."

Michaela cleared her throat. "That's probably a good idea. Can I ask how you got involved in this?"

He paused. "I wanted to wait and tell you at the barbecue, but considering this situation . . . I became certified as a state vet, Mick. That way I can vet at the track. I thought it might be an interesting challenge. Yesterday when Halliday sustained the injury, I happened to know the vets on the surgical team and was invited to take part in performing the surgery. Since I was with him for the ride down and saw the injury happen, I wanted to be here with him. The vets have been kind enough to allow me to be involved."

"Wow. I had no idea that you wanted to vet the track. That's great." She considered telling him about Audrey. It was obvious he didn't know. Sooner or later he would, but he seemed genuinely happy at that moment — he was pretty sure Halliday would recover and he and his wife had a baby on the way. He'd be upset over Audrey's death, and Michaela didn't want to put a damper on his day. She also did not want to go to the barbecue–baby shower deal.

"I've got some other good news: We found out the baby is a boy."

"Oh, Ethan, I think that's wonderful. You're going to be a great dad."

"I hope so. I'm looking forward to it. One of the other vets told me about this baby store close by the center. I thought I'd stop on my way home and pick something up for him. Who would have ever known I'd get all mushy over a kid?"

"I knew you would."

"That's not saying much, you know me better than I know myself."

She laughed. "Probably so. Okay well, I'll see you Friday, then, if not before. And keep me posted on the horse. Hey, by the way, does Kathleen Bowen know about Halliday yet?"

"I've tried calling a few times and got no answer. I finally left a message on her answering machine to call the center for an update. It's surprising that she hasn't made the trip down here. Maybe she's on her way."

She doubted that. For all the concern Kathleen had portrayed about Halliday the day before, Michaela had to wonder if she was off taking care of what she considered more important matters, like delving into her daughter's affairs. "Maybe."

"Hey, Mick, you're not still planning on taking care of this horse's bill?"

"Yes, I am."

"I don't get that."

"Tell you what, I'll explain it all to you when I see you."

"You'd better."

■ ■ ■ ■

Michaela turned into her place before 1 p.m. and found Joe and Genevieve standing out by the barn. Oh no, she'd forgotten that she was to give Gen a lesson that afternoon. Part of her wanted to cancel it, take time to think about Audrey. She hadn't mourned her loss; not really. But she couldn't do that to Gen, and working with the little girl would be therapeutic for her as well. It would be what Audrey would want her to do. She got out of the truck, spotted Audrey's overnight bag still in the backseat, and sighed. She'd deal with it later.

"Hey, I'm sorry. I forgot about today. I've been in L.A. . . . and oh God . . . anyway, I'm sorry."

Joe looked at his watch. "I was ready to send one of my cousins out after you." He laughed. "Never knew you to be fifteen minutes late for nuthin'. You okay?"

"Sure. A bit of traffic, that's all."

"And you couldn't pick up that cell phone you got glued to your ear half the time?"

"Joe. Stop it." She smiled at him. "Hey, by the way, I need to talk to you about your cousins."

"What you need?'

"Some information on a guy named Bob Pratt. He's a veterinarian. I thought one of your cousins might be able to find something out about him."

"What gives, Mick?" He bent down to Gen. "Go get the horse a carrot, sweetheart. Daddy and Miss Michaela are gonna talk for a minute, okay?"

Gen nodded and walked toward the feed room, where she knew Michaela kept the veggie drawer in the fridge stocked with carrots and apples.

She sighed. "His sister was a friend of mine and she was murdered yesterday. Bob is missing. Has been for the past four or five days."

"Oh no. I'm sorry about your friend, but you don't need to go messing into this. I'm smelling trouble here."

"Please. All I want to know is if the guy has fallen off the wagon. He's had a drinking problem in the past, and his sister helped him get back on his feet. I find it hard to think that he might be involved in her murder, but with him incognito it does not look good. The police seem to think he killed her and is on the run. I'm actually hoping he's on a bender somewhere. And, that's where you or one of your cousins might be able to help out. That's it. Just want to know if he is okay. That is all I need to know, and then I'll drop it. Promise." She crossed her heart.

"Where was he living? And, what about where he worked?"

"L.A."

"Okay, got some cousins in L.A. that might be able to help me out. We'll see. But that's it. *Capisce?* No more this crazy you-playing-Miss-P.I. business. Hear?"

"You got it. Thanks."

"Okay, so the guy lives in the City of Angels. You know any of his pals? Where he works? His address, phone number? I gotta have something to go on."

Michaela gave him the information that she had, which wasn't much, other than his employer, that he worked the track, and had been to rehab at Betty Ford within the last year.

"That's a start. Now you gotta do me a favor." She knew this was coming. "You gotta call that director over at Genevieve's school and tell her that you want to organize the riding program. I've done a lot for you, Michaela." He crossed his arms over his wide chest.

"You sure know how to guilt a girl, don't you?"

He smiled. "You know and I know that

you are perfect for this." He took out his wallet and handed her a card. "Call this gal, tell her you'll set it up."

She sighed. "Okay, Joe, I'll give it a shot."

"Good woman. I knew you'd do it." He pointed a finger at her. "Now go and work with my kid. I'll see what I can find out about this Pratt dude."

Michaela looked at Gen walking back to them, carrot in hand, her dark, curly hair pulled into a low ponytail in order to fit her helmet over it, her big brown eyes staring straight ahead. She took the little girl's hand. "Thanks."

Joe bent down and gave his daughter a kiss on the cheek. "I'm proud of you, pretty girl. I know you're going to be great up there today. Miss Michaela will take good care of you. Daddy is gonna come up and watch soon. I have to make some phone calls." He winked at Michaela.

Michaela put a halter around Booger. He was perfect for Gen. Calm, well behaved, with no intention of moving any faster than a walk. The new horse she'd purchased from Hugh that morning, Geyser, would be the right addition for Jude's daughter. Katie was up for the challenge of a horse that would eagerly move out.

Together they brushed the horse. Michaela placed a hand over Gen's on the brush and they stroked Booger's coat. She spoke in calm, hushed tones. "That's good. See how clean he's getting?" Michaela asked. "What a good job you're doing, Gen. Look at how pretty you're making Booger. He likes that a lot."

Once Booger had the therapeutic saddle on him and Michaela slid a headstall over his ears, she kept him on a lead line and, after putting Gen up on him, led him up to the arena. There, Booger did as Michaela asked him, and Gen finally smiled from ear to ear when Michaela put Booger into a jog on the lead line. "Look at you ride Booger. You have a great seat. Stay with the horse. Keep your bottom in the saddle. Wow. Nice job, Gen. Really good."

After they finished their lesson they headed back to the barn, where Michaela had Gen get the carrot out of the groom caddy. Michaela broke the carrot into threes and reminded Gen to hold her palm flat so the horse couldn't nip her fingers or hand. "He wouldn't mean to do it," Michaela said. "But it could happen. So, we hold our hand out like this." She held out her palm flat then, with the other hand she smoothed Gen's hand out, placing a carrot in her hand and putting her own hand underneath the child's to keep it stable. Booger took the carrot gently and Gen smiled again. Peace and a genuine feeling of happiness came over Michaela for those few minutes alone with the girl. This was what life was about. The moments where a real connection happened.

While Michaela put Booger back in his stall, she told Gen that there was a treat for her inside the tack room. The girl knew what that meant. It had become a ritual since she'd started working with her. Katie was also aware of the cookie jar. Michaela made sure that she baked a new batch every few days for the girls, and when they were done with a lesson they could have one.

Joe came into Michaela's office while Gen ate her cookie. "I'm still checking this dude out, seeing what I can get on him. I'll give you a call when I know something."

"Thanks," Michaela said, hoping inside that Joe and the cousins would find out what had happened to Bob Pratt.

SEVENTEEN

After Joe and Gen left, Dwayne showed up. He'd had Rocky, who appeared to have recovered from his bizarre "attack" the other day, out on the hot walker. Michaela kept her fingers crossed that it had been an isolated incident.

"You doing good with that kid," Dwayne said.

"Thank you. How is Rocky doing?"

"He be okay, you know. No more problems. The vet call me and say he had some higher testosterone levels than normal. She say that could be causing him a problem."

"Interesting. Did she know what might be causing it?"

"No. She ask if you give the horses any kind of bute or steroid."

Michaela laughed. "Oh, sure. I'm all about drugging these animals up. Why would she ask that?"

"Dunno. I think she trying to figure it all

out. She say that she have Dr. Slater take a look when he get in tomorrow. She don't seem to know. Say maybe something with his pituitary gland."

"Hmm. Okay, well, I'm glad Ethan will be taking a look; if anyone can figure this out, it might be him."

"Michaela, you okay? You looking tired."

She sighed. "No. I'm not okay." She told him about Audrey.

"Oh, lady, you been through a lot these last coupla years. Losing Uncle Lou, then old Cocoa passing on," Dwayne said, mentioning her chocolate lab, who she'd lost in the spring to old age. "Now your friend." He shook his head. "Must be good things on the horizon for you. Hawaiian spirituality tell us that when there are tough times to be grateful, cause there are nothing but good things coming around the corner. Everything happen for a reason and it serve you."

She touched his shoulder. He was good to have around.

"Hey, hey! I'm ready for my riding lesson."

Michaela turned to see Camden bounding down the breezeway. Holy cow! Was she actually wearing Wranglers and a pair of riding boots? "Whoa! What is going on here?" Michaela stifled a laugh as she remembered the last time Camden got on a horse and nearly broke her tailbone falling off the other side.

"Oh, hey you. Didn't know you would be back so soon from L.A. Yeah, well I decided that if I'm going to live on a ranch, I might as well learn how to ride. And Dwayne is teaching me." Camden flashed a smile at him.

"Huh. Really?" She glanced at Dwayne, who had turned a shade darker than his native skin tone. He nodded. Okay, something was up between these two.

"Yes. Really."

Michaela bit her tongue and for some comic relief watched Camden in the arena while Dwayne gave her a riding lesson. To her surprise, Camden did well up on the horse. She'd been on a horse more than a few times of late, because there was no way that the Camden Michaela had out on a horse a while back was the same woman on her mare Macy right now. She shook her head, confused, and decided to let it go for now. But later, when Camden had filled up on margaritas, she planned to ask her what in the world was really going on. She'd never shown an interest in horses and she'd been living with Michaela for almost two years.

She let the two of them finish their lesson and went on down to the house where, to her surprise, she found a dozen pink roses in her kitchen. Camden and her admirers. She picked up the card and saw that they were for her: from Hudson Drake. *Looking forward to Saturday.* "Great," Michaela said out loud. "What the hell am I going to do?"

"About what?" She jumped and looked up to see Jude Davis leaning against the kitchen doorway. "Sorry, it was open and I saw you standing there. Didn't mean to frighten you. Who are the roses from?" He walked into the kitchen.

He smelled good — kind of tropical, coconut maybe. He looked good, too. He always looked good with his blue eyes and rugged features, and he dressed how she liked a man to dress — simple; jeans, nice shirt. No sport coat today. Sunday was his day off. She set down the card. "Oh, um, just this guy who . . . well, I met him at the races and he knew some of the same people that I know and I don't know, I gave him my card and I kind of offered to do him a favor."

"Favor? Must have been a pretty good one." Jude smiled and rocked back on his heels. It was a nervous habit that Michaela had noticed.

"Wait, no, it's nothing. I only told him that I'd relay a message for him." She thought back to the conversation she'd had with Hudson and her plans to inform Audrey about Bob. It was not something she wanted to get into with Jude, the cop.

"Must have been some message."

"Jude!" she implored.

"Hey, no big deal. So, some guy sent you a dozen roses. I'm not dumb. Men are going to pursue you. And I personally don't mind a bit of competition."

"You don't?" She wasn't sure how she felt about that. "Why?"

"Because I plan on coming out the winner."

"Really?"

"Really."

He walked over to her. His eyes reflected a bright intensity. "I think I can top the flowers." He pulled her into him and kissed her. The touch of his lips, his hands on her waist, all of it shocked her, but she didn't resist. The kiss was sweet, smooth, and really nice. It shot a surge of electricity through her as her heart raced and what felt like a thousand butterflies fluttered in her stomach. Wow. She hadn't been kissed like that in a very long time. In fact, she wasn't sure she'd ever been kissed like that at all. She pulled away from him. "Yeah."

"Yeah what?"

"That was better than roses."

He pointed at her and started to leave. "There is more where that came from."

"Wait. Where are you going? Why did you come by?"

He smiled. "Just to say hi. And see when you'd like to go out for dinner. How about Friday?"

"Friday? Oh, uh . . ."

"Oh no, no. You just told me that the kiss beat out the roses."

"It did. Definitely. Hands down. It's that, um, it's Summer and Ethan Slater's baby shower–barbecue thing on Friday. God, I don't even know exactly, but it's kind of this couples thing, and I thought . . ."

"Yes, I'll go."

"I didn't ask."

"You were going to though, weren't you?"

"Maybe."

"So we'll have dinner another night. Friday we'll go to a baby shower–barbecue instead." He laughed. "See you Friday."

"See you Friday," she uttered, bringing her fingers up to her lips, still burning from Jude's touch.

EIGHTEEN

Michaela tried to make light of Jude's kiss, but it stuck with her for the rest of the day. Why did he have to go and do that? It only made everything that much more confusing. But confusing about what? she chided herself. He liked her, she liked him; maybe they could have something together. Why did that have to mean *confusion?* Why couldn't she be more like Camden and just go with it, and if it didn't work out . . . well, then it didn't. But she wasn't like that. As much as she thought she'd like to be, she simply wasn't, and therefore Jude's kiss caused her confusion, some stress, as well as a smile when she thought about it.

What wasn't making her smile and was also making her crazy was Audrey's murder, and she wondered if the police had made any headway at all in the investigation, other than focusing on Bob as the killer. She hesitated to pick up the phone and call

Detective Merrill. What kind of questions could she ask him anyway? She did want to know if they had discovered anything new. It probably wasn't such a good idea to call Merrill, and she knew she should drop it anyway. She was doing what she could by asking Joe to help her out, and he'd promised to give her a call if he found out anything.

The sun was going down, which meant it was time to feed the animals and make herself some dinner. She'd let Dwayne have the night off since he'd covered for her while she was in L.A. Funny, she hadn't seen Camden *or* Dwayne since the riding lesson. She couldn't wait to quiz Camden about her newfound interest. Where had they disappeared to?

She filled the wheelbarrow with several flakes of hay and distributed it to her "kids." She then went back into the feed room and filled buckets with supplements for the handful she fed them to. Rocky nickered as she came to his stall with his bucket of treats. She dumped the contents into his feeder and he immediately dove in. "It's the good stuff you like, isn't it?" She laughed, and then stopped as she thought she heard someone else laugh. Where was that coming from? There it was again. Definitely laughter.

It was coming from the tack room.

Michaela walked into the tack room and the words slipped out at the spectacle she saw. "Oh, my God."

Camden immediately started buttoning her shirt. Dwayne pulled his shirt back over his head. He turned crimson. "Oh, oh. I'm sorry. We uh, well, we uh . . ."

Michaela held up a hand. "That's okay. I think I know what you were doing." She turned and started to walk away.

"Wait, Michaela. Stop," Camden called out. "You were going to find out one way or another. We planned to tell you."

"What in the hell is going on?" Michaela asked.

"We're in love," Camden said, beaming. "And I'm moving in with Dwayne. Look." She held out her left hand; on it she wore a ring with a small diamond.

"Is that what I think it is?"

Camden jumped up. Dwayne put his arm around her. "Cammy girl and I, we be gonna get married, island style, you know. We thinking a wedding on the big island. My home and all."

"It'll be beautiful," Camden gushed. "And, we're going to have a margarita bar, doesn't that sound great? And you have to be my maid of honor!"

"Cammy girl?" Oh boy, these two were intimate. "That's great. A real wedding, huh?" That would be a first for Camden, whose first three marriages were by elopement. She could not believe what she was hearing. Her friend and employee were not only getting it on together, they were getting married! "So, tell me, how long have you two been keeping this from me?"

Michaela looked at Dwayne. He smiled. "You know, it be like three or four months."

"Three or four months! Jeez, I must be blind."

"No. We were just good at hiding it," Camden said.

"We are in love. I feel it in my heart. Never met no one like my Cammy girl."

"Oh, I'm sure of that. I suppose that's what the riding lessons are all about. I figured you were dating someone new and didn't want to tell me because I'm always lecturing you on your poor choice in men, but I can't think of a bad thing to say about this guy." She pointed at Dwayne.

No, actually in this situation it was Dwayne who Michaela might have to worry about. Camden could be a heartbreaker when she wanted, and the last thing Michaela needed was a heartbroken horse trainer. Not to mention she wouldn't want to lose Dwayne. He was the best, and if it didn't work out between him and Camden he could very well quit his job. She cringed at the thought, but when she eyed the two of them, she could honestly say that she'd never seen Camden look at anyone the way she was looking at Dwayne, and vice versa. Maybe it was true love, and they'd gotten away with it right under her nose. She started to laugh.

"You aren't mad?" Dwayne asked.

"No, I'm not mad. I'm not your mother. You two are weird. Why would you think I'd be mad? I love you both. I want you to be happy and if you're happy together, I think it's great. A little strange, but great."

"I certainly never expected it," Camden said.

"You. What about me?" Dwayne laughed.

"Why don't you come have margaritas with us? We'll celebrate and make wedding plans."

"I've got to get the horses fed, so I'll take a rain check. Go back to what you were doing, but maybe take it over to Dwayne's — or can I now call it your place, too?"

"Not officially. We'll go the traditional route and I'll move in after the wedding. I mean if it's okay with you, considering it is your property."

"I may have to raise the rent, you know."

"You do that," Camden said.

"If it were anyone else but you, I would."

"Come on, honey, let's go to your place. Our place." Camden took Dwayne's hand.

"Have fun," Michaela yelled after them.

She watched them walk away hand in hand. She shook her head. Compatibility. Who knew those two would wind up together? Strange combination. Michaela prayed that it would work between them. She'd wondered how Summer and Ethan would work out, too. They didn't exactly seem compatible, but she was no one to judge. They were expecting their first child, and Michaela could not believe that she would be taking Jude with her to the baby shower. That thought reminded her that she needed to call Hudson Drake. She'd thank him for the roses but explain to him that Saturday was out. Maybe she could meet him for lunch when she went to Los Angeles tomorrow to pick up Geyser. No. That wasn't a good idea. Well, she would have to give him back the key. "Ugh," she said aloud as she went back to taking care of the horses. Now that was something she could do, do it well, and have it all make sense —

take care of the animals. Humans made no sense, while animals made perfect sense.

As she finished feeding and started back to the house, a horrible realization hit her. She could not believe that she hadn't thought of it earlier. Oh no. *Francisco.* Audrey's ranch hand. Had he heard what happened to Audrey? She knew how much Audrey thought of the man. He needed to be told.

Instead of going into the house, she got into her truck and drove to Audrey's place.

As she pulled in to the ranch, everything seemed quiet, until she got out of the truck and heard whinnies from the barn. She walked over to the stalls, which looked like they'd recently had a fresh coat of paint applied. The horses grew further agitated seeing her. She quickly realized that they hadn't been fed. She looked at her watch. It was past seven. Where was Francisco? She tossed them each a flake of hay, not knowing what else Audrey fed them. She walked over to the house and used the spare key that Audrey had given her to the back door. She stopped. There were voices. "Francisco?" she called out. She realized that the voices were coming from a TV upstairs. The guest room. Maybe Francisco had dozed off watching a show earlier. She'd better wake him and let him know about Audrey. Plans would have to be made for the animals. "Francisco?" she called out again as she climbed the stairs.

The door to the guest room was cracked. Francisco appeared to be asleep on the bed. "Francisco? Hello?" She went into the room, irritated that he hadn't woken up and bummed that he hadn't been taking care of the animals the way he was supposed to. "Francisco," she said, this time louder. She stepped toward the bed. *Paint. Next to the bed. Different color from the barn. Red paint, not beige.* Michaela touched Francisco's shoulder. *Cold. Really cold.* She shook it and realized, as his body turned and he stared blankly up at her, with dried blood on his chest, that he was dead. She backed out of the room and ran down the stairs, nearly stumbling at the bottom. As she picked herself up, someone reached out for her and she screamed.

NINETEEN

Michaela fell back onto the bottom stair, terrified. She picked herself up, still screaming. "Michaela? It's me. It's me!"

"Olivia!" she yelled. "What the hell are you doing here?"

Olivia took a step back. "I . . . I came here to feel close to Audrey. I wanted to get away from my mom, too. I thought it would help me feel better."

Michaela grabbed her arm. "We have to get out of here now!"

"What?" Olivia shook her head. "What is wrong with you?"

She tugged on the girl's arm. "Come on. We have to call the police!"

"You're scaring me."

Michaela stopped, looked at her and said, "There is a dead man upstairs. I think he's been murdered and we have to get out of this house and call the police."

"Oh shit!"

They ran outside. "Get in," Michaela told Olivia as they approached her truck.

"You think that the killer is still here?" Olivia asked.

"I don't know what to think." Michaela grabbed her purse from the floorboard, retrieved her cell phone, and dialed 911.

The operator asked her some questions and told her to stay put and on the line as the police were dispatched to the ranch. In a matter of minutes the sheriffs' cars started pulling in.

Michaela and Olivia got out of the truck as men and women in uniform quickly swarmed the place. Two deputies approached them. One was a young, pretty woman, her dark hair pulled back, brown eyes trained on them. The man next to her was older and stocky with a graying mustache. He looked as serious as the woman did.

"I'm Deputy Garcia," the woman said. "This is Deputy McDaniels. We're going to take your statements. We have officers securing the grounds."

Michaela introduced herself, then Olivia, who fidgeted nervously. The police had a way of amplifying an unnerving situation, but Michaela couldn't help wonder if there was more to Olivia's reaction than the situation at hand. Had she really come out to Audrey's ranch to *feel* close to her?

Garcia asked Michaela to come with her so she could take her statement. McDaniels stayed with Olivia. After half an hour of going over her story twice, Garcia looked up from her notes. Something caught her eye because her demeanor changed almost abruptly from questioning, hard-line cop to . . . mmm, what was that . . . womanly? Michaela turned around to see Jude approaching. *Oh no.*

"Detective Davis, this is Ms. Bancroft," Garcia said.

"Yes. I know, we've met." Jude crossed his arms.

Garcia looked from one to the other, then stepped aside. "Okay, well, I just finished taking her statement —"

Jude cut her off. "Thank you, Deputy. I'll take it from here."

"Of course." Garcia stepped away.

Wait a minute. She batted her eyelashes. No she did not. Oh yeah. Yeah, she did. Michaela stood up straighter. *What was that all about?*

Jude lowered his voice. "What is going on, Michaela? What are you doing here?"

She sighed. "It's not what you think."

"Oh, you don't know what I'm thinking."

"Okay, well you better not be thinking that I had anything to do with Francisco's death, murder, whatever."

"He was murdered, all right. A gunshot through the chest."

Michaela winced. "Oh no. He was a good guy. Audrey cared about him."

"Speaking of . . . you did not tell me that you knew Audrey Pratt."

"No, I guess I didn't. I know a lot of people."

"Michaela, I was just at your place earlier today. Why didn't you tell me about your friend being killed? I've only received sketchy details at this point, but what were you thinking?"

"Huh? What was I thinking? I don't know, Jude. You didn't give me a lot of time to think. If I remember right, you kind of took my breath away." She glanced behind him and noticed Garcia eyeing them. The deputy quickly went back to jotting something down in her notepad.

Jude blushed. "Took your breath away?"

"Jude!"

"Davis, need you in the house," one of the detectives called. "Looks like one of the rooms has been torn apart. May have been a robbery gone bad."

Michaela didn't buy that theory. It all

187

seemed way too coincidental that Audrey had been killed the day before. *Someone had been looking for something.*

"We're not done with this. I know you. I know how you think, and I don't want you getting mixed up in this investigation. I don't want you hurt. Please."

She didn't comment.

"Davis!"

"I'm coming," he yelled back to the other detective. "I mean it, Michaela. We're not finished."

"Can I go now?"

He shook a finger at her. "Garcia, you finished with your statement?"

"Yes, sir."

He nodded and looked back at Michaela. "I'll see you later."

She found Olivia, who had just finished with McDaniels. "Oh my God, I was like totally bombarded by that cop. I told him like five hundred times that I just got here. I didn't even know there was anyone dead."

"Would you like to go have a cup of coffee or a bite to eat?" Michaela asked. She wasn't sure she felt like eating but she didn't feel like being alone either, and she had some questions she wanted to ask the girl.

Olivia looked down at her watch. "Uh, sure, okay. But I don't have a lot of time."

"Didn't you just drive a couple of hours to be around Audrey's things, her house?"

"Yeah. I did. But a friend just called me and wants to get together tonight, so I figured if I can't stay here, I might as well head back."

"It's almost nine."

"Right." She shrugged and didn't offer up any other answers. "So, coffee? Where?"

Michaela told her to follow her to the coffee hut she liked — The Honeybear. Once seated with a cup of decaf and Olivia fidgeting in front of her with some kind of fancy specialty coffee, she couldn't help herself any longer. She set her cup down and leaned in. "I'm kind of confused, Olivia. Maybe you can help me here. You drove out here to feel close to Audrey?"

"That's what I told you. Look, it may sound crazy to you. I know that cop was thinking I was full of crap, but I'm not." Tears filled her eyes. "I wanted to be here. I thought maybe if I drove out to her place that I'd feel close to her, like she was still here."

Michaela softened at the sight of Olivia crying. Maybe she was simply hurting over the loss of Audrey and was telling the truth. "Are you okay?"

"I don't know. No. Not really. My mom

told me about Halliday, and with Audrey being killed . . ." She sobbed. "I can't believe it. I loved her so much and she would know what to do right now. I don't know what to do. I want everyone to leave me alone."

"To do about what, Olivia?"

"That stupid Callahan guy is leaving me messages on my voice mail."

"Frederick Callahan?"

"Yep."

"The guy who runs that men's magazine *Pleasures*?" Michaela recalled Callahan standing next to Bridgette Bowen, over Audrey's body. The thought caused a shiver to snake down her back.

"That's the one," Olivia replied.

"What does he want?"

"He's been bugging me to do a spread in his magazine. Says I can be dressed, just a transparent blouse. He wants me to wear a pair of breeches and — this is the best part . . ." She wiped her face. "He tells me a crop in my hand would look good, kind of do a jockey thing."

"Creep."

"I've told him no way, but he still keeps calling. Then Marshall Friedman, Steve Benz's manager, suggests I do the magazine and that Steve would like to do the photos

190

with me, and together he thinks we would make a great pair."

"Jerks."

"Yep. But wait, the biggest jerk of all is my mother. I told her what they proposed and she said that I should do it. It would be good for my career. She says that as much as she loved Audrey and as hard as it is that she's gone, I have to think about moving on, and Audrey was holding me back. Can you believe that?"

"Oh my God. That is so cold. What the hell is wrong with your mother?" she blurted. "I'm sorry. I didn't mean to say that."

"No. You're right. My own mother wants to sell me out. Wants me to pose half naked with some asshole pop star in hopes of me making it huge for her."

It looked like Josh was right about Kathleen likely being the one to set up the meeting between Olivia, Friedman, and Benz after the races. She'd kept it from both Audrey and Olivia, maybe fearing that they would veto the queen and her ideas. "What did you tell her?"

Michaela also couldn't help wondering if Olivia was aware of her mother's financial troubles. Michaela had dealt with her own difficulties when it came to finances, but when it had happened in her life after her ex left and stuck her with thousands of dollars in medical bills incurred from failed in vitro fertilization attempts, Michaela had changed her lifestyle — slowed things way down. Not that she ever really lived beyond her means anyway, but she knew how to tighten up when necessary. That was clearly something Kathleen Bowen was unable to do, even while going down the tubes. Appearances meant more to her than honesty and reality.

"Nothing. I left. You don't tell my mom anything. It's not worth the fight. She'll wear you down."

"Is that why you haven't told her that you want to be a jockey?"

"You know about that?"

"I do. Audrey told me."

"Ah." Olivia crossed her arms. She looked paler tonight than she had the other day. Granted, she had ivory skin, but she appeared more gaunt and unhealthy. "That would be nice. Dreams are nice but they're bullshit."

"Is that why you left the races with Benz and Friedman? Why you were willing to discuss a contract with them?"

"Look, I did that because I was mad at Josh. He'd been a jerk to me earlier and I didn't want to be around him or my mom. Benz and Friedman came to see me after the show in my dressing room. We started talking and decided to go party somewhere else."

"Did you have anything to drink?" Michaela remembered Josh telling her that according to Olivia she'd only had a couple of drinks and they'd been before she'd left the races. He'd suspected that Benz might have spiked the drink.

"Yeah. I had a beer, maybe two. I don't know. It's kind of a blur now. We were talking and then Benz said he'd grab a few beers. Friedman hung with me while Benz got the drinks and then when he came back we downed them and took off."

Those moments that Benz went to get the drinks: He had the opportunity to spike Olivia's beer then. He also might have had opportunity to kill Audrey. He had threatened her only a couple of hours before with Olivia changing management camps. The timing seemed right to Michaela for Benz to have done it. Maybe Josh had good reason to distrust Benz. Not only was he trying to scam the girl he cared about, but could Josh have a gut feeling that Benz was even slimier than what he put out there. Could Josh suspect that the guy was evil enough to kill? "Josh seems to be pretty protective over you."

She nodded. "Yeah, so? He's cool. I know he has a thing for me." She shrugged. "I kind of like him, too, but my mom would freak, and I don't know what my dad would say."

"You are an adult."

"Right."

"You are, Olivia. Maybe you should try acting like one."

"What the hell does that mean? Oh forget it." She looked at her watch again. "I have to go. Thanks for the coffee."

"You hardly drank any."

"I know. But I need to get back." She stood, her demeanor changing.

Olivia obviously did not want to talk about the prospect of being a jockey, or acting like an adult, and she'd begun fidgeting again. Her cell rang. She took it out of her purse and answered, waving good-bye to Michaela as she walked out. Michaela shook her head in bewilderment. The young woman certainly was confused, and confusing. She sat there and sipped her coffee. The waitress came over with her bill.

"Oh, hon, looks like your friend forgot something; maybe it dropped out of her purse." The waitress reached across the booth and handed her a tiny envelope, the kind that typically holds a card attached to flowers.

"Thank you." Michaela took the envelope and couldn't help but look inside. No card, but there was something. Crushed chalk? No. Flour? Powder? *Oh damn.* A sickened feeling struck Michaela, for she doubted that the substance was anything of a legal nature. She felt pretty sure that what was inside the tiny envelope was cocaine.

TWENTY

"You look like hell," Camden said when she walked into the kitchen the following morning and found Michaela trying to jump-start herself with a strong cup of coffee.

She hadn't been able to get to sleep until the wee hours of the morning and then it wasn't exactly restful, as nightmares invaded her dreams. "Thanks. Not all of us get to sleep in the arms of a loved one, all warm and cozy. I am still mad at you, you know." Michaela poured herself another cup from the carafe. She had to hit the road if she wanted to reach Los Angeles early and get out before the late afternoon traffic kicked in. She took a bag of bread from the cupboard. "Toast?"

"No. I'll have some cereal, though."

Michaela served up her friend's favorite cereal — Fruit Loops. *How fitting.* By the time she finished waiting on Camden, her toast was ready. She slathered it with peanut butter and sat down. "Aren't you going to say anything?"

Camden set her spoon down and shrugged. "Look, I knew that you would discourage me from a relationship with Dwayne. And I know what you're thinking, that I'll dump him, leave him brokenhearted and he'll hightail it back to the islands."

"You got it," Michaela replied.

Camden reached across the table and took Michaela's hand. "I know I've been a flake. I know I've been unlucky in love and that's why I'm here with you. You always warned me with each guy I've brought around that it wouldn't work, that he wasn't good enough. That he was some superficial moron. And that's what's different this time. You know as well as I do that *superficial* is the last thing Dwayne is. He's unlike all the men I've fallen for in the past. There isn't a phony thing about him, and material gain isn't what he wants."

"You're right. And that's what worries me. I don't want Dwayne to be the flavor of the month or year because he is different. Camden, you like material things, and you can be phony." At that comment, her friend scowled. "You can and you know it."

Camden nodded. "I love him." She looked up at Michaela, tears in her eyes. "I can honestly say for the first time in my life that I am in love with a man and he loves me. It's not about anything else but that, and I want your blessing. Please."

Michaela squeezed her hand. "Okay then. But don't ever keep something like that from me again. I feel like an idiot. I can't believe that I didn't notice."

"I won't. Thank you. It's not hard to believe that you didn't notice, though. You've been busy with the horses, running this place, Joe's kid, and that hot detective's daughter. Hell, I feel like I haven't seen you much these past few months."

Camden was right. She had been busy. They hadn't spent much time together lately like they used to. "We need to change that, don't we?"

"We'd better, considering we'll be planning a wedding together."

Michaela smiled. "Should be a good distraction for me."

"What do you mean?" Camden asked between bites of cereal.

Michaela sighed. "Dwayne didn't tell you about Audrey?"

"No."

She began the sordid tale. "Oh my God." Camden brought her hand up to her mouth. She stood and wrapped her arms around

Michaela. "I am so sorry. Is there anything I can do?"

"I don't know. Last night after finding Francisco, I asked Olivia to have coffee. She was acting really strange. Then she took off and left something behind. It must've fallen out of her purse."

"What?"

"A small envelope of cocaine."

"Ah, jeez. Not good."

"Poor Hugh. I should tell him."

"Oh no. You need to stay out of this. None of this sounds good at all. I know how obsessed you became when Lou was murdered, and you almost got yourself killed. Promise me you're not off trying to piece it together. Let that family unravel without you being stuck in the middle. You're a good person, you don't need outside hassles getting in the way of running your life. That's your problem: you're always trying to solve everyone *else's* problems. Take care of yourself for a change."

"All I'm doing is trying to find some answers."

"Michaela," Camden implored. "Run as far away as you can from those people."

"Joe is checking into a few things for me and that's it. Then I'll drop it. I even promised him."

Camden shook her head. "Stubborn. Very stubborn. Now you got Joey Pellegrino involved. I knew it, and I bet your cute detective is aware of your activities and he probably is not too happy about it."

Michaela looked up at the clock. "Oh, would you look at that, gotta run. I have a horse to pick up."

"Michaela."

"I'll be back tonight."

"Michaela!" Camden yelled. "Stay out of it. Please. You have a lot of people who love you."

"I love you, too. Thanks for caring. Have a good day."

With that she shut the door behind her. Camden was right. Leave all the dysfunctionals back in Hollywood. She'd do that tomorrow, she promised herself. Today she had to go and pick up Geyser. So asking a few more questions couldn't hurt, now could it?

Twenty-One

Before heading out, Michaela stopped off at Audrey's place to make sure the animals were all okay. Jude had left a message to call him. She was going to give that some time. She wasn't ready for the third degree. At Audrey's, she found Deputy Garcia holding down the fort. She sat on her porch swing looking beat tired and bored out of her mind. She eyed Michaela up and down.

"You know, technically you're not supposed to be here. I do know that Ms. Pratt was a friend, but I have my orders, straight from Detective Davis," she said as she glared at Michaela. Maybe it was her imagination, but did Garcia have a bone to pick?

"I understand. I only came by to feed the animals."

"The animals will be fine. Arrangements have been made for the Humane Society to pick them up. That's why I'm still here. I was off two hours ago, but they send in the rookie to do this shit."

"Oh, no! Not the Humane Society. I have room for the horses. Please give me a day."

"You'll have to take it up with the Humane Society. Or maybe your boyfriend." Garcia stood up from the porch swing and crossed her arms.

Something about her intimidated Michaela. Maybe it was the fact that she carried a gun. That might have been it. But her comment was way off base. "I don't know what you mean."

"You and Detective Davis. I saw the way you were looking at him. You two *do* know each other."

"Yes, but we don't have anything going on."

"Can't blame you. He's a hottie. That's for sure. More power to you, girl. But let me just say that you've got all the women around the station a little peeved at you. They've all been competing to spend some time with Davis."

"Peeved about *me?*"

"Word is that you and Davis have a thing. It's the gossip around the station. I'd be careful if I were you. He's got the womanizer thing down. You can ask anyone in a skirt back at the station. He and I have even spent some time together." Garcia winked at her.

"You can go back to the station and tell the ladies there that Detective Davis is more than available," Michaela said.

"You sure about that?"

"I'm sure. Now, can I go and check on the animals? Feed them? They have to be hungry and it's best if I turn some of them out to pasture."

"Why not?"

"Thanks." Michaela stormed off and could have sworn she heard Garcia chuckle under her breath. What was that all about? She did not like being the subject of gossip. And to even have become that subject, Jude must've told someone that they were seeing each other, or something like that. *Whatever.* And what was that comment that he and Garcia had spent time together? Was Jude different from what she'd thought? Could he be another womanizer? God knew she had a knack for picking them, and then getting blindsided like a deer caught up in headlights. Had she fallen into another man's trap? No, she had not. She wouldn't let Jude get the best of her. If he wanted to chase the skirts back at the station that was just fine. But she wasn't about to allow him to get under her skin and feed her lies. No way.

She made her way to the barn and started feeding the horses. Then she went out to the pasture and brought the roving ones to their stalls and fed them. Audrey had about twenty head. By the time she was finished, it had taken nearly forty-five minutes. As she was locking up, her cell phone rang.

"Mick, it's me, Joe. I got some info for you on that Bob Pratt dude. Seems he had a girlfriend named Cara Klein. She lives in San Diego. That's all I've been able to get so far. I'm still working that angle." Michaela made a mental note of the information. "Also, he liked to hang at this bar up in Malibu. Place serves good fish and chips, my cousin told me. Anyhow, he was in there a couple of weeks ago."

"Drinking?"

"Only Cokes, according to the bartender."

"Was he by himself?"

"No. Says he was with a couple of younger men, both Hispanic. He said that one didn't seem as friendly as the other, was kind of an ass to the bartender and it made Pratt nervous. The other guy seemed okay. The bartender also said that guy was a short dude."

"Interesting. We've got to find out who

those men were that he was talking to. Can you do that?"

"You're getting sucked into this, Mick."

"Joe, do it. And I know you will. You know why?"

"Cause you're working with my kid."

"Nope. Well, maybe that, but it's also because you love this cloak-and-dagger stuff."

He didn't comment for a few seconds. "I'll call you back. Be careful."

"Always."

Michaela went into Audrey's office to see if she could find a pen and something to write on. She wanted to jot down Cara Klein's name. She doubted she'd forget it, but she wanted to be certain.

She opened the top drawer and found a pen but no paper. The third drawer down, she located a stack of legal pads as well as an 8×10 envelope addressed to Audrey. But what caught her eye was the return address: that of her brother, Bob.

TWENTY-TWO

Okay, so she shouldn't have done it. It was impulsive. Michaela knew she should not have done it. But she had. She'd walked out of the barn with the large envelope, keeping an eye out for Garcia, hoping the deputy wouldn't spot her and ask her what the envelope was about. She knew she was taking something that didn't belong to her. Maybe she should've passed it on to Garcia. Heck no. Why do *her* any favors? She set the envelope in the backseat and headed west. Besides she had a feeling that this was the envelope Audrey had mentioned the other day. The one that she was to give to Ethan. It didn't belong to the police or her. It belonged to Ethan. Right? That is, if it was the right envelope. Michaela could not be sure about that without opening it. And, she didn't know how she felt about opening it. But she certainly couldn't give it to Ethan to open and then have it be something he would have no clue about. She'd have to ask him if he'd gotten Audrey's message about it. She'd also have to tell him about Audrey, if he hadn't already heard. Detective Merrill had told her that he would be needing to speak with Ethan and ask if he'd spotted Audrey on the track after Halliday had broken his leg.

Over lunch: Maybe that's when she'd take a look at what was in the envelope. She would have to eat lunch today. And she'd be in Los Angeles at lunchtime. Hudson Drake came to mind. But she was pulling a horse trailer. It might be nice to have lunch with him, her treat. Ah, who was she kidding? She was irritated that Jude might be talking about the two of them as if they were a thing. They were *not* a thing. And she didn't like feeling suspicious that he might be playing her and another woman, or women. That she did not like at all. She recalled his almost egotistical attitude about coming out the winner yesterday when he'd kissed her. Was he like that with all women? She'd discovered that the kind of man who exuded the kind of self-confidence Jude did around women indicated he'd traveled the path to a woman's heart or bed more than a few times. But did she have a right to feel that way?

She picked through her wallet where she'd put Hudson's card and gave him a call. He told her that he'd love to have lunch with her, and since she was pulling a trailer they could meet at Duke's, a nearby restaurant. "It's laid-back there. Not the jet set in and out, and the parking lot is huge. They've seen trailers come in there before," he said.

"Great. Noon work for you?"

"Sure does."

She wondered if he'd had any luck with the private investigator he'd said that he hired to look into Bob's disappearance and intended to ask him about it. Lost in thought, Michaela at first didn't see the flashing lights in her rearview mirror. When she did, it took her another second to realize that she was being pulled over. What had she done? She wasn't speeding. She hadn't cut anyone off, had she? Oh brother! She didn't have time for this right now. She pulled off to the side of the road and cut the engine. A highway patrolman approached the truck. "Hi, Officer," Michaela said. "I'm not certain why you pulled me over."

He faced her, eyes covered in dark sunglasses, a serious expression on his face. This could not be good. "Can I see your driver's license, ma'am?"

She removed her wallet from her purse. "Sure, but can you tell me what I did wrong?"

He opened up his ticket pad and took the license from her. "I'm going to have to write you a fix-it ticket. Did you know that the lights are out on your trailer?"

"Oh no." She sighed, relived that it wasn't anything more than that. That sounded like an easy fix. "Are you sure?" He frowned. *Stupid question.* "I will definitely have that fixed." He finished writing the ticket and tore it off. "Have a nice day," she said taking the ticket. He walked back to his car. Damn. She was only thirty minutes from Hugh Bowen's place. She'd have to get the trailer fixed. There wasn't a way out of it. She couldn't haul a horse back without those brake lights working.

She called ahead to the Bowen ranch. Hugh told her that someone should be around who could fix them, that she should just pull on in and either find Josh or Enrique. "I have some errands to take care of. I don't think I'll be around by the time you get here. Hopefully you can get the trailer fixed quickly and be back on your way. I know it's quite a drive."

"True. I'm sorry that I won't see you."

"Me, too, but you'll be at the charity event

on Saturday. We'll catch up there. I'd actually stay and wait here for you, but I need to find out when Audrey's body might be released. We have to plan a proper service for her."

Michaela recognized the emotion in his voice. How had she not thought of a service for her friend? Of course, something needed to be arranged. She thanked Hugh for his willingness to take care of it and offered her help in any way that she could.

When she pulled into the ranch, the gate was open. She parked the truck and trailer near the main stables. She looked around but didn't see anyone at first. Then a Hispanic man in jeans, T-shirt, and leather gloves came toward her. "Hey," he said. "I'm Juan Perez. You Ms. Bancroft?"

"Yes."

"Yeah. Okay, Mr. Bowen said you would be by. He said that your trailer's light are out."

"They are." She frowned.

"I'll unhook it for you and see what's going on, okay?"

"Thank you. That would be great. Quiet around here this morning?" she said as Juan started unhooking the trailer.

He nodded. "Josh and my brother, Enrique, had to take care of some business with the American Quarter Horse Association. I think they're in the office on the phone or something."

"Oh."

"And most of the grooms are on break, but I'm trying to get ahead, you know. Mr. Bowen, he just give me this job, so I'm doing the best I can."

Michaela couldn't help but remember what Hugh had said about Juan — something to the effect of him having been in some trouble. She also couldn't help wondering who it was that Bobby Pratt had been talking to at the fish and chips bar in Malibu a few weeks ago. She suddenly wondered if it was possible that the two Hispanic men he'd been hanging out with were Juan and Enrique Perez.

"Hey, Juan, do you know Bob Pratt?"

He stood up. "Who?"

"The vet. I know that Mr. Bowen uses him at times, and that they're friends. I'm sure you heard about the murder at the races."

"Sure, yeah." He nodded emphatically. "I heard 'bout that. No good, you know. My brother tol' me, and he say it was real bad. Mr. Bowen pretty upset 'bout it."

"Me too. The lady who was killed was a good friend of mine."

"Oh no. I'm real sorry."

211

"And, her brother is Bob Pratt. He's been missing for several days now."

Juan clucked his tongue. "That's too bad."

"So, you don't know him? Never met him?"

He shook his head again. "I don't think so. I only work here on and off, you know. I haven't been here for about three months, maybe. My brother got my job back though. Mr. Bowen is a good man. He's helping me out. I don't want to mess up, you know? But the vet, no. I wouldn't know if I did see him because a lot of people come here and look at horses. I just fix stuff."

"Right. Thanks. Hey, is there any water down here? I'd like something to drink."

"You know, I gotta fix that, too. The faucet in the tack room got all messed up. You can maybe go in the office where Josh and Enrique are. There's a refrigerator there."

"No, I don't want to bother them if they're on the phone."

"You can take the golf cart up to the house. Mr. Bowen, he has a fountain in the garden."

"That's okay. I can just get a drink out of the hose. I was only looking to quench my thirst a bit. No biggie."

"Might as well go up to the gardens and see it anyway. It's gonna take me some time to find the problem here. And it's real pretty up there. Take a cruise around the place. It's nice. And the water is much better than from the hose." He laughed.

"Okay. Thanks." She really didn't have time to kill, but she also had no choice. She climbed into the golf cart and cruised around the ranch. Either Juan Perez was lying or he really had no clue who Bob Pratt was, and the men he'd been with at the place in Malibu were two different people than she'd guessed at for a second. Another thought struck her: What if it had been Francisco, Audrey's ranch hand? He'd met a horrible, untimely demise as well. Michaela could not believe that his murder was not somehow connected to Audrey's, and she was also pretty sure that Bob's disappearance was what tied everything together. She realized that both thoughts were kind of out there. After all, there were quite a few Hispanics living in Los Angeles. What type of business would Bob Pratt have had with Juan or Enrique or Francisco? Just because they were all Latino didn't mean anything. She realized that she was grasping at straws here.

As she jetted around on the cart, she took in the opulence of the place. She passed the practice track, the stables, and palm tree—

lined pasture, which had a beautiful pond in the center of it where ducks lazed through the water. The facility was magnificent and seeing it all made Michaela sad, knowing that Audrey would have enjoyed living here. She would have appreciated the ranch and she would have been happy with Hugh. "Oh, Audrey," she whispered as tears stung her eyes.

She approached the garden, complete with the English hedge maze that Juan had mentioned. Unsure exactly where the water fountain was located, she got out of the cart and took a walk through the garden. Various rosebushes gave off their soft floral scent as hummingbirds dipped in and out of water feeders. A large fountain, with a statue of an angel atop a horse, sat in the middle of the garden. The artwork was gorgeous. She finally found the fountain off to the side of a path that led into the hedge maze. She took a long drink. She decided it might be fun to take a walk through the maze. Apparently there was time to spare. Why not?

Michaela started in through the maze, taking in the sounds and smells. It really was like an English garden. As she wound herself farther into the maze though, some anxiety came over her when she'd heard something — a rustling in the maze. Probably birds.

No need to get spooked. She glanced around. She wanted out of there. Her nerves buzzed with the idea that if someone were inside the hedge watching her, she certainly wouldn't be heard if she screamed. She backed away. She had to get out of there. Her brow started to perspire as she tried to wind her way back through the route she'd come in. A few minutes later she was at the entrance of the maze. Thank God. Then she heard the rustling noise again. She inched toward one of the Spanish moss trees that lined the gardens. There it was again — only now, she also heard a voice. A woman's voice. She stayed close to the shadows and tried to make out where it was coming from and who was talking. She caught a glimpse of blond hair as a person walked through the hedge and then out of the maze. Bridgette. Had she spotted Michaela? She'd been walking the maze at the same time? She must have been on the other end, because she didn't seem concerned, or to be looking for anyone herself. It was obvious to Michaela that Bridgette did not know that she was there.

Michaela watched, intrigued, as Bridgette headed toward the rosebushes, cell phone to her ear, and then sat down on the bench. Michaela kept out of sight, and she could now hear the woman quite a bit better.

"I have to see you." She smelled one of the roses. "No. Look, I know it's not a good idea, but please. I need you right now. If Hugh knew what was going on . . . What we did. Oh God, I could lose everything. Everything. Dammit." She paused. "No! I need to see you now. This is a big deal. It's a huge deal. What we've done, well . . . if anyone knew. Please, lover. Please. We can just have lunch. That's all I'm asking. Okay. I'll meet you at the restaurant then. Shutters. Half an hour. Thank you, love." She turned off her cell.

Michaela moved even closer to the tree. Bridgette glanced in her direction. Oh no. Don't see me. *Don't see me.* Bridgette stood up and started walking toward the house. Oh God, what about the cart? Michaela had parked it off to the side, but if she saw it, she'd wonder who had driven it up here. She might look around. Michaela watched as she veered off to the other side of the garden. She finally dared to breathe, knowing that Bridgette hadn't discovered her.

So, who was the good Mrs. Bowen off to meet? And what was this business about losing everything? And who was she calling *lover?* Furthermore, what had they done that Bridgette seemed to want covered up?

216

Did it involve Audrey? Michaela jumped back in the cart after waiting a few minutes to be sure Bridgette didn't spot her. She knew what Shutters was: a luxury hotel down in Santa Monica, about thirty minutes away if the traffic was working with her.

She found Juan. "I need to take my truck and run some errands while you're working on the trailer. When do you think it'll be ready?"

He laughed and held up a handful of shredded wires. "Something tells me you got a rat problem at your place. Not so good. They chewed through a bunch of the wires. I think it's gonna take me a while. Why don't you call the ranch around four? I'll see what I can do."

She nodded and started her truck. She didn't have time to wait around Los Angeles all day hoping her trailer would be fixed, but it appeared she didn't have a choice. And since she didn't, she made her way down the Pacific Coast Highway to see if she could find out exactly who Bridgette had been speaking to on the phone in the garden.

TWENTY-THREE

Michaela felt like she couldn't breathe as she headed down the 101 toward Santa Monica. A ton of thoughts rushed through her mind, and her anxiety levels soared — Audrey, Francisco, Hugh, Olivia, Kathleen, Bridgette — all of them blurred in her mind.

She reached the luxury hotel shortly after Bridgette pulled in, noticing that the valet was parking the woman's Mercedes. Michaela parked her own truck, not wanting to be seen. She counted on the fact that Bridgette Bowen would not exactly be looking for her. What was Michaela's goal here anyway? How had she become some real-life Jessica Fletcher? She didn't have time to ponder that thought, as she noticed Frederick Callahan climbing out of a white Rolls-Royce. Now, wasn't that interesting? He was an easy one to spot, with that bad toupee. Her mind churned. She pondered what to do as she watched Callahan go through the front doors of the hotel. What in the heck was she doing? Jeez — spying, that's what! As the thought crossed her mind, an eerie feeling swept over her: The kind that says you, too, are being watched. She glanced to her left and caught a very tall man with a large build — almost like a football player — dark hair, and olive skin, eyeing her with deep-set brown eyes. His eyes turned away when she made contact with him. He glanced back as he headed for the front of the hotel. He smiled slightly, then picked up his pace. That was odd.

Okay, if she was going to play this out like one of her old favorite TV detectives, she knew she'd have to go in.

The valet greeted her as she breezed past him; she asked him where the restaurant was. The conversation Bridgette had had with Callahan — assuming it was Callahan she'd been speaking with — was about having lunch. Interesting that they also chose a high-end hotel to have lunch in. Michaela guessed that there was more than just lunch plans on the agenda. The valet told Michaela that there were two restaurants inside, one a more upscale place, the other an al fresco café out near the bike path. She first looked inside the formal restaurant, spotting only an older couple and a younger man. The al fresco café held quite a few people, and she spotted Callahan and Bridgette in a corner, tucked in tightly near a large potted plant. So, it *was* Callahan that she'd been talking to! Mmm, she would love to be a fly on a leaf of that potted plant.

"May I help you?" the maitre d' asked. She didn't answer right away, and he persisted. "You are here for lunch?"

"Damn!" She clapped her hand over her mouth. The maitre d's eyes widened. "Oh, I'm so sorry, I . . ." She held up her hand. "I'll be right back." Surely the man thought she was crazy, and as she started to flip around she spotted the same tall, intense guy she'd seen out in the parking lot. He was seated at the opposite end of the café, but in sight of Bridgette and Callahan, and he was watching them. Yep, he definitely was studying them. He held a pen, an expensive ballpoint, which he clicked off and on. Now, her mind reeled. This spy thing was getting to her. Was that guy using one of those pen cameras to take photos of Callahan and Bridgette? Oh, boy! Could it be? Was there even such a thing as a pen camera? Michaela shook her head and hurried into the lobby, where she quickly called Hudson, hoping he had not already left his office. She was supposed to meet him for lunch in only half an hour. She quickly explained to him that her problems with the trailer were worse than she expected. She didn't go into any details but said that she'd have to postpone the lunch. He sounded disappointed. "Are you sure?" he asked. "You can't make it?"

"No." She could. She knew she could. But something was going on inside that café and she wanted the skinny on it, if there was any way to get it. Then on impulse she said, "You know, it does look as though I'll be here for the afternoon. How about an early dinner?"

"That would be great. Let's do five. Duke's still?"

"Perfect." And, it was, because if the trailer was fixed, then she'd have time to load Geyser and get down to Duke's. The horse wouldn't mind waiting for an hour. She'd be sure to give him some extra feed, and she'd pay the parking attendant a bonus to keep an eye on him.

After hanging up, she sat in the lobby for a few moments, not sure what to do. She was kind of hungry. She went back to the maitre d' and asked for an inside table. She wanted to position herself to see both Bridgette and Callahan, but she could only see his face and her back. She ordered a bowl of soup and tried to be inconspicuous. She could not see the weird guy, who sat to her left and behind her on the patio. Callahan's facial expressions at first showed concern, maybe even anger, but then they mellowed as he picked up his phone. Who was he calling? She also noticed after he hung up that he moved from his chair to the other side and sat next to Bridgette, where he put an arm around her. The around-the-arm thing could just mean he was comforting her about something. No, that didn't fit. There was something going on between these two. That much was obvious.

They finished their meal. She waited a couple of minutes after they paid their bill and left before following suit. She didn't want to lose them, but if Bridgette spotted and recognized her, what was she going to tell them — that this was where all the horse trainers went to lunch when in town?

Outside the restaurant, she spotted the couple going up in an elevator. So, they *had* gotten a room. Sneaky snakes. Poor Hugh! After losing Audrey, his problems with his daughter . . . now a cheating wife? She wasn't sure what to do. Some of her questions had been answered. Maybe it was time to quit the spying act. She started to walk out of the hotel when she spotted Steve Benz walking in. Now what the hell was *he* doing here? Coincidence? Before he could see her, she ducked behind the large floral arrangement in the lobby and opened her purse, pretending to be looking for something. *Please don't see me.* Would he remember her anyway? She heard Benz say, "Hey." Oh no, had he seen her? She glanced up. No. He stood near the elevators, on his cell. "It's me, Cal, what room you two in?"

Cal? This was getting shadier by the minute. Was Benz going to pay a visit to Callahan and Bridgette? Michaela didn't know what else to think, but she decided it best to go and wait in her truck. What if someone else who might recognize her showed up for this little get-together?

Almost to her truck, she heard footsteps at her heels. Oh no. She spun around and stood face-to-face with the weird guy. That dark look he'd had when he'd eyed her earlier? Well, it was much darker now.

TWENTY-FOUR

"Hey!" Michaela yelled as the guy grabbed her arm. "What the hell are you doing? Let go!" She pulled free of the strong man's hold.

"I could ask you the same thing. Would you mind lowering your voice?"

"What? You're lucky I don't scream." She noticed the valet watching and was relieved. Who was this nutcase?

He quickly pulled a card from his wallet and handed it to her. "Dennis Smith? Private investigator?" she read.

"Exactly. What I want to know is why you're so interested in Bridgette Bowen and Frederick Callahan."

She shrugged. "I'm not."

He rolled his eyes. "Lady, I am a trained investigator."

"And why do *you* want to know? You investigating one of them?" He didn't respond. She clapped a hand over her mouth and then pointed at him. "Holy . . . You *are* investigating one of them." A warm ocean breeze blew across the parking lot. "Wait a minute, wait a minute . . . Hudson! Did he hire you? Hudson Drake?" That made sense to her because of the conversation she'd had with him at Hugh's ranch the other day. Smith said nothing, just eyed her. She pulled herself up tall. "Listen, I don't know you, and you haven't told me jack about why you noticed me supposedly watching those two, but I'm not saying another word until you start talking, too." She crossed her arms as he took a step back. Then she gasped as her focus turned to the front of the hotel.

Smith turned to see what she was looking at. He grabbed her arm again. "Get against the truck, as if we're talking."

"We *are* talking. Well, I'm talking anyway, and you're still a freaking stranger. A tall freaking stranger!"

"I'm not a threat. Hugh Bowen hired me. Now do what I say," he said in a rush. "We are having a nice chat with each other, as if we're lovers."

"I don't think so."

"Okay, friends."

Steve Benz had just emerged from the hotel and sauntered toward his Lexus, which the valet had brought around. She watched Smith. He took a tiny camera from his coat pocket — definitely one of those devices that only a private investigator or someone in law enforcement would use — and started taking covert shots of Steve Benz. "Hugh hired you?"

"Yes," he said, still snapping.

"What are you doing? Why are you following Bridgette and Callahan?"

"I could ask you the same thing," he replied. "You know my name, now who in the hell are you, lady?"

"Wait a minute. Does this involve Audrey's murder?"

He stopped taking photos as Benz got in his car. "Murder? What are you talking about?"

"My friend. She was murdered the other day, and she was close with Hugh."

"Oh." He stuffed the camera back into his pocket as Benz pulled out of the lot and sped away.

He studied her. "Go on . . . Wait." He held up his palm. "Can I get a name?"

"Michaela Bancroft."

He shook her hand. "Sorry for earlier. It's my business to be perceptive, and you were far more than just curious about those two. You were definitely searching for some kind of answer."

She nodded; emotion rose in her throat, as his question conjured up her last memory of Audrey. He raised his eyebrows. "Well?"

She sighed. "Audrey was a good friend. She was killed at the races the other day, and like I said, she and Hugh were close. This morning I was up at the Bowen ranch and overheard Bridgette having a conversation that sounded suspicious, as if she had something to hide. Obviously, it was Callahan. She mentioned meeting at Shutters. I followed. I wanted to know who she'd been talking to, and what it was they were trying to hide."

"You thought they might have had something to do with your friend's murder."

She nodded. "Hugh didn't tell you about Audrey?"

He shook his head. "He hired me three weeks ago to follow his wife. He suspected that she was having an affair. I haven't spoken with him in days. I am supposed to report to him tomorrow."

Michaela didn't quite know what to make of this. Why would Hugh care if Bridgette were cheating? He was getting ready to leave her and marry Audrey. Unless, of course, it would make him look better to a judge during court proceedings. That made sense.

But, what it didn't do was prove that Bridgette or Callahan had anything to do with Audrey's murder. It only cemented the fact that they were messing around. And how did Benz fit into this thing? Why had he shown up at the hotel? He certainly hadn't stuck around for long. If the three of them had some weird sex thing going on, someone must've changed their mind. "What about Benz, how do you figure he's involved?"

Smith didn't have time to reply as the sound of sirens drowned out their conversation. An ambulance pulled into the front entrance of the hotel. They turned to see what was going on.

"What do you think that's all about?"

"I don't know. But here's our girl," Smith said.

Bridgette walked out the front door, looking dazed and quite pale. Her demeanor certainly was different from when she'd gone into the elevator with Callahan. Something was wrong. She handed the valet her parking stub. Smith started in again with the photos.

"Callahan should be right behind her," he remarked. "Typical." He shook his head. "I've seen this kind of thing go down way too many times. The woman leaves first and then a few minutes later, the man follows. But man, they were quick. Guess that happens when you're with a woman who looks like her." Smith chuckled.

Michaela didn't find his comment amusing. But Smith was right. Callahan did exit a few minutes later, only he was on the EMTs' stretcher. She turned to the private investigator. "You see that very often?"

TWENTY-FIVE

"Can't say that I have," Smith replied.

Michaela remained fixated on the scene as she watched the paramedics load Callahan into the ambulance. What was going on? Why had Benz taken off so suddenly, and then Bridgette? Had they killed Callahan, or tried to? He looked to be alive. In fact, from where she and Smith stood, the paramedics appeared to be speaking to him before closing the back doors and speeding off.

"What in the hell?" Smith muttered.

"I've got the same question."

"Look, it's obvious that Callahan is on the way to the hospital. What those two did to him is a mystery. It's also obvious that you have a stake in finding out who killed your friend. I have a stake in getting paid by Bowen, but this little scenario ups the ante quite a bit. Do you know what a scandal like this is worth in this town? I could sell these photos to the tabloids and take a five-star vacation in the tropics." He paused. "Want to get some coffee? Maybe share some thoughts on this?"

She considered it. "Yeah. Maybe so."

"Good. Let me make a phone call and see if I can find out where they're taking Callahan and how bad off he is. We'll start there. I know this place probably costs ten bucks a cup, but . . ."

"My treat," she interjected.

They walked back into the café and ordered coffees. Smith made a call, inquiring about Callahan. "He's headed to Cedars-Sinai. No word yet on his condition, but I'll get it. So . . ."

"So?" Michaela said, still shaken by what she'd witnessed.

"Your friend who was murdered . . ."

"Audrey."

He nodded. "You mentioned that Benz threatened her."

Michaela told him about the races the other day and what had occurred inside Olivia's dressing room.

"That guy is an ass."

"Do you think the three of them could be involved in Audrey's murder? Why else would they be meeting? Maybe to talk business, I suppose."

"There are other possibilities. A hotel room? One woman, two guys . . . although typically, it's usually the other way around — two women."

Michaela brought her hand up to her mouth. "No. Don't even go there. That's disgusting. The three of them . . . together?"

"It's possible. I doubt Benz came here for a drink. But there is another possibility. Maybe I know the reason Benz paid a visit to the lovebirds. And if my guess is correct, it might have caused the old geezer to have a problem with the ticker."

"What's that?"

"What if I told you that Steve Benz has been known to supply Mrs. Bowen with some good old-fashioned cocaine?"

"Oh." Michaela thought about Olivia and what had fallen from her purse at the coffee shop the night before. This was twisted. Olivia using drugs, Bridgette using drugs, Callahan trying to get Olivia to pose for his magazine, Benz possibly the supplier and maybe — just maybe — Audrey somehow got caught up in the middle of it all, and they'd killed her. Or one of them might have killed her. But Benz was a real up-and-comer on the country western scene. What about his career? Why would he jeopardize what he'd worked so hard at? "How do you know this?"

"It's the nature of the business. When things get slow, I start snooping and I sell some of my information to the tabloids. This situation here might have taken on an entirely different angle for me, and an added bonus. I know a guy at one of these rags who has it in for Benz. Says he had a one-night stand with his girlfriend after some bigwig Hollywood party. He's asked me to pass any information about Benz on to him. He knows that I work for the people who run in fast circles."

"What about Hugh Bowen? Would you exploit him if you found out that his wife is not only cheating on him, but might be linked to the murder?"

"If that's the truth, someone will discover it and put it out there. Besides, if that *is* the situation, he's a victim here. And so is Audrey. What was her last name?" She hesitated. "I won't lie to you, I will be checking into this thing. If Callahan, Benz, and the latest Mrs. Bowen are up to no good, I will exploit it. You want justice, don't you?"

"What if it's the wrong path?"

He shrugged. "It's a starting point."

"Okay, I'll tell you what I know, but you need to give me some of your insight. About Benz."

Dennis produced a notepad and repeated Audrey's name as he wrote it down. "Okay. Steve Benz is a party boy who started out in this town as a pool boy."

"Pool boy?"

"Yeah, you know, cleaning pools for the rich and famous. He met Bridgette on the party circuit before she hooked up with Bowen. They liked to hang together. Then, Bowen and Bridgette hooked up and he put her in rehab, right after the two of them got married. They tried real hard to keep that hush-hush, and for the most part Bowen's money did a good job of it. Money can pretty much buy you anything in this town. But people *do* talk. So, Mrs. Bowen's stint in rehab was one of those unspoken things amongst the rich and spoiled."

Michaela thought about Bob Pratt, his stint at Betty Ford, and a possible link between him and Bridgette Bowen, as well as the fact that Bob was now missing in action. Could it be coincidence, or was it linked to what had happened to Audrey? Was it possible that Bridgette and Bob had been in rehab at the same time? "Tell me then, or at least confirm if I'm on the right track."

"Go on."

Michaela's theory came from the center

of her gut. "Bridgette went through rehab, tried to stay straight. That didn't happen. She's back at it with Benz as the supplier, because she trusts him and she knows that with him in the limelight, he'll keep things quiet. She likes rich and powerful men, thus her rendezvous with Callahan. Benz brings the party favors for the two of them, and in return uses Callahan and Mrs. Bowen to become a superstar. Because from what I hear, Benz is looking to do a magazine spread with Olivia Bowen for *Pleasures* magazine. He thinks that Callahan can help put him on the map. Maybe he also thinks that Bridgette has some kind of in with her stepdaughter. Although, that's the furthest thing from the truth from what I understand."

"What did you say you do?" Dennis asked, placing his elbows on the table.

"I didn't. Why?"

"Because I think you'd make one hell of an investigator."

"Not everyone would agree with that," she replied, thinking of Jude. "I'm a horse trainer."

"Horse trainer? Really? Nah."

She didn't reply.

"Oh, shit. You're serious. You're really a fucking horse trainer? Sorry for my trash mouth. I pegged you for a bored, rich housewife, or maybe a mistress."

"Oh. Thanks, asshole. Pardon me for my trash mouth; I'm not used to being insulted."

He laughed. "I gotta say, you are a breath of fresh air. You are in a town knee-deep in bullshit, and here you are going around just trying to get the truth by telling the truth. You may have to change your ways to ever really find the truth. Nothing wrong with a bit of whitewash to get what you need."

"Sorry, lying isn't my style."

"Did I say lie? I said whitewash."

She couldn't help but smile. As offensive as this Dennis Smith seemed to be, there was something about him she was warming up to. Maybe the no-nonsense part appealed to her. Whatever it was, she wasn't in that fear-for-her-life mode around him any longer.

"Where did you hear about Olivia Bowen posing for Callahan's magazine?" he asked.

"The horse's mouth."

"Is she going to do it?"

Michaela shrugged and decided to go ahead and tell him about Kathleen Bowen's possessiveness over her daughter, and how she seemed to be the one behind the girl's career. Michaela decided to hold one piece of information back from Smith, not certain if it was important and not completely trusting him yet.

"They are a strange bunch. You see it all in this town."

"Looks like it. What do you think happened to Callahan in the room?"

"Possibly a heart attack, or maybe Bowen's wife and Benz had it in for him and it backfired. But *someone* called the paramedics. I can't imagine that if either one of them were up to no good where Callahan was concerned, they would've placed that call. He might have been able to do it himself, but the timing of Bridgette leaving the room doesn't work for me. I'm not sure, but trust me, I will find out."

"She seemed different when she left. Kind of like she'd had the wind knocked out of her. But why leave behind Callahan when something bad had obviously happened?" Michaela asked.

"That might have been a necessity. You said that she was jumpy on the phone earlier with Callahan. Maybe after whatever happened up there, she figured to save her own skin, she'd have to pull herself together. I'm sure she didn't want to have a chat with the paramedics or the hotel management. That would certainly get back to her husband."

"Yeah, but what she doesn't know is that it's already going to get back to her husband."

Dennis held up the camera. "Yep. Listen, you're a nice lady and I'm sorry for first scaring you in the parking lot, and then insulting you. My bad. But can I give you some advice?"

"Something tells me that you're going to give it to me anyway."

He ignored the comment. "This crew you're keeping tabs on, they've got a lot of cash, and if any one of them has something to hide and finds out that you're trying to uncover their dirty laundry, you could get hurt."

"Trust me, I've heard this before."

"Well, then . . . be careful. Here's my card. I'll see if I can't get anywhere with what happened to your friend, and not only because I want to sell a big enough story so I can head out on the next flight to Tahiti, but because I can tell you really cared about Audrey, and I think you deserve answers."

She took his card. "Yeah, sorry about the asshole thing. I don't usually call people names."

He laughed. "Are you kidding? That's a compliment. Trust me, I've been called worse. By the way, do you need directions to Cedars-Sinai?"

"Why would I need that?" She tried to play dumb.

"Fresh air. That is what you are." He stood and shook a finger at her. "Just take my advice and watch your back, horse trainer. Watch your back."

TWENTY-SIX

Michaela had had one of those lucid moments while speaking to Smith at Shutters, and because she still had plenty of time before dinner with Hudson Drake, she figured there was no better time to check her theory. Marshall Friedman had flown under the radar during this entire thing. But everyone knew him. Everyone involved had a connection to him. He sent Benz to make a nasty threat to Audrey at the races. He was using whatever tactic he could to pressure Olivia into signing with him as her manager. He obviously had business ties to Callahan. She didn't exactly know how Bridgette Bowen was connected to him, but she had a sense that Kathleen Bowen was somehow in his inner circle.

It was the last minutes of the day at the racetrack that hit her: minutes that at the time had gone by in a blur, and she hadn't stopped to really consider them. But now she had a hunch that she was right. Kathleen Bowen had asked her to call the chauffeur. She'd told her to press five. When Michaela had, she'd gotten a man, but not the driver. When she looked down at the call that had been made, the initials *MF* had come up. It had struck her as odd at the time, and she believed it had been just a mistake on Kathleen's part. It could be someone else with those initials. Michaela was aware that she was betting against the odds, but it made sense to her. The name *Marshall Friedman* had popped up in the course of conversations between her and Kathleen, her and Josh, her and Olivia, and her and Hugh. Marshall Friedman was lowlife Steve Benz's manager, and they were in cahoots over signing Olivia to a recording contract with them, and then some — like baring herself for Frederick Callahan's sleazy magazine. Who was this Friedman, anyway? How well had he known Audrey? As Michaela thought back to earlier that day at the races, she also recalled Benz's threat — or what had now, in retrospect, sounded like a threat. Weren't his exact words something like, *"Audrey's days are numbered and that Marshall Friedman will have Olivia under contract in a matter of a week."*? Interesting how things had gone down after that.

She dialed Information and was connected to Friedman's office. She made up a story that she was with one of the major hotel chains that she was in town on a quick trip and wanted to speak with Mr. Friedman about contracting some of his talent for entertainment in their larger hotels. "I don't have much time, and I promise I won't take much of his. I need ten minutes. I'd really like to speak to him. This is a major opportunity." She was told that he was in a meeting for the next half hour. She asked where the office was located. It was off the I-10 in Century City.

The secretary hemmed and hawed for a second, then finally agreed to allow Michaela to meet with him. Okay, she'd taken Smith's suggestion of whitewashing to heart. And, she'd apparently learned a thing or two from Joe. What would he say? What was *she* going to say when she came face-to-face with Friedman? Oh well. She would come up with something. She had to give it a try. Audrey's murder wouldn't stop haunting her.

By the time she made it to Century City and got out of the truck, she was perspiring and her nerves were shot. Was she crazy? It sure felt like it at the moment. What the hell. She'd never have to see this man again, and if he gave her any answers to satisfy her curiosity, it would be worth it.

She started toward the building just as two familiar figures emerged: Kathleen and Olivia. She called out to them, but with the din of the traffic they didn't hear her. They slid into the back of a limo before she could reach them, and it pulled away. She felt relieved that Olivia was okay, relatively speaking. But what were they doing there? They must have been there to see Friedman. Had Kathleen convinced Olivia to sign an agreement with him?

Michaela found his office on the eleventh floor. The receptionist took her name and eyed her. She knew she didn't exactly look the part of a traveling businesswoman.

Michaela eyed her back. She was just a little slip of a thing and Michaela had no doubt she could take her if she wanted to. "I'll let him know that you're here," the girl said.

"Thank you."

She came back a moment later and said that Mr. Friedman would see her. She followed, and was led to a well-appointed office where Marshall Friedman sat behind a huge desk, one devoid of papers and files and the normal clutter of a busy man.

He stood. "Good afternoon, Ms. Bancroft."

"Good afternoon." Her stomach became one nauseating wave.

"Have a seat."

Michaela sat down in a plush leather chair opposite him.

"You're from Starwood Resorts, my secretary said. It's unusual to schedule an appointment on this short a notice. How can I help you?" Friedman was bald with a big nose and light blue eyes.

This was the tricky part. Michaela shifted in the chair and tried to sit as tall as she could. "I've heard quite a bit about you."

He gave her an odd look. "Many people have. Again, how is it that I can help you?"

Beating around the bush was going to get her nowhere. "I was with Audrey Pratt, Olivia Bowen's manager, at the races the other day. The day that Audrey was murdered."

He held a finger up. "Ah, yes. You mean former manager, don't you?" He smiled slightly . . . or maybe it was a smirk. "Is that what brought you to our fine city? The races? You knew Ms. Pratt, huh?"

What a jerk. "Excuse me? The *former* manager? That seems callous, considering what happened."

He held up what looked to be a contract. "I don't mean to be disrespectful. My apologies, if you knew the woman. However, I've recently acquired Ms. Bowen as a client."

"That's convenient, isn't it? Audrey Pratt is murdered and the singer you've been after to sign with you for some time now is suddenly available."

Friedman shifted in his chair. "What are you getting at, Ms. Bancroft? It's obvious that you didn't come here to speak about entertainment for the Starwood Resort chain. Why are you wasting my time?"

His asinine comment about Audrey and his overall pompous attitude pushed her buttons, pressing her to go for the jugular. "I'm here because you represent Steve Benz, who was one of the last people to see my friend before she died. He said something to her that I'll be sure to mention to the police — or maybe the tabloids — since you represent such an up-and-coming star." His face flushed. "It was something like a threat actually, about how Audrey didn't have much longer to manage Olivia, that she'd be signing a contract with you within the week. I'm also aware that when the two of you were with Olivia after the show, Mr. Benz stepped out to grab drinks. To me that feels like he had time and also motive. Maybe that motive is directly tied to you."

"I barely knew Ms. Pratt. Steve is full of hot air at times. Whatever he said to Ms. Pratt does not concern me. Steve is certainly no killer, and if you are implying that I would ask him to murder a woman because I have a business-related issue with her, or for any reason for that matter, I'd say you are full of shit, lady. Certainly the reason I am representing Miss Bowen now is because she is wise enough to make an intelligent career choice —"

"I'd like to know how and why you took Olivia Bowen from the races."

"I don't think that's any of your business. It's time for you to leave." His face flushed once again.

She stood. "I'm sure that the police will probably find it as interesting as I do that you now have Olivia as a client only a few days after Audrey was murdered."

He shrugged. "Business is business. I'm sorry about your friend, but you are delusional. Now get the hell out of my office before I call security. And if you ever bother me again with your bizarre accusations, I will have you arrested."

"On what grounds? I wasn't accusing you of anything."

"Trespassing and harassment. I have a lot of pull in this town."

"I'm shaking." Michaela walked out of his office, baffled and if she admitted it, a bit shaken. She didn't trust Friedman at all. She also found it awfully strange that Olivia, who had been disgusted by the prospect of being his client the night before, would have signed that contract.

Twenty-Seven

Michaela had just about stopped shaking when she got into the truck and her cell phone rang. It was Joe.

"I got some more info on your friend Bob Pratt."

"What did you find out?"

"I worked the Betty Ford angle."

"The treatment center?"

"Yep, and it paid off. I got a list of people he spent time with there at the BFC."

"How did you do that?"

"I got a cousin who has a friend whose wife works in the cafeteria there."

"Of course. I should have known."

"I did some research on Bob and Audrey and who they are associated with. The name Bowen ring a bell?"

"It does."

"Uh-huh. We're gonna have to have a powwow, so I can learn what else you know about this guy, if you want me to help you the best that I can."

"I'll be home tonight. Late. Or you can come by tomorrow."

"I'll call you after I get the kids to bed. Maybe I can swing by; otherwise I'll stop by your place in the morning. You need to be thinking about everything that you know about this Pratt dude. Everything."

"I will. Promise." She sighed. What had she really gotten herself into?

"Deal. Check this out. What would you say if I told you that Bob Pratt and Mrs. Bowen spent some time together in rehab and they got pretty close there?"

"Bridgette?"

"The one and only."

A lightbulb moment happened as Michaela tied in the idea that Bob and Bridgette were in treatment at the same time. It could give Bridgette even more motive to want Audrey dead. Maybe she was afraid of what Bob might share with his sister. Not only that, what if she had done something to Bob? What if Bridgette was hiding something horrible that she'd confessed to Bob, and once out of rehab with some time to ponder, Bridgette knew she needed to get rid of them both? "What do you mean by close?"

"Hard to say. My cousin's friend's wife

didn't know if there was any hanky-panky going on. Those types of places really frown on fraternization, plus Mrs. Bowen was already married."

"What was Bridgette Bowen in Betty Ford for? Alcohol, too?" She already knew the answer to that one, but wanted to see if Joe could confirm it.

"Nope. She had a problem with the white powder."

"Cocaine?"

"Yes, ma'am."

Michaela didn't respond.

"Mick? You there? You okay?"

"I'm here. Just thinking, is all."

"Want me to see if I can find out anything else about the little scenario at rehab?"

"Would you?"

"You know I will. You was right when you said that I loved this stuff. But have you called that gal over at the autism center?"

"No. I'm sorry. I will, though. I promise. I think I may have some new horses coming in soon for the center." She thought about Audrey's horses. It was likely there were a few in that group that might work for the kids. She'd have to make a call to the Humane Society, too.

"Get on it, Mick, or I'm gonna stop this Colombo business for you."

"Thanks, Joey, you're the best. I'm on it."

Michaela turned off her phone. Bridgette Bowen and Bob Pratt? Tight? Odd combo. Looked like Michaela would be having a discussion with Hugh's wife. Should she come right out and confront her about what she'd seen at Shutters? And then ask her about her time in rehab with Bob? What if the woman was a cold-blooded killer? Oh dammit. Then, there was Callahan to consider. He'd been with Bridgette when she *found* the body. Maybe the two of them had something to do with Audrey's murder. And what about Callahan anyway? She wondered if he was okay and if Bridgette was responsible for him being in the hospital.

It was after three and she wanted to know if her trailer was ready. Juan had suggested she call after four. She was already in Century City. Cedars-Sinai was within a couple of blocks. She'd never guessed when she started out that day that it would become a fact-finding and info-gathering trip. A part of her almost felt like she was being directed to do this. Was Audrey somehow guiding her through this maze of lunacy and lunatics? She'd always believed in angels. It somehow comforted her to think that Audrey might be one, and that she was watching over her, helping her to find the justice she so deserved. Maybe it was a silly notion, but it comforted her all the same. If only she could also find out what had happened to Audrey's brother.

Even with the hospital nearby, the afternoon Los Angeles traffic made it difficult to maneuver through the surface streets in her truck. She graciously received the middle-finger salute by some kid whipping around her in a battered Honda.

She was happy that she made it to the hospital in one piece, and although she didn't know Callahan from a hole in the wall, she was relieved to learn that he was in good condition and able to see visitors.

She walked into Callahan's hospital room; he looked half asleep, but sat up when he saw her. "Well, hello. And, who may I ask is calling?" he sputtered. "Do I know you? Wait." He snapped a finger. "Miss April 2003? Great photo shoot, wasn't it, love. You were divine. Roses draped over you. Ah, what a dream. I am right, aren't I? I still have my memory intact."

She tried not to laugh as his toupee was askew and to the side of his head. "Keep dreaming. I am hardly Miss any month, nor do I intend to be."

"You break an old man's heart."

"Looks like someone else already took

care of that."

He shook a finger at her. "She's funny, too. I should have had an affair with you. What are you, a reporter? I thought my assistant was keeping you fiends away."

"There was no one outside your room."

"I knew I should have fired that moron long ago. Doesn't do a damn bit of good to have an assistant if they can't even keep the vultures at bay. But you're so lovely, I may talk to you. Maybe when I get out of this place we can have dinner together or something."

Yuck. I don't think so. "I'm not your type. Trust me."

"Oh, baby, you're all my type."

"I've noticed."

Michaela moved the newspaper that had been left on the chair next to Callahan's bed. She handed him water from his tray.

"Why are you being so nice? I already told you that you could be in my magazine. Give up the tabloid reporter gig and make some real money. Come pose for *Pleasures.* I can make you a star."

Michaela sighed and took a seat. "Listen, I'd love to tell you that I'm here as a reporter, but I'm not, and I'm not here to land my ass in your magazine. I feel terrible about what's happened to you though, and

I want you to know that." Maybe a little sympathy would go a long way with him.

"Gee thanks, sweet cheeks, I think." He laughed. "Can I ask you, if you're not with the paper and you aren't a nurse, then what are you doing here? And, how did you find out I was here? News couldn't have spread that fast."

Another sticky situation. Hell with it. If she could get through the Marshall Friedman thing earlier, she could handle a sick old man lying in a hospital bed. "Don't ask how. But I saw you at lunch today with Bridgette Bowen. I saw you go up in an elevator with her at the hotel. I also saw Steve Benz come and go, and then I watched as the paramedics wheeled you out shortly after Bridgette Bowen took off, which wasn't too long after Benz made his getaway."

"Not with the tabloids, huh? Because I could sell you the story for a ton of money. You do seem to know all the players."

"I don't want money. I don't plan to take your story and sell it or anything. I want answers. I was a good friend of Audrey Pratt. Does that help make my reasons for being here any clearer?"

"Audrey?"

Michaela nodded. "I think there is a lot

more to what happened to her than that her brother may have killed her after drinking too much over some sibling issue, and made his way out of town. I knew Bob Pratt and he and Audrey might have had issues like most siblings, but they loved each other. And I don't know what to think after what I saw today. I had to wonder if Benz and Bridgette hadn't poisoned you."

He laughed, then placed a hand on his chest. "Oh dear, no. It was nothing like that. Bridgette didn't try to kill me and neither did Steve. I was being a foolish old man, doing things I have no right to be doing at my age. Then I felt a burning in my chest. Thought I was having a damn heart attack. Turns out I shouldn't have eaten the Mexican shrimp dish I had for lunch. Just some acid reflux is all. At the time I didn't know what the hell it was. Bridge called the emergency crew and I told her to get out of there before her presence raised any questions."

Smith had been right about that observation. He'd mentioned that might have been the case. Callahan obviously had a soft spot for Bridgette. "And Benz. Why did he pay you a visit?"

He clucked his tongue. "You are an inquisitive one. I think we should let it all die down."

Michaela shook her head. "I wish I could. But my friend is dead on a cold slab at the morgue waiting to be buried properly, her brother is missing, and there are a lot of people around her who I simply find crazy. Sorry to say, but you're one of them."

He smiled. "I like you. You've got spunk. Are you sure we can't just do some test photos? Being a *Pleasures* girl can do a lot for you."

"Mr. Callahan —"

"Frederick, please."

"Fine. Frederick, I don't want to go to the police with what I saw, because I seriously doubt that you are a killer. I do wonder if you know who killed Audrey, though."

He took another sip of water. "Benz came to our room to give us some party favors."

"Drugs."

"Yes. I know, it's very stupid to do, and I do know better, but Bridgette can be quite persuasive and she was feeling upset, so I indulged her."

Another point for Smith. He'd been right about Benz being a supplier. "Why was she upset?"

"Isn't it obvious? She and I have been

256

fooling around. It's what we were doing at the races, out in one of the stalls, way on the back forty. Afterward, she left first and came upon Audrey. I ran when I heard her scream and soon after a crowd formed . . . Wait a minute, you were there. That's where I saw you."

She nodded. "So Bridgette was upset that the two of you might get caught. Don't you think that this will all come out? I'm sure that I'm not the only one who saw you two at the hotel. You weren't exactly discreet. And it's possible you were spotted at the races."

He laughed. "I suppose we weren't too careful. Sometimes that's a part of the thrill. I probably do owe Hugh a phone call, before the shit really hits the fan."

"Probably so. He's been through a lot. Can I ask you, why Bridgette? You have lots of women in your life. Why choose Bridgette Bowen?"

"You've seen her. She's damn gorgeous, and for the record, I didn't choose her, she got her hooks in me and wouldn't let go."

"She pursued you?"

"Does that surprise you? Look, I've seen Bridgette's type around and if you ask me, I did Hugh a favor and in time he'll see that. Bridgette is one of those women who are opportunists to the nth degree. She had a wealthy, wonderful husband in Hugh, but when he started paying more attention to other things, she became angry or sullen like a spoiled child. Men like us are busy people. To get his attention back, or to get any attention at all, she looked to another man. These women typically look to other men who have more money or power than the one they're with. I happened to be that man."

"Looks are one thing, but aren't you and Hugh friends?"

"Men like us don't have friends. It's healthy competition."

Michaela raised a brow. "Healthy, huh?" She scanned him up and down.

"Not this go-around, I suppose. And, maybe I deserved it. Little scare to knock some sense into me, I suppose."

"No comment. You mentioned that Hugh had other interests besides his wife. Do you mean the horses and his businesses?"

He laughed. "You are such a treat. Is that naïve streak in you for real? Or do you like to play coy?"

She rolled her eyes at him. "I actually like to think the best of people. See, in my world, it's not totally common for people to go around screwing other people's spouses behind their backs." Okay, so that wasn't completely true. Her own ex-husband had played around on her, but Callahan did not need to know that. Maybe she *was* naïve. Hell, she'd rather live in a rose-colored-glasses world than this seedy place she found herself in currently.

"It's in everyone's world."

She felt her face heat up. "What is this about Hugh and other interests?"

"Hughie boy had his own love on the side, but his was a bit more serious than just a fling."

Michaela uncrossed her legs and leaned in.

He nodded and for a second, as he gazed outside his hospital window, his face took on a faraway look. "I was in love once. Beautiful emotion."

Okay, there was no time to go down memory lane with Mr. Pleasures. "Who was he in love with? Who was Hugh seeing?" Michaela knew the answer, but wanted to confirm it with Callahan. If he said who she thought he would say, then that meant there were more people who were aware of Hugh's real feelings. Could Hugh's feelings for Audrey have caused someone else to murder Audrey other than Bridgette?

"The woman he's always been in love

with. The one he should have married. Audrey."

She still couldn't find any words for a while. "How do you know this?"

"I think almost everyone knew. Back in the day when Hugh opened his place in Malibu and we would all hang out, I'd see the way Audrey would look at Hugh, but he missed the signals. Everyone knew they should have been together. Everyone but Kathleen . . . or if she did, she would make certain it didn't happen for them. Kathleen Bowen gets what she wants, and she wanted Hugh. And Kathleen was a gorgeous woman, too, back then, before the bitterness set in. She came on to Hugh like a mare in heat and didn't let go. Audrey, being as gracious as she could, stepped away. But that love never died and when Hugh realized the mistake he'd made, he tried to set it right."

"What did he do?"

Callahan started to cough. Michaela stood and gave him a sip of water. "Thank you. How would you like to be my personal nurse?" he asked and winked at her.

"You are bad."

"So they say."

"How did Hugh try to make things right?"

"Recently Bridgette came to me in tears.

260

Said that she'd found a ring."

"A ring?"

"She found it in Hugh's private safe. The naughty vixen got into the safe. Don't know how she did that. But there are many things she does that I haven't been able to figure out how." He smiled.

Michaela wished he'd stop with the innuendos and memories of his sexual escapades with Bridgette Bowen. It was pretty disgusting.

"The ring wasn't just any ring. It was a princess-cut diamond and on the inside of the band it was inscribed *To Audrey, my forever love.*"

"Oh."

"Oh, ho!"

"An engagement ring?" The ring that Hugh had mentioned to her. It was all true, then. Hugh and Audrey had been deeply in love for years.

"It does look that way now, doesn't it?"

Michaela took a minute to absorb what Callahan was telling her. "Do you think Bridgette would have killed Audrey out of jealousy, or worry that she wasn't going to get the payday I'm sure she'd expected from Hugh?"

"No. Bridgette may have a naughty streak, but she's no killer. A killer in the sack, sure, but no. She may not have had a prenup, but if Hugh had left her, he would have treated her right. She was dumb to keep pursuing me, but maybe she saw a bigger payday where I was concerned. Hell, though, I wouldn't have married her. She is what she is — an expensive whore, plain and simple. She was playing all the angles. Crapshoot if you ask me, and the stakes were high. I'm pretty sure Bridge has lost it all by now. If Hugh doesn't know what was going on yet, he will. Sad thing is Hugh would have treated her right, though, if she'd just kept her cards a bit closer to her chest or not even ventured outside the house. Like I've already told you, I'm never one to turn away a hot piece of ass. But Bridge didn't off Audrey. No, if anyone killed Audrey out of jealousy it wouldn't have been Bridgette. It would have been Kathleen."

"What?"

He waved a hand at her. "You bet. The woman always had this competition thing going with Audrey."

"They were friends."

"Friends! That's a joke. Maybe Audrey *thought* they were friends, but Kathleen espoused the idea of keeping your friends close but your enemies closer."

"Okay, say that's so, then why bother after

Hugh left Kathleen for Bridgette and not Audrey. Why keep up the charade then?"

"Control and power."

"Excuse me?"

"Oh, that damn Kathleen is a control freak. She likes to have control over anyone she knows, and she lost it with Hugh. Look at the way she treats her daughter. The kid doesn't blink an eye without asking Mama, and I think Audrey was the same way. And Kathleen enjoyed that. Kathleen plays the beaten mouse, but trust me, there is a monster lurking inside and if she winds up being arrested for killing Audrey, I won't be a bit surprised."

"That's horrible."

"Life isn't always nice, sweet thing."

"You're saying then that it's possible Kathleen killed Audrey because she was jealous that Hugh was always in love with her."

But if Kathleen murdered Audrey, could there be other reasons for the savage brutality? Could it have been more about Olivia than anything else? Maybe Audrey did know about her drug problem and wanted to help Olivia. Maybe Kathleen didn't want to take the risk of having Hugh involved, and silenced Audrey before she had a chance to go to him.

He nodded. "There's that fine line between love and hate. For Kathleen, I think that means something."

"You're filled with all sorts of clichés, aren't you?"

"I'm an old man. What do you expect?"

"I'm not sure what I expected. But for now, I think I've had more than I can take."

"Thanks for stopping by. Anytime you want to come on over to my mansion in Bel-Air, give a ring. We all have a swell time there."

Michaela didn't even acknowledge the comment and left the perverted old fart behind.

TWENTY-EIGHT

Michaela called the Bowen Ranch and got a recording. She decided to drive over there. Someone should be around. Hopefully, the trailer would be ready to go; she could load Geyser and meet Hudson for that quick dinner without any more bizarre turn of events. She didn't know if she could handle anything else for the day.

It was half past four when she pulled into the ranch. Climbing out, she heard hooves from the practice track. She noticed a bay coming around the backside, tail in the air, looking like a fierce machine. It seemed late in the day to be running.

She stood against the rail watching as the horse opened up into full stride. What a spectacular animal. Quite an athlete. The rider knew how to handle him, and Michaela wondered who it was. It didn't appear to be Josh. She jumped when she heard a voice behind her. "Hey!"

She turned to see Josh, hands on hips, staring at her. "Oh, hi. So, it's not you up on the horse."

"No. It's Olivia."

"Oh!" Michaela was a bit shocked by this revelation. She wondered if Josh was aware that Olivia had been using drugs.

"I know what you're thinking."

"I'm not thinking anything," Michaela said.

"Really? So, you aren't wondering why she's riding with the knowledge that her mom would freak out?"

"Okay, maybe."

Josh faced her. "Olivia needs help. I know it, Audrey knew it, and her mother is in denial about it."

"I don't know what you mean." Maybe he was aware of the drugs. She was waiting to see if he'd spell it out for her.

He ignored her reply. "My way of helping Olivia is by seeing that she gets to do what she wants with her life, and that's riding."

"Okay."

"Okay," he repeated.

What was it with Josh? Why was he acting so pissy toward her, like he had a bone to pick? Maybe he did that with anyone connected to Olivia. Not that hers was a huge connection, but the trainer appeared aw-

266

fully protective over the young woman, always prepared to come to her defense. "Hey, can I ask you something?" At this point Michaela had lost her inhibitions about asking questions. She done it with the slick, asshole entertainment manager, Smith the asshole — sort of — and Callahan the dirty old man, so it certainly couldn't hurt to talk to the horse trainer. They at least had something in common.

"What about?" His tone had a definite edge to it.

"Bob Pratt. You knew him, right? He came here to vet last Monday, Hugh said, and that you helped with the horses. What do you think of him taking off and the police saying he's their prime suspect in his sister's murder?"

He shrugged. "Not sure what I can tell you. I don't know Bob all that well. Yeah, I helped him out last week with the horses. That's not unusual. We might have had an occasional drink in the past. It's the horse business. You know, birds of a feather and all. He's a good vet. I like him. He doesn't drink anymore, and I'm not a big drinker so yeah, we'd grab a Coke once in a blue moon and shoot the shit."

"What do you think about his disappearance?"

"I don't know what to think. Didn't know him well; I already told you that."

"Obviously you knew him well enough to grab a Coke and 'shoot the shit,' as you put it."

"Come on. I'm a guy, so is Bob. We don't do deep-therapy types of discussions like you women do."

Michaela took a step back to blow off his pissy attitude. "Did Bob ever talk to you about his sister?"

"Not a lot. I know he thought a lot of her, but he was busy with his new job at Eq Tech and with his new girlfriend."

"Girlfriend?" She wondered if this was the same woman that Joe had gotten a bead on.

"I didn't stutter."

"I'm sorry." Michaela decided to placate the man. Maybe being sweet would get him to open up. She had a feeling that Josh Torrey was hiding something about Bob, maybe Audrey, too. Or, if he wasn't hiding anything, the information he might have, which he didn't know he had, could lead her down a path that could help her figure out who had murdered her friend and why. "I wasn't aware that Bob had a girlfriend." Michaela thought it best to hold her cards close. The less that anyone knew she was putting her nose into places that she probably should not be, the better off she figured she was. "Audrey and I had a lot of those womanly talks, you know, about relationships, that sort of thing, and she mentioned Bob quite a bit. This is the first I've heard anything about him having a girlfriend." She was getting good at this whitewashing tactic Smith suggested.

"I don't know. I think she was a girlfriend. I know they worked together at Eq Tech. She was one of the chemists there. At least I know they hung out. I met her one night when he made a vet call at the ranch. Pretty lady. Nice, too. Bob seemed into her and vice versa."

"You don't know what to make of him just not showing up for work, or that no one can find him?"

"No, I don't. I know what the papers are reporting and that everyone is thinking he fell off the wagon and had something to do with his sister's murder. But I don't believe any of that shit. Bob might have had problems in the past, but from what I know of him, he's solid and was headed in the right direction. He also mentioned to me that he was going to go see his girlfriend for the weekend, that she wasn't feeling too well. I don't know, maybe he took off early to be with her."

"He would've been in touch with someone, contacted somebody, if that was the case. Don't you think?"

"Yeah. I'd think so." Josh raked his hand through his hair.

"Then maybe it's foul play."

"Maybe it is."

"Do you know of anyone who would want to hurt Bob or Audrey?"

"No."

"What about his girlfriend? Do you remember her name?"

"Carla, something." He snapped his fingers. "No. Cara. I didn't catch her last name."

"She still working for Eq Tech?" It looked to be that the woman Joe had discovered and the one Josh was referring to were one and the same.

"I don't know. When I met her, she mentioned something about the commute and how she hated it; even took the train pretty often, she said."

"Where was she commuting from?"

"Down near San Diego, if I remember right. Maybe Del Mar? I honestly don't know. I really don't know what to tell you, but it sucks. The whole thing does. Wish I had some insight. But I don't, and I hate to cut this short, but I've got work to do."

"I understand."

Michaela needed to call Joe and give him this information, see what he could find out before they hooked up. Maybe this Cara had heard from Bob. She watched as Olivia dismounted. When the girl spotted Michaela, she turned away. Maybe she'd figured out that her drugs had been found. Michaela approached her, but Olivia abruptly turned to Josh. "I've got to go. Sorry."

Michaela thought about confronting her but changed her mind. She would be talking to Olivia or her dad about discovering the cocaine, but not now. There were still some parts of this puzzle in regard to little Miss Olivia that she wanted to put together.

Josh looked baffled as Olivia ran off. He turned back to Michaela, leading the horse in her direction. "Look, I'm sorry about Audrey and I don't know what to think about Bob. It's a shame, that's what it is. A damn shame."

Michaela nodded. "Is Hugh around?"

"No. He's not. I don't know what happened up at the house a little while ago, but there was some shouting going on and then Bridgette took off with Hugh speeding down the drive behind her."

Looked like the cat was out of the bag.

"Hey, aren't you here to pick up Geyser? Juan told me about your trailer." Josh pointed at it in the distance.

"Yeah, is he around? I've got to get on the road."

"You're not going anywhere with the trailer."

"What?"

He frowned. "Sorry. Juan told me that he had to get some more parts to fix it, and what he needed he wasn't able to find at the hardware store in Malibu."

"When did he say it would be ready?"

"He didn't. He's gone for the day. I'm sure he'll have it taken care of in the next few days."

"Few days. Damn. It's not like I live down the road, you know."

"Tell you what, I'll find out for you, and once it's fixed, I'll get someone to transport the horse out there for you."

Now he was being Mr. Nice Guy. What was it with these people that Audrey hung out with? They were cold one minute, warm the next.

She gave Josh her number and looked at her watch. Happy hour with Hudson was fast approaching, and if she didn't head out now, she'd be late.

TWENTY-NINE

Hudson Drake turned out to be as delightful as Michaela remembered. She also discovered that they had a lot in common.

"Grew up on a ranch, too," he said. "My dad taught me how to ride. I don't ride like I used to, what with work. It ties me up quite a bit," he said, the candlelight bouncing off the sparkle in his blue eyes.

They'd started with a glass of wine and appetizers during happy hour and their conversation carried them through dinner. Michaela decided against any more wine, knowing she had more than a two-hour drive home. But his company made her feel giddy, almost as if she'd drank more than she really had. He looked as handsome as he had the other day, only toned down now in a gray V-neck sweater and jeans. She'd thought about telling him about her ridiculous day, but decided against it. His conversation was far more upbeat. She had mentioned the horse trailer fiasco and he'd laughed heartily, then apologized.

"I'm not laughing at your expense. Okay, maybe I am. That stinks. What did you do all day? Why did you have to cancel lunch?"

"I had to take care of some business." She'd leave it at that. "And, no offense taken. Come to think of it, it is kind of funny. Stupid rats. I'll have to set some traps."

He didn't make any moves on her, which was nice. No flirtation, just nice conversation. She felt oddly at ease with him. Jude made her kind of nervous, left those butterfly feelings in her stomach. Now she was just plain angry and irritated with him. Ethan . . . well, he was another story. He was her best friend and that was all, and she wanted nothing but the best for him. Their relationship was comfortable, almost too much so for friends at times. She knew it had to bother Summer that they were as intimate as they were, what with all they'd shared growing up over the years. Those childhood ties could never be broken, and Michaela comforted herself with that thought quite often.

Hudson was interesting and fun. "How are you doing? After everything that's happened?" he asked.

"It hasn't really sunk in; I can't believe that my friend was murdered. But I'm keeping busy. That's all I know to do. Damn!"

"What?"

"I forgot to call the Humane Society. I wanted to talk to them about taking in some of Audrey's horses."

"That's nice of you."

"She would have done it for me. She was like that. A really kind, good-hearted woman. I hope they find who did this to her."

"Me, too." He picked up her hand and squeezed it. "I have a guy working on finding Bob."

"You do? So, you called in the private investigator that you were talking about?"

"I did, but so far, he's got nothing."

"Nothing at all?" Hmm, maybe Joe's cousins were better at this than any private eye.

"No, nothing. You better get on the road if you're going to make it home at a halfway decent hour. It's already past eight."

"You're right."

"By the way, you did get my roses, didn't you?" he asked.

"Oh, my gosh, I'm sorry, I meant to thank you. Yes. They were beautiful. I loved them. Um, but about that . . ."

"Oh no, you are not going to back out on me now."

She sighed. "It's just the timing and all the driving I've been doing and I really need to get back into the swing of things."

"Do it next week. We'll have a great time, forget your worries for a night. I won't take no for an answer. Besides, all the 'in' crowd will be there." He rolled his eyes. "The Bowens, Fredrick Callahan, who owns *Pleasures* magazine and several winner's circle horses, and just about anyone who is a player in the racing arena."

She might have had enough of all of them, but she thought about Jude and how angry she was with him and she agreed that she would see Hudson on Saturday.

He walked her to her truck, gave her a peck on the cheek, and held the door open for her. "I had a nice time this evening and I'm looking forward to Saturday night."

"Me, too. But, I have a question: What do I wear?"

"Dress to the nines. This thing is quite an event."

"The nines, huh?" He nodded. She knew she'd have to raid Camden's closet to find something. When she looked in her rearview mirror, she saw Hudson waving. She smiled and headed home.

THIRTY

The next day Michaela played phone tag with Joe, who hadn't been able to make it by between the hardware store, one kid's doctor's appointment, another one's soccer game, and some other event. She did leave him the message about this Cara person who had worked at Eq Tech with Bob Pratt. She wanted to know if he'd been able to find out anything more on that front.

She'd also placed a call to the vet who had seen Rocky over the weekend. It was already Tuesday and she didn't understand why it was so difficult to get any answers. Granted he appeared to be fine, but she was still concerned and wanted to know what his labs reported. She would have to track Ethan down; the last she'd heard, he was still in San Diego with Halliday. She was planning on stopping by his and Summer's house that evening. She needed to tell them she was not going to attend Friday night's baby shower. As for Jude, Michaela planned to leave him a message through the receptionist at the station, because she didn't want to talk to him yet. The last thing she wanted to do was show up sans half of a couple at a couples' baby shower. Not that she and Jude were a couple anyway. Sheesh! Who ever heard of a couples baby shower? That had to be Summer's idea. Sure they were in vogue now, but *come on,* as if the men really enjoyed sitting around with a group of women oohing and aahing over baby clothes and toys. That was a scene she wanted to miss. She already had a gift for the baby — a bath set and a teddy bear. Generic, but useful.

Since neither the other vet nor Ethan had called, Michaela decided to speak to Dwayne about Rocky. It was feeding time and Dwayne was mixing the grains and supplements for the horses. Camden hung at his heels, which was kind of annoying, because it wasn't as if Camden knew a damn thing about horses. However, being around Dwayne, maybe she thought that she'd gained a master's of equine through osmosis.

"Maybe he needs to be turned out more. You know, he is a stud and they need to roam, feel like they're in charge of their brood," Camden said, winking at Dwayne. "Didn't the vet say that Rocky's testosterone levels were high? Maybe he just needs to get out and about more. Burn off some steam."

"From what I understand, this is a medical situation and not so much about lifestyle," Michaela shot back as she walked up. Her friend looked genuinely hurt, which made her feel bad. Camden was trying, and the bottom line was that she'd been her friend for years. So why was she feeling so irritated by her? Did it really have to do with Camden trying to express her limited knowledge about horses? Or, did it have more to do with the fact that Camden seemed to have found true love, and Michaela . . . Well, she was still struggling with the idea of whether or not such a concept even existed.

"Michaela is right, Cammy girl, Rocky not too worried about running with mares right now. He be a happy boy, but this thing he got going on has something to do with his insides."

Camden nodded. "You know what, why don't you two talk about it while I go and make some dinner?"

Dinner? Now that was a first indeed. Michaela might have expected Camden to say she would be going to make margaritas. But dinner? Michaela had been the cook over the last couple of years. Sure, Camden might have popped in a Lean Cuisine once in a blue moon, but dinner? That sounded fishy. She eyed Dwayne as Camden walked away. "Dinner?"

He shrugged and grinned. "She's taking cooking classes. She not so bad, you know. A little bland, but she be trying."

"You two are really in love, aren't you?"

He nodded. "She want your approval. She want you to be happy. She worry about you so much."

Michaela nodded, feeling the back of her throat swell with emotion. "I am happy. I'm just shocked. Surprised, you know. I already told her that I'm happy for the both of you."

"I know."

Michaela took a deep breath and asked, "So what do you think could be going on with Rocky?"

He shook his head and scratched the toe of one of his boots into the dirt. "I thinking about it a lot, and I don't know. Really don't. I seen lots of problems in horses over the years, but not like this. I been taking his vital signs and writing them down because the vet asked me to, and I see nothing crazy. I think we be worrying 'bout a onetime thing, until last night and again this morning." He walked into the office, brought out a sheet of paper with Rocky's vitals, and handed it to Michaela.

She didn't like the sound of that. "Why didn't you say anything if you thought there was a problem?"

"I wasn't so sure at first and didn't want to scare you. You been going through a lot, and I think I better be real sure before we go and get worried again, plus he didn't have no more spells like the other day."

"Dwayne! This is my horse. My kid. You can't keep anything from me. I don't care if it'll cause me worry. I love this animal. Dammit, don't try and protect me."

"Thought I was doing right."

"No. You weren't." She looked at the sheet where Dwayne had recorded Rocky's vitals, blood rushing through her, angry with her assistant. From the records Rocky's heart rate and blood pressure looked like they elevated at about eight in the morning and eight at night. "This looks like it happens about two hours after feeding," Michaela said, tucking away her anger.

"Right," Dwayne said.

"I don't get it. And I'm irritated that I can't get a hold of this vet. I'm going to see if Ethan is back from San Diego." She used the office phone to call Ethan's cell, but it went straight to his voice mail. She hesitated but decided to call his house. Summer answered.

"Oh, hi, Michaela. Are you calling about Friday?"

"I am. Um, something has come up. I'm terribly sorry, a commitment I forgot about. But I was wondering if I could stop by and drop off a gift for the baby."

"Sure," Summer replied, and Michaela could have sworn that the woman sounded as relieved as she felt about her nonappearance at the baby shower.

"Is Ethan going to be home? I need to talk to him about one of my horses the oncall vet saw on Saturday."

"He should be. He's on his way home from San Diego now. I'm expecting him any time."

"Okay, I won't be long." Michaela hung up the phone and sighed.

"You going to see Ethan?" Dwayne said standing in the doorway. Michaela nodded. "That's good. Call me tonight at home if you get an answer. I got to go and check on my girl. I am sorry about Rocky. I'll never do something like that again."

Michaela hugged him. "It's okay. I understand and I do appreciate it, but I'm a big girl." She pulled away and socked him lightly on the shoulder. "And as far as you and Camden go, I am happy for the two of you. I really am. You're good for her."

"Thanks. She good for me, too."

Michaela grabbed the gift for the baby and was heading out the door when the phone rang.

Damn! She should let it go. She wanted to get over to Ethan's, talk to him about her horse and get home quickly. Maybe it was Joey though, with some word on Bob Pratt. Her caller ID didn't register. Probably a damn solicitor. She grabbed it anyway. The phone crackled loudly. No one seemed to be on the other end, as she didn't get a response when she first answered. She started to hang up, when a man's voice on the other end said, "Is it true?"

"Is what true? Who is this?"

"About Audrey?" His voice sounded distant.

"Who the hell is this? What do you know about Audrey?"

Again, no answer. "I said, what do you know about Audrey?" she yelled.

Finally the man said, "Terrell Jardinière." Then the line went dead.

THIRTY-ONE

"Oh, Michaela, we're so glad you could come by," Summer said, a little too unconvincingly as she opened her front door in all her pregnant glory. She still had her perfect ivory skin and shiny red hair sleeked back in a ponytail. On top of all her perfectness she had that pregnancy glow, and she hadn't gained a ton of weight, except for her tummy. It seemed as if there were a perfect basketball resting inside her. "I'm only sorry that you won't be able to make it Friday night. Why don't you stay for dinner this evening?"

"That sounds lovely, but really I can't."

Ethan appeared next to Summer, his rugged, chiseled features quite the contrast to his wife's delicacy. "Hey Mick, what's this I hear you can't come on Friday?"

"I'm sorry, it's, well, I have to . . ."

Ethan interrupted her, sensing her panic. "I know, if I remember right, I think you said you were doing something with Joe Pellegrino's little girl."

She nodded. "Yes. Gen. It's a party at Joe's and since I'm her riding instructor and am going to be working with more of the kids in her group, I thought I'd better go."

She smiled at him, secretly thanking him. He'd saved her. That was Ethan. She knew he understood that it was not easy for her to be at a baby shower. She was sure he didn't quite grasp the fact that it also had a lot to do with the fact that it was *his and Summer's* baby shower, but that was okay. He understood enough. He'd been there through the years when she'd tried to get pregnant to no avail while married to Brad, and he knew how badly she wanted a child.

"That's great," Summer said. "Ethan mentioned that you were working with her. She's autistic, right?"

Michaela nodded. "Yes, and Joe and his wife, Marianne, have asked me to run a riding program for other autistic children. I plan to take that on soon. I'm getting a great horse from Hugh Bowen — should be here in a day or two — and I placed a call to the Humane Society today. They picked up Audrey's animals, and I'd like to adopt the horses. I think she had quite a few that would work out well for this program."

"That's terrific, Mick. Man, I am so sorry about Audrey. I just can't believe it."

"Me either."

Summer smiled. "Oh, I'm sorry, can you excuse me for a minute?" She glanced at Ethan. "I'm making one of Ethan's favorite's — veal cutlets in a lemon caper sauce and au gratin potatoes."

"Sounds and smells delicious," Michaela said, somewhat jealous, knowing that her culinary expertise didn't extend much past barbequed chicken on the grill — with sauce from a jar. She could make a mean hamburger, too, though.

"Thank you. I'll be back in a jiff." She scurried into the kitchen.

"Oh, here," Michaela said when Summer walked away, and handed Ethan the baby gift.

"Thanks."

"No, thank you, for covering for me."

"That's what friends are for. I know it isn't easy for you, and as much as I want you to be here on Friday, I understand why it's hard."

"You're not upset?"

"No. I am kind of upset that you didn't tell me about Audrey. I know what she meant to you. I had some cop call me — a Detective Merrill — and ask me if she'd

286

been down on the track right after Halliday had the break. I was in shock to hear the news, but no, I didn't see her on the track."

"I'm sorry that I didn't tell you. I wanted to, but I knew — know — that you have a lot on your plate right now. With Summer getting ready to have the baby, and your new job, all of that has to be on your mind. The last thing I wanted was to burden you."

He took both of her hands. "Shut up. You've been my friend for what? Almost thirty years? And you think by telling me about what is going on in your life and the pain you're dealing with is a burden?"

She shrugged. It might not be a burden to him. She knew that. But what she didn't want to do was come between him and his wife. He was married to Summer and she respected that his wife was not super keen on their friendship, even though it had been one from childhood.

"You or what you're going through is never a burden. Got it?"

She nodded. "Got it."

"Now, Summer said that you needed to talk to me about a horse. What's up? Come on in and sit down."

She followed him into the family room, which was floral, feminine, and delicate in pastel shades of green, rose, and yellow. Michaela almost laughed seeing Ethan plunk down on the rose-patterned sofa. To recall what his bachelor pad had looked like! This was all *so* Summer.

"Talk to me," Ethan said.

Michaela explained to him about the vet coming out to see Rocky, what the labs had shown, and how she'd been having difficulty getting a hold of Dr. Burton for further explanation.

"She's new. A little overwhelmed. I'm trying to get her to take on more, since I've taken on the track appointment, but it's been difficult being in San Diego so much. I'm going back down on Thursday morning to check on Halliday when they change his cast and then hurry home to help with the preparations for the shower. I'm sorry to say that I have not seen Rocky's labs, but when I get into the office tomorrow, I'll take a look."

"Do you have any idea by what I'm saying as to what it might be?" Michaela asked.

"Not without examining him. He's six now, and it's possible that he could have some type of degenerative heart thing going on. The one thing I do find kind of interesting is that from what you're telling me, the initial labs that were reported are sounding similar to Halliday's labs."

"What do you mean?"

"Come on. I'll show you what I have in his file. I brought it home with me to go over again. It's up in my office. First, I want to show you the baby's room. I finished painting it a few days ago."

"Sure." They walked up the stairs of the very formal, almost museum-like home, passing his and Summer's bedroom, all done up in peach and gold. Puke. But when she took a second look, it really wasn't barf material at all. It was as tasteful and beautiful as Michaela figured it would be, though she didn't get a sense that it would be easy to relax in all that perfection.

Next door was the baby's room. "Oh my gosh! This is amazing! You did all this?" she asked. He nodded, a huge grin across his face. Was he blushing, too? Ethan was obviously proud of all he'd done.

"I didn't paint the horses. Summer had a pro do that. But I set up the crib, and painted the background colors. I even helped sew the curtains."

Michaela crossed her arms. "Look at you."

"I know. I can't wait for this kid to be born."

Michaela gave him a hug. "I'm so happy for you. And for Summer. You two will make great parents." She *was* happy for him. She knew how much Ethan wanted to be a father. His own dad had abandoned him before he was born and only recently had he even discovered the true identity of his father. She knew that he felt a certain obligation to be the best father ever, and she was sure he'd live up to that. The room was painted a light tan with an amazing mural of wild horses running through the desert; the ceiling was a blue sky with billowy clouds, and the drapes and baby's comforter were red with a cowboy pattern on them.

"Thanks. We're excited."

She followed him to another museum-quality room with some of his degrees up on the wall. He went up to an ornate mahogany desk, grabbed a file, and handed it to her. "Look at this and tell me what you think."

She opened the file. "I'm not a vet, Ethan."

"No, but you know quite a bit. Remember all the times you've helped me study? And it's not like you haven't had your fair share of illnesses on the ranch. Plus, I'm looking to see if any of this sounds like what you or Dwayne has seen going on in Rocky."

"I'll try." She studied the results. "His testosterone and cortisol levels are high, like what we're seeing with Rocky, and it looks like he has a spike in blood pressure after meals. Might be a thyroid problem. I meant to bring you a sheet that Dwayne has been keeping on Rocky. It resembles this almost to a tee, with his pressure rising after meals. Do you think it could be steroids in Halliday? I know it isn't in my horse, but it's a possibility with a racehorse."

"He was tested prior to the race and he didn't have any steroid, bute, *nada,* in his system."

"Maybe they were masking it somehow."

"Maybe. I am concerned though. I noticed this afternoon that his heart rate and blood pressure were up again, this time not after eating. First we suspected an infection. I don't know. I had him started on a course of antibiotics because you can't be too cautious after a leg break like the one he's suffered."

"Could this diminish his chances for survival?"

"It might."

"Oh no."

"Ethan?" Summer yelled from downstairs.

"We better go down. She hates to climb stairs if she doesn't have to these days. I'll let you know what happens."

"Okay. Did Kathleen Bowen ever turn up

at the center?"

"Nope." He shrugged. "Maybe she figures since you're footing the bill that she can ignore him. I still think you need to reconsider that."

"I know you do.

"You know what, I almost forgot." Michaela smacked herself on the forehead. "Did Audrey call you and leave you a message about a file that Bob asked her to give to you?"

"Yeah, she did. She called me last week. I called her back and we played phone tag. Then I got busy and forgot about it. Now that you mention it though, I remember. I have no clue why she would have one of his files. Especially one that he thought I might need. I have to think about and look at some of my cases. I know that we've conferred on some things together, but I can't recall anything lately. But I've had a lot on my mind. How did you know about it?"

"Audrey mentioned it to me the other day. She thought it was strange that he asked her to give it to you, but apparently he said that it was because the two of you were in close vicinity and he thought you might get it faster from her. They'd had dinner last week together."

"Huh. I still don't know what it's about."

"I have the file."

"You do?"

"I think I do, anyway."

"Michaela?"

"I took something from Audrey's desk that was in an envelope that came from Bob."

"You did what?"

"I figured that it was for you."

He rubbed his chin. "Okay. Where is it?"

Thank goodness he didn't press her on it. She didn't want to admit that she'd left Audrey's ranch with the file right underneath the nose of one Officer Garcia. "I left it at home. I meant to bring it with me tonight, but was kind of in a rush to get over here." She didn't want to tell him that the reason she'd lost her focus was the mysterious phone call she'd received before leaving. "I'll get it to you."

"Ethan," Summer called again.

"Come on."

They walked down together. Summer stood at the bottom of the landing, frowning. "What were you two doing?"

"I was showing Mick the baby's room."

"It's gorgeous. You two have done a wonderful job," Michaela said.

"Thank you," Summer replied. "It's time to eat. Are you sure you can't stay?" She smiled sweetly at Michaela, but there were

293

daggers in Summer's eyes aimed right at her heart.

"No, but thank you."

Michaela left their place with a ton on her mind, from Halliday's and Rocky's conditions to Audrey's murder, and of course, to the very strange phone call she'd received before heading over to Ethan and Summer's house. Had it been a prank call from someone who knew that she and Audrey were close? If so, that was sick. Terrell Jardinière. That's the name the caller had said. Who in the hell was Terrell Jardinière? Michaela didn't have a clue, but she knew she'd be up late into the night trying to figure out who this guy was, or if he was anyone at all.

THIRTY-TWO

Even though sleep had eluded her much of the night, Michaela rose early the next morning. She'd worked the Internet for about an hour after getting home from Ethan's and found out a little about Terrell Jardinière, a guy living in Los Angeles — a boxer who'd had a stroke but had survived. It wasn't much, and it felt like a dead end, but when she and Joe finally hooked up after Gen rode that afternoon she passed on that information, plus everything else she'd learned about Bob Pratt.

"Getting info can take some time," Joe said as they sat on Michaela's porch watching Gen hold Booger's lead line while he chewed on a patch of grass.

"I understand. I feel like there is no way Bob did this horrible thing." She felt her throat tighten. "Even if something bad has happened to him, I want to know. It seems as if Audrey wants me to get to the truth and vindicate him, find justice for her."

Joe patted her on the back. "You may have to accept that it might not happen. The cops seem focused on Bob, and you vindicating him might not be in the cards."

"You're going to keep helping me though, aren't you?"

He nodded.

She had told Joe about discovering Francisco, and then the story about Olivia and her odd behavior afterward at the coffeehouse. "There is more to this than that Bob went nutso. And how would it tie into Francisco being killed at Audrey's? Doesn't it make sense that both of the murders have some kind of connection?"

"It does seem like that."

"Can you do something for me?"

He laughed. "Mick, if I had a dollar every time you asked me that question, I'd be able to send all my kids to private school."

She went inside and brought out the envelope she'd found in Audrey's office when she'd gone back the day after Francisco had been killed. "I've had this for two days now. I think it's something that was meant for Ethan, but I'm not sure. I don't know what's inside, or if it's even important, but it does have Bob's address on the return."

"And you want me to open it."

"Would you?"

"Girl!"

"I know, Joe. Please."

"Mail fraud. Or tampering or something like that. What the hell." He tore it open.

Michaela had not been able to bring herself to do it, and with everything else that had been going on, she'd left it in the truck, but now she knew she needed to find out what was in the envelope. She wouldn't give it to Ethan until she knew it was meant for him.

Joe pulled out a file, opened it. "Don't know what it is. Here's a note on it though." He handed her the file.

She read the note. *Dear Sis, Please give this to Dr. Ethan Slater, as I asked. Love, Bobby.* Michaela studied the sheet on the inside. Names that appeared to belong to horses, and all sorts of numbers, percentages. They were labs. Huh. No big deal. It made sense that they would be sharing lab information. "I'll get these to him. He did say that they conferred on cases from time to time."

"Okay. I'll keep on seeing what I can learn. Get some rest. You look tired."

"Thanks."

After Joe left and Michaela finished up for

the day, she sat down at the kitchen table and looked over the labs again. The phone rang. She could see from her caller ID that it was from Jude. She'd let it go.

The machine came on. "Michaela? Where are you? I've been calling and you're not returning my calls, then I got this message that we're not on for Friday. What is up? Please call me. And how about Katie? She's asking to come for a lesson. Can you at least call me about that?"

She reached for the phone, but he'd hung up. She knew it wasn't right to treat him this way. But what if he was playing her? What if Garcia was right about Jude being a womanizer? She'd been down that path with her ex-husband. She hadn't seen the signs at all. She didn't want to make that same mistake. But she did owe Katie her time. Definitely. She'd call tomorrow, after the girl was home from school.

She put her dinner in the microwave and the labs on her kitchen counter. Okay, so it was normal for vets to pass information, especially because they were both track vets. But why would Bob have sent the labs to Ethan?

Without taking her food out of the oven, she grabbed the files and once again drove to Ethan's place.

Luckily he was the only one home. Summer was out shopping for the shower. She explained to him how she'd come into possession of the file.

"Thank you," he said. "I thought about it after you left last night. The only thing I can think of is the information in here is about a case that we worked on together a few months ago with a horse at the track." He looked them over. "I'll see if I can't figure them out." He closed the file. "Listen, I want to take Rocky down to the Woodward Center with me tomorrow. I called you earlier but didn't get you, so I'm glad you came by."

She sat down. "What do you mean? Why do you want to take him?"

"I want to run some more tests, and there isn't a better facility around than that."

"Ethan, you're scaring me."

He placed his hands on her shoulders. The familiar warmth that came from him traveled through her for a second.

"I'm not trying to scare you. I don't know that there is a real problem, but I don't like the labs that I've seen with Halliday, and I don't like the comparison with Rocky's. I know how much you love the boy, so let me take him down tomorrow and see if we can't get to the bottom of it."

"I'm coming with you."

"No. You're better off running your day. Let me do my job and if there is anything significant I'll call you and you can come then."

"Like hell. I'm going. I want to be with him. You obviously think there is a problem. I need to be there."

"Please, Michaela, you know that I wouldn't do anything to hurt Rocky or you. You're going to worry yourself sick while we do an exam and run more tests. Tell you what, if you'd like to come on down in the afternoon, fine. But while the vets are taking care of him and doing what they need to, just trust me on this."

With tears in her eyes, she agreed to let him take Rocky. "You better call me if there's a problem."

He wiped her tears. "You know I will. I don't anticipate one."

She nodded, silently praying that he was right.

THIRTY-THREE

Ethan arrived early the next morning with his truck and trailer. It took everything Michaela had in her not to get in that truck with him.

"Promise me he'll be okay," she said, after they'd loaded Rocky into the trailer.

Ethan hugged her. "I'm only taking precautions here, Mick. It's a few tests, that's all, and I'll call you the minute I know anything."

She smiled through her tears. Silly really, she knew that. She didn't need to cry. Rocky was in good hands. The best. He'd be fine. But dammit, he was like a kid to her. All of her horses were.

Before leaving, Ethan said, "Stop worrying your pretty head. Do your thing. You've got other animals that need you. I'll call."

She nodded and watched as he drove down the dirt road until the trailer was no longer in sight. He was right. She'd work hard today and before long she'd know what was going on with Rocky. There was plenty to do after her trip to Los Angeles. Work would keep her mind off of Rocky and Audrey. She planned to give Hugh a call today to see what he'd learned about the coroner releasing Audrey's body, and when they might have a service for her. She also needed to find out the status of her trailer. First she needed to work Leo, her two-year-old. He'd just been started under saddle and she expected a champion reiner out of him. Reining was a real art form as far as she was concerned, where horses performed routines with various elements including spins, sliding stops, turns, and a gamut of difficult feats. It was her goal to win the big futurity held in Columbus, Ohio, annually. Leo had it in him to be a winner. Working with him did take her mind off of everything for a bit, as she had to place all of her focus on the young horse.

As she was putting Leo up, she heard a car coming down the road. She peered out of the breezeway and spotted Joe's minivan. He drove fast. After pulling up he rushed over to Michaela. "What are you doing today?" he asked.

"Um, what I usually do. I'm working the horses. Why? What's up? You're acting like you got a bug up —"

"No horses today. Get your purse. We're taking a trip."

"Joe! What is going on?"

"I got a lead on Bob Pratt and I knew you'd want to be in on it. You coming or what?"

"Hell yes." She jotted down a note for Dwayne that she'd be gone for a while. He was out running errands with Camden. "We'll take my truck." Joe frowned. "Come on, minivan is not my style."

"You're no fun. I thought you liked to live on the wild side," Joe replied.

"Guess I'm not quite that wild."

"You're a snob. Okay, but I'm driving," Joe said, and she tossed him the keys.

"What's this all about?" Michaela asked as they headed onto the highway. "And where are we going?"

"Malibu."

"Ugh," she replied. "Maybe I should rent a place in L.A.; I've been there, what, twice already this week. Want to fill me in?"

"Bob hung out sometimes at that fish and chips biker place up there in Malibu, right?"

"Yeah."

"The manager who was working the last time Bob was in is there today. He told one of my cousins that he thought Bob was acting strange that day he saw him with a couple of other guys. He didn't say anything else but my cousin got the feeling the bartender knew more than what he was saying. I figured that maybe I ought to go and see this guy. I figured you'd want to go, too. I know what it means to you to find out what happened with Audrey."

"Thanks, and you're right. I definitely want to find the truth. Since we're headed there anyway, maybe we could also check into this Terrell Jardinière." She'd left him a voice message yesterday about the mysterious phone call she'd received.

"Yeah. I got an address where he used to box. It's a gym in Venice. We can head there, too."

"One more thing."

"Now what!"

She laughed. At least she'd be able to take her mind off her worries around Joe. "Right. My trailer is at the Bowen ranch, plus a horse that was going to be delivered to me. Maybe if my trailer is fixed we can grab them, too."

"Whatever."

The traffic was miserable, but the company good as she and Joe chatted about his kids, her horses, his wife, politics, and his cousins. The lively conversation filled the three hours it took to finally get through the traffic, into Los Angeles, and up the PCH.

They parked in front of Mermaids. Michaela took Joe's arm and they walked into the place. Greasy, divey, with a slight musty smell, Michaela mused over the thought that this was where Bob liked to hang out. Maybe the food was good.

A handful of patrons already in various states of drunkenness at a little after twelve noon sat at the bar partaking of their choice of poisons. A couple of them looked at Joe and Michaela when they entered. The others didn't bother. The bartender, a man with long hair pulled back into a ponytail asked them what they wanted to drink. Joe ordered two beers.

They waited until the bartender put their drinks in front of them. After a few sips and some small talk between him and the bartender, Joe asked, "Is Pete around?"

"I'm Pete."

"The manager?"

"Yep."

Joe reached across the bar and shook the man's hand; he looked bewildered or irritated, maybe both. "Joe Pellegrino. You talked to my cousin Anthony. He said that you was here when Bob Pratt came in last." Joe produced a small photo of Bob.

Michaela looked at Joe. He was good.

"Yeah, so?"

"Yeah, so. My cousin says that you said Bob was acting kinda weird that day."

"Oh, you know, that just might have been him having an off day. We all have 'em."

"Right." Joe leaned back and laced his fingers together, stretching them out and cracking his knuckles. "I'm thinking that you might know if there was another reason for Bob to be acting *off*."

Pete hesitated. "You know I don't like to talk about people."

"Sure, sure. I understand." Joe stared him down.

The bartender caved. Michaela figured she would have, too. Joe had one piercing, mean look. "Bob was saying some weird shit, you know?"

"No. I don't. Was he drunk?"

"Nope. Not as far as I could tell. He was drinking a Coke, eating fish and chips, hanging out, but he got on this kick about his girlfriend —"

"Cara," Michaela interrupted. Both men looked at her. "Sorry."

"I think that was her name. Anyway, he was saying that she's got cancer and how he knew it was all a conspiracy. That someone gave her the cancer."

306

"Cancer's not contagious," Joe said.

"Right. See why I didn't want to say anything? The man was talking crazy and he seemed really upset. My shift was over before he left."

"And that's it?" Joe asked.

"That's it." The bartender turned. "Hang on, someone else needs a drink." He pointed to the end of the bar, where a man and woman had just sat down. Joe nodded.

"Odd," Michaela said.

"You guys talking about Bobby Pratt? The vet?"

Michaela and Joe turned to see an older man looking at them — silver haired, dark brown eyes, lines on his face that made him look far older than his years. He reminded Michaela of an ancient-looking medicine man. "You know Bob Pratt?" Joey asked.

"Maybe. Who wants to know?"

Joe lowered his voice. "You ever hear of the Pellegrino and Torrino families?"

The man's face turned white. He wrapped his hand tightly around whatever it was he was drinking — whiskey, maybe some kind of rotgut. "Yeah, I heard of them."

"Thought you might have. Anyway, they wanna know."

"Oh," the man whispered.

"Well?"

"Let's get a booth."

They followed him to a corner booth across the room, where the vinyl seats were torn and cracked. Michaela slid in next to Joe, opposite the old man. "Well?" Joe said again.

"I heard that some not so good things happened to Bob."

"Do you want to elaborate?" Joe asked.

The man glanced around nervously. "I heard that some dudes took him down to Mexico and sort of . . . dumped him."

"Sort of dumped him. I don't know what that means."

"You know, I think they hurt him pretty bad like."

"You know who these guys were?"

He shook his head. "No, sir. Don't know."

"I don't believe you."

The man's eyes widened more. Michaela shifted uncomfortably in her seat. She hadn't witnessed Joe playing the heavy before, and it made her nervous, but she trusted that he knew what he was doing.

"I swear. That's all I heard."

"Right. Let's try something different. Where did you hear this — or wait, who did you hear it from?"

"Some guy. I don't know him. Swear I don't. Look, I'll tell you what I know, okay, but don't hurt me."

"I wasn't planning on hurting you, but I got a lot of cousins."

"That's true," Michaela said before she could catch herself, then decided to sink back into the booth as Joe glared at her.

"I get the point," the old man said. "There's this place up in the hills here. You go up a few miles. Street is called Vista Cielo, go right. It's the only way you can go or you take a trip into the drink."

"I got that," Joey replied. "Go on. What's this place?"

The man lowered his voice. "It's a barn, a place where . . . things go on."

"What kind of things? I'm losing my patience."

The man cleared his throat. "Cockfighting. They got cockfights up there."

Michaela gasped. "What? Roosters? There are people who really do that?"

The man nodded, his craggy lips formed in a slight smile. She wanted to reach across and wring his scumbag neck. So much for the medicine man impression.

"That's sick."

Joe shot her a look that told her to shut up, and she figured that was probably a good idea right about then. What she wanted to do was *throw* up. The thought of that kind of cruelty nauseated her.

"Go on. Tell me where this place is and who you talked to."

The man finished the directions. "But, like I said, I don't know the guy. Some Mexican dude. There was a lot of tequila going around. Lots of people there, and I really don't know him."

"What exactly did he say?"

"I ain't so sure what he said, but know it was sumthin' like Bobby Pratt got dropped off outside of TJ and he wasn't coming back."

Now Michaela was sure she'd vomit.

Joey grabbed her hand. "Come on."

"Where are we going?" she asked as they exited the bar, leaving the man sitting there in shock.

"We're going to the cockfights, babe. We are gonna get some answers about what happened to your friend's brother. Cause that guy knows more than he's telling us."

"How do you know he's hiding something?"

He rolled his eyes at her.

"Dumb question?"

"Yeah. Wish I had a cousin close by."

"You don't?"

"Closest one is in Venice Beach. Might have him send someone out to have a talk with the geezer. But something tells me he'll be long gone the minute he sees us pull out of here. I would have shaped him up if I had it in me. But I don't believe in violence."

Michaela started to laugh.

"I don't, but even more than that, I can't stand when someone hurts an animal. I don't care if it's just a rooster. That's plain wrong."

She patted his shoulder. "And, that's exactly why we're friends."

"Let's go see if we can save some roosters."

"Let's," she replied.

THIRTY-FOUR

"I liked the tough guy act in there," Michaela remarked on the way to the rooster ranch or whatever the place they were headed was called.

Joey blushed. He definitely was a good guy, connected cousins notwithstanding. And, as far as she knew they weren't really *connected,* they just knew a lot of people. "Yeah, well."

She scowled. "What kind of person operates a cockfighting ring?"

"That's no person. It's savage. That's what it is. Man, I hate to see anyone hurtin' animals. Since having Gen, I guess I have softened a bit. And you know she loves animals, and I love watching her with them. Hey, did you call that gal yet at the autism center?"

"I've had a lot on my plate this week. You know that. And honestly, I still don't know that I'm the right person for the job. I appreciate your faith in me, but I'm so afraid I might damage one of the kids."

"Bullshit. You're afraid of how much you'll grow."

She was taken back by his words. "What do you mean by that?"

"Mickey, we've always been honest with each other. I like you. You're a good woman. But since your ex-husband made off with the rodeo queen and you weren't able to have a baby, you've been living half-assed. I know it's been a rough few years. I do. But the Michaela I remember growing up with was balls out. Pardon my mouth, but it's the truth. And lately, I've watched you let life kind of go on automatic. Start living again. Try this. You can do it. Gen loves you and the horses are good for her. They'll be good for other kids, too."

"Talk about not holding back." She looked out the window. Was he right? Had she been in auto-pilot mode? She didn't say anything for a few seconds. "Since you know how to lay down the perfect guilt trip, I suppose I could give it a try. Maybe it is time to *grow*, as you put it. Time to live."

"Damn straight. Hey, here's our turn."

The place was hard to find after they made the initial turn, because the road they were traveling up wound in and around with various dirt road offshoots. She wasn't sure they were even on the right road, but Joe seemed certain. Michaela started to think that the old man back at the bar had led them on a wild goose chase. Then again, he did seem to know exactly who Joey's "cousins," were, and he'd either have to be stupid or ballsy to lie.

"There it is." Joe pointed out a dilapidated house, and off to the right of it a large, but mostly rotted-out barn.

"You sure?" Michaela asked.

He nodded. "I'm sure."

They drove on past and parked. "We'll walk down and see what we can find out." It didn't look like anyone was there. No lights. No cars that she could see. Nothing. But as they neared, Joey led them off the road. "We'll go in this way."

She wanted to laugh seeing Joe all Ramboed out, as he'd even seemed dressed for the occasion in a pair of combat boots, black T-shirt, and army pants, but she knew that they could be in real danger. Maybe she should pretend that she was a secret agent spy. One who was going to rescue a bunch of roosters.

They came up behind the house. As they did, Michaela squinted her eyes to see because of all the trees, which thankfully

314

shadowed their movements and much of the property. "Get down," Joey said. "There's a car in the drive."

"There is?"

"Yup. Nice one, too. Lexus, I think."

"Lexus?" It was getting weirder. What kind of freakazoid drove a Lexus and ran a cockfighting operation?

"Let's go over to the barn."

They rounded the back side and went in through an area that had rotted out.

"Oh no," Michaela said, looking around. Feathers were strewn everywhere and several crates were crammed full of the poor roosters.

"Assholes," Joey muttered.

They started toward the cages when they heard voices.

"Get down, Mick. They're coming in here." Joe took her hand and they hid behind some crates. He held a finger to his lips. She rolled her eyes at him. She wasn't so stupid as to alert whoever it was coming into the barn.

Through the dim light, she could barely make out two figures. "I don't like it, man. We ain't been paid for taking care of jack. You know that job wasn't easy. You need to go and see the boss man this time. You got more pull than I do with him," one of the men said in Spanish. She thought that she recognized the accented voice — Juan Perez?

Joe looked at her and shrugged. He obviously didn't understand Spanish. She was thankful that she'd picked it up so easily as a kid.

"You know, you think I got a better connection with him, but I can't make him pay me, or you. He knows he got us, man. We the ones doing the dirty work. And what about your deal you got us into with *pinche vato* Benz." It was Enrique Perez. Michaela was shocked. Wasn't he supposed to be the good brother? Hugh had told her of his doubts about Juan but praised Enrique. Why would a jockey of Enrique's stature go and get involved in something so seedy?

"He's good for the *dinero*. He don' want no trouble. He got a lot to lose, man. I not worried 'bout him. He easy, we give him drugs, he pays us, and that's it. He don't want me to beat his ass and he don't want me to go tell the news he really a loser druggie. No man, he's no big deal. What I don't like is the boss is loaded and we been doin' a lot of bad shit, you know, for him, and he don' give us nuthin' yet."

"He'll pay. He gonna pay us, bro. I know the man real good. He good to me and the money is on the way. He promise me," Enrique said.

Michaela squinted to get a better view. Juan went over to one of the cages and took out a rooster. "You know what's gonna happen if we don't get paid. You know what, lil' bro. I gonna be real mad and the shit will fly. I tell everyone it was you who did that guy in."

"What?"

"Yeah. You better take care of it, or else."

Joe covered Michaela's eyes as she heard a loud crack. Her stomach flipped. The men left the barn a minute later, still arguing. They heard the sound of an engine, and figured they were leaving.

"You didn't want to see that," Joe said as they stood up.

"Right." Michaela glanced at the dead rooster and thought that she and Joe just might have stumbled onto the largest piece in this mystery yet. Her gut told her that not only was Benz more of a lowlife than she'd figured, but that Juan and Enrique Perez had something to do with Bob's disappearance and Audrey's murder. However, they obviously weren't the only ones involved. The sick feeling in her stomach worsened, as she had to consider that the boss they were referring to was none other than Hugh Bowen.

THIRTY-FIVE

"Mick, those are not good guys back there," Joe said after she told him what the Perez brothers had discussed. They were making it back to the highway, winding down along the coastline. "So, you know them?"

"Sort of. I've met them." She explained to Joe how Enrique was Hugh's jockey and Juan, his brother, worked around the ranch.

He shook his head. "You gotta tell Hugh Bowen about this."

"I can't."

"Why?"

"They were rambling on about a boss man. It just might be that the boss man . . . is Hugh. I hate to think it, but it adds up. What doesn't add up is his sincerity over being in love with Audrey. I really believed that he loved her. I can't imagine why he would kill her. It makes no sense."

Joe shrugged. "None of this is making sense. The only thing that does is you heading back to Indio with me now, and forget-tin' this whole mess."

"Can't do that. We're close. I can feel it. Maybe it is Hugh who caused Bob's disappearance and killed Audrey. I just don't know anymore. I have no clue what to think. But those two bastards back there *do* know who it is, or at the very least they're up to no good, and I suspect that it all ties in to what happened to Audrey. And Benz? He might be a part of this after all."

Joe asked her about Steve Benz and how he played into everything. She shared her thoughts on him and what a creep he was, how he also connected to Olivia, Callahan, and Bridgette, not to mention the weirdo Friedman. There were too many paths she could wind her mind down, and she had no clue which one to take.

Joe's cell rang. "Hang on. Yep." Michaela could hear the high pitch of a frantic woman on the other end. "Now calm down, Marianne. It's okay." He held the phone away from his ear.

"It's *not* okay!" Marianne yelled. "Get your ass back here now before we have a lawsuit on our hands."

"You gonna have to take it down a notch, hon, and explain to me what this is all about." The shrillness in Marianne's voice did not subside, although Michaela couldn't make out what she was saying. "Uh-huh," Joe said. "Dammit! What in the hell! That's it. He's grounded forever. Tell him that. I'm in L.A. No, I can't get back right now! I told you I was gonna be gone all day, that I had business in the city to take care of. No I didn't mean Riverside. C'mon, honey. Can't you take care of this? Marianne?" More yelling from the other end. "Okay, okay. I'll be there as soon as I can. Tell them four o'clock. Now honey, calm down, please. It don't do any good to get so upset." He shut off his phone. "Little shit!"

Michaela cringed. "Do I dare ask?"

He sighed. "Little Joe has a bit of a temper and if someone looks at him cross-eyed he takes it upon himself to kick the crap out of that kid. I've tried everything from taking away the PlayStation to making him clean the toilets. Don't know what to do."

"I don't like the sound of this."

"Today, he went too far, broke a kid's nose on the playground. The parents are threatening a lawsuit, and the principal wants all the parents in his office as soon as possible."

"Guess we'd better head back, huh."

Joe nodded and grew silent for a minute. "No. Take me to my cousin's place down in Venice. It's not that far. I can borrow one of his cars. Won't be a problem. I know you want to go and handle a few more things. I shouldn't let you. But my gut tells me that as soon as you took me back home, you'd be back here to see what more you can find out."

"Joe."

"Michaela? Am I wrong?"

"Okay. Maybe, I would like to figure a few of these angles out. Like I said, I think we're close and I do want to hunt down that boxer. Terrell Jardinière."

"What if I send a cousin to talk to him?"

"No. Audrey was my friend. I need to do this."

He nodded, gave her directions to his cousin's place, and then handed her a Post-it with the address of the gym where Jardinière supposedly worked out. "Careful. Call me when you get back?"

"Thanks, Joe. You know I will. I'm sorry about the kid."

"Nothing we can't handle." He shook a finger at her. "Be careful. And here, take this." He reached into a backpack he had with him and took out a small can.

"What's this?"

"Some mace, Mick. I make Marianne carry it, and my sisters. Don't know why I hadn't thought to give this to you 'til now, but I want you to have it. Use it if you need to. Even if you aren't sure if you need to but feel scared or threatened by someone, pull it out, keep your hand on the trigger."

She smiled. "Thanks, Joe." He was the closest she'd ever come to having a brother. Michaela watched him as he ran up the front steps of a condo on the beach. Apparently the cousin wasn't hurting for cash. Out of curiosity, she wanted to see what one of Joe's cousins was like, but decided against it. Maybe she wasn't ready for that part of Joe's world.

She took her Thomas Bros. map out of her glove box and thumbed through it to get directions to the gym where Terrell Jardinière worked out. Down near Muscle Beach. Then she was on her way, in hopes of putting one or more of the pieces to this puzzle together.

THIRTY-SIX

The articles Michaela had found by searching Google for Terrell's name, along with what Joe had discovered about him, gave her the same information. Terrell Jardinière was once an up-and-coming boxer out of Los Angeles in the late nineties. He'd apparently had a stroke and, although he survived, he'd retired from boxing.

The gym near Muscle Beach occupied a two-story building a block from the water. She could hear and smell the gym before she even opened the door. Nothing like the odor of sweat and the sounds of groans and grunts to make a woman's heart go pitter-patter. Inside, the gym turned out to be pretty much what she expected of a gym in Venice: from muscle men obviously on boatloads of steroids, to serious boxers in the ring, dodging and punching each other out. Who actually considered boxing a sport? The idea of two men going rounds in attempts to beat the crap out of each other made her queasy, and seeing it in action even more so.

"Can I help you?"

Michaela turned to see an older, rail-thin black man. At first she didn't respond, because she hadn't planned this thing out very well. Here she was, one of maybe three women in the gym, and the other two were working out — boxing, actually. The man stuck out his hand. "Brian Dell. I own this place. And you are?"

"Hi. Sorry. Just kind of watching." She'd have to wing it, which she was getting good at anyway. Brian Dell seemed like an okay guy. "Michaela Bancroft."

"Morning, Ms. Bancroft. Are you here to find out about our self-defense class, or are you interested in taking up boxing?"

She started to laugh when she realized he was serious.

"Neither, actually. I'm looking for someone and I think he used to train here."

"You the ex-wife looking for back child support or something? Cause if that's the case, I hate to tell you, I won't be giving out any details."

"No. I think this man knew a friend of mine who was killed."

"You the police?"

325

"No. I'm only trying to find answers concerning my friend's murder."

"Murder, huh? Well, if one of the boys here gone and killed someone, I certainly don't want them in my place. Who we talking about?"

"I don't think this man killed my friend. I think he knew her. That's all."

"Alrighty then, like I said, who we talking about?"

"Terrell Jardinière," Michaela said and brushed her hair back behind her ears.

Dell glanced at the fighters in the ring. He didn't answer her for a few seconds, his face taut and filled with what appeared to be sadness. "No, Terrell certainly could not have killed your friend. Terrell had a stroke a few years ago. I used to train him."

"I know about the stroke. I'd like to talk to him."

Dell shook his head. "You can't. Terrell's been living in a home for the last few years. He can't do a lot for himself anymore. Such a shame. I go to see him occasionally. Good guy. Good fighter."

"He lives in a nursing home?"

"Yep." Dell's expression changed from one of sadness to what Michaela thought was anger. His eyes darkened, and the brow on his forehead creased. "State takes care of him now. Man, it's not good, you know."

"I'm sorry. It sounds like you're close. He must be a good man."

He nodded. "The best. Terrell was always good to everyone he knew. He lived in South Central all his life. He started boxing and I discovered him, got him set up in a place here in Venice. I wanted him away from some of those guys he grew up around. You know, he didn't need any bad influences. He was winning fights and making money. He don't deserve to rot in that nursing home."

"Can I ask what kind of money Terrell was bringing in?"

"You could, but let me ask you, why all the questions about Terrell? What's this story you got going with your murdered friend?"

Michaela sighed. Truth time. She told him about Audrey and the phone call.

"Sounds like a mystery to me," he said. "No way Terrell could've called you. The man can't eat on his own. No way on God's green earth that he could have picked up a phone. You would have known something was wrong with him by his speech. To answer your question about how much Terrell pulled in, it was getting close to six figures. And, everyone knew he was a rising star, destined to make millions. He had an aunt who kinda raised him, and she blew all of it away once he wasn't able to control it."

She shrugged. "That's horrible."

"The world can be a cruel place. Man like Terrell doesn't deserve what happened to him. He did do a few print ads for some vitamin company and a boxing glove outfit. But he didn't make a wad of cash doing that. Maybe a couple thousand bucks or so."

"Hey, Brian," one of the boxers in the ring called out.

"Yeah. Be right there." He told Michaela, "Wish I could help you out and I'm sorry to hear about your friend, but there's no way in hell Terrell made that call to you. No way. I better get back at it."

"No problem. Just one more thing: You have an address for the nursing home where he lives?"

"It's called Sheltered Palms. It's in the mid-Wilshire district. Don't bother going to see him though. Like I said, he can't tell you anything."

"Thanks."

Michaela left the gym. The same question kept playing out over and over in her mind: If it wasn't Terrell Jardinière who'd called her last night, then who was it, and why?

Furthermore, why had he used this poor ex-boxer's name?

THIRTY-SEVEN

Sheltered Palms was a concrete institutional building with a decent-sized water fountain out front and a handful of palm trees that weren't exactly sheltering. The grounds were nice, though, in a parklike setting of grass and flowerbeds. A dozen or so patients lounged outside by the water fountain and another half dozen were either walking on the lawn or sitting in wheelchairs, some accompanied by caretakers.

Michaela figured she might not have an easy time getting in to see Terrell. She was already running a story in her head. Once inside the building, which smelled of disinfectant and age, she found the front desk, where an older nurse sat behind a glass partition. Nurse Ratched came to mind, the scowling woman's eyes boring into Michaela as if to say *What the hell do you want?*

"Yes?" was what she actually said as she slid the window open.

"Hi," She gave the biddy her best smile. Not even a flicker of pleasantry emanated from the woman. "Um, I'm here to see an old friend. I'm from out of town, and it's important that I see him."

"Did you make an appointment?"

"No. I didn't know that was necessary."

"It's necessary." The nurse slid the window shut and looked down at her paperwork.

Michaela rapped on the glass. The nurse frowned. "Please," Michaela said.

The woman slid the window open. "What?"

"This is important. I've traveled a long way and I'm only here for the day. I really need to see my friend."

The nurse sighed. "Name?"

"Michaela Bancroft."

"There's no one here by that name." She started to shut the window again.

Michaela stopped it with her hand. "No, that's *my* . . . Do you have a manager? Someone who is in charge?" She was pissed now.

"What's your friend's name?" she asked, ignoring Michaela's question.

"Terrell Jardinière."

The woman looked up at her and smirked, shaking her head. She handed her a badge.

"Put this on. He's in room 306. Third floor. But if he's a friend from the past, he won't remember you. Elevator doesn't go to the top anymore, if you get my drift."

"I'll take my chances."

Michaela rode the real elevator to the third floor, passed a nursing station and walked down a long, dingy hall. Entering room 306, she saw a man in a wheelchair, his back to her, looking out barred windows. "Mr. Jardinière?" He didn't respond. She came around, letting him see her. "Mr. Jardinière?" His fingers moved slightly and he seemed to be trying to focus his gaze on her. "Can I talk to you?" No response. Maybe Brian Dell and the nurse were right: This was probably a waste of time. But still, she was here and she had to try and see if he could communicate in some way. She turned his wheelchair slightly so that she could sit in a chair opposite him and hopefully be able to decipher any body language or sounds he might make. This was definitely not the man who had called her. He was still a big man. He had on a tentlike patient gown and a pair of sweatpants. His brown eyes, although distant, expressed sadness.

"My name is Michaela Bancroft. I know that you used to be a great boxer. I spoke with your trainer, Brian, today." Terrell tilted his head slightly and his eyes seemed to light up. "Yes. He says that you were great." Michaela sighed. Why in the heck was she here? Whoever had called had only used this man's name for some reason. None of it made sense. She decided to tell him her story. She found herself crying again when she talked about Audrey and everything that she'd gone through in the last few days. Terrell didn't respond, but she believed that he was listening, and it felt good to let it all out; then, she felt ridiculous to do so in front of a stranger. A man who was ill, at that. "I'm sorry, Mr. Jardinière. I thought you could help me. Someone called me the other night claiming to be you, and asking about Audrey. But it obviously wasn't you. I wish I could figure this all out. Who murdered Audrey and why her brother, Bob, disappeared."

Terrell made a noise. She looked at him. He was trying to say something. It was difficult for him. Michaela couldn't make sense of the sounds he uttered. "Did you know Audrey? Did you call me?" Terrell shook his head . . . barely. "No. What is it? What is . . . ?" Here she'd told him the whole story, but he hadn't reacted until that moment. What had she said that triggered him? Wait a minute. "Bob? Did you know Bob Pratt, Mr. Jardinière?" He became further agitated, trying hard to speak. "You did, didn't you?"

At that point a caretaker who looked like a linebacker walked into the room. "Hey, Terrell, pretty visitor today." He smiled at Michaela, who smiled back. 'What is it, T? You lookin' a little off. Time for your meds." He glanced back at Michaela and then at Terrell. "What's going on in here? He's usually very subdued."

"We were just talking."

"Uh-huh. I'm going to have to ask you to leave. It's time for his medications."

"Oh no, please."

"Are you a relative, Blondie?" She frowned. "Yeah, don't look like you two are cousins. I need you to leave."

"One more thing." She looked at Terrell. "Do you know what happened to Bob?"

Terrell became extremely agitated this time and was trying hard to say something. But all he could get out was the word *Bob*.

"You need to leave, miss, or I'll call security."

"I'm going. I'm so sorry. I really am." She reached out to touch Terrell on the shoulder. The caretaker pushed her hand away.

She walked to her truck, upset and baffled,

but convinced that somehow Terrell Jardinière knew what had happened to Bob Pratt.

THIRTY-EIGHT

Michaela headed toward the freeway after leaving Sheltered Palms, almost in tears again, thoroughly frustrated and not knowing where to turn or what to do next. It was peak traffic time, and the last thing she felt like doing was trying to make her way home amid the sea of cars and smog. She pulled over and called Ethan to check on Rocky. Although she'd kept busy, he'd been on her mind and it had taken all of this craziness to keep her from losing it.

She was relieved to hear Ethan's voice. He sounded upbeat. "Hey, Mick. I told you that I'd call as soon as I knew something."

"I know. I'm just checking in."

"I don't have any answers so far, but he's happy and comfortable."

"That's good."

"I guess you've taken my advice," he said.

"What do you mean?"

"About Halliday."

"I'm confused. I don't know what you're talking about."

"I received a message from Kathleen Bowen today that she would be taking care of the expenses."

Michaela didn't know what to say. The woman had said she was bankrupt. "This is the first I've heard about it."

"I don't know. You may want to give her a call and find out. She's a strange one."

"I'm aware. Thanks. Call me, okay?"

"Sure. Are you okay? You sound upset."

"No. I'm fine. Worried. That's all."

"Quit worrying. He's fine. Now, go rest or take a ride, or do something to get rid of that anxiety."

"Right. Bye." She didn't divulge that she was well over a hundred miles from home.

She sat back in the seat, traffic whizzing past her, somewhat relieved to hear that Rocky was doing well. But she wouldn't feel completely at ease until he was back home in his stall with a clean bill of health. She also knew that she wouldn't truly be able to relax until Audrey's killer was caught, which made her wonder about Kathleen.

What was it with Kathleen Bowen? How had she come up with the cash to pay for Halliday's bills, and why hadn't she contacted her? Michaela didn't bother trying to answer the question herself. She got back on the road; what was a few more miles? She wanted to hear the answer straight from the horse's mouth.

The sun had started to set, casting a rose-colored haze across the sky, but she couldn't revel in the beauty of it, because the traffic was migraine worthy. Her blood boiled by the time she made it back up the PCH. She'd been cut off, flipped off, and nearly run off the road. There was a reason she lived out in the middle of nowhere: It was called serenity.

A silver BMW Roadster stood parked outside Kathleen's beach house. Michaela rapped hard on the front door. She was tired of the games these people played, and she wanted some answers. Kathleen Bowen came across as a victim in her bizarre world, but Michaela had her doubts. Kathleen didn't come to the door; rather, Olivia opened it. Her nose was red and running, her eyes bulging. She tried to slam the door when she saw who it was, but Michaela pushed it open and walked inside. "Where's your mother?"

"I don't know. She said that she was going out of town for a few days. Why? What do you want?"

"What do you mean, she's out of town?"

"Duh. She's gone. Like I don't know where. Maybe Italy, Paris. Beats me."

Michaela trembled inside. "You're high, Olivia. You need some serious help."

"And you, babe, need to seriously mind your own damn business," Steve Benz said as he appeared from another room.

Michaela crossed her arms. "Figures. You know, your name keeps coming up in all the wrong places, and now you are actually *in* the wrong place." She looked back at Olivia. "Can't you see what this guy is? He's no megastar. He's a lowlife drug dealer, and he's got you hooked. And if I were to bet on it, I would say that your mom has been crying poor to you. You did the good daughter thing, and agreed to sign with Marshall Friedman and pose with this creep here for Callahan's magazine to help her out of debt. My guess is she's just come into some cash, and that cash is yours. Now, I don't know if she's aware that you are doing cocaine. She's likely stuck her head in the sand due to her selfishness. But trust me, this scumbag and his no-good manager knew exactly what they were up to; you sign with Friedman, and you do their bidding, and they keep you high."

Olivia stared blankly at her. Was any of this getting through?

"Hey babe, you're ruining a good time here. You really are. Why don't you just leave?" Benz said.

Michaela ignored him. "Does Josh know this guy is with you? Does he know about the drugs? Would he let you get back up on a horse knowing you're stoned out of your mind? No, I don't think he would. I believe he cares about you. What are you thinking, Olivia? You have dreams to be a jockey. You can't do this to yourself. Come with me, okay? We'll find you some help."

Olivia shook her head. "I think you better go. Please."

"No. I'm not leaving."

Benz walked over and got in her face. "She asked you to leave. You deaf, bitch?"

Michaela knew she shouldn't be messing with this crazed, drugged-out rocker, but she also knew the right thing to do when it came to Olivia — what Audrey would have wanted her to try and do. "Let me tell you something, jerkoff, I've found out quite a bit about you and what you do to make extra cash. Oh, and I also know who you visited at Shutters the other day. Bridgette Bowen ring a bell? How about Frederick Callahan? Freddie boy told me that you deliver party favors for friends in need. I'm sure that Callahan wouldn't think twice, if it came down to causing him a problem or ruining your career, as to what he might tell the media — or the police for that matter. I wasn't the only one who witnessed your visit with Bridgette and Callahan. Let's just say, you look good on camera."

"What the . . ."

"Right. Here's the deal. You're going to leave now if you don't want those pictures to surface." Michaela knew she was telling him something she had no control over. She was pretty sure that Smith was at work offering the photos to the highest bidder in the tabloid realm. "So, you go on your way, while Olivia and I stay here." Michaela stood her ground. "Oh, and come to think of it, I've also heard your name mentioned in regard to Audrey's murder." She was stretching that one, too, and she knew it, but this asshole had it coming. She had not forgotten though, what Olivia told her about the fact that Benz had gone to retrieve beers while at the races, and the timing looked to coincide with Audrey's murder. She knew she might push him over the edge with her comments, but she needed to see his reaction. As far as Michaela figured, Benz might have killed Audrey for his own needs — to boost his career by having Olivia away from Audrey and under his manager's wings, which would mean a profit all the way around — or he might have murdered Audrey at Friedman's behest. She still didn't know where or how Francisco's death played into it, but right now she only wanted to get Benz out of the house. She knew she was taking a huge risk, but if he was a killer, she was prepared. She had her hand stuck down into her purse, wrapped around the vial of mace Joe had given her earlier, and she'd use it if need be.

"You are freaking psycho. I didn't kill anyone, and what's the big deal? If people want to party once in a while, how does that hurt you?" He looked at Olivia and shook a finger at her. "This is your mother's fault if you don't succeed. I had nothing to do with any of this. She's the one taking all your cash, babe. Call me when this bitch leaves!" He grabbed his wallet off a side table and walked out, slamming the front door.

Yep. Michaela was not making any friends in this neck of the woods. She had to wonder what Benz's comments meant about Kathleen. But before she could question what he'd said, she needed to try and help Olivia.

She turned back to see Olivia still staring at her. "Why are you doing this?" Olivia snapped. "Go away."

"Because you need help. And because Audrey loved you and I loved her. These people are ruining you. They're taking away your dreams. Are you going to allow your mother and her lackeys to control your life? Is that what you want? You can ride, Olivia. You're good. I watched you on the track, and you can do it, but not like this. Not wasted. I think we should call your father."

Michaela didn't know if she trusted Hugh any longer, but she believed that the man loved his daughter. That was a strange thought, especially since she figured that he could also be a killer. This was not good.

"No. I can't call my dad!" Olivia started to cry. "I don't want him to know. He's already been through this with Bridgette. I'm fine. I don't need help. Go away."

"You *do* need help. Do this for Audrey." Olivia wiped her face. "You have a long life ahead of you. Don't ruin it because you didn't follow your own dreams, or because someone took advantage of you."

"I do have dreams," she sobbed.

"I know. Now get smart. You can get help for this, and you'll be fine. You'll get better and then you can pursue your dreams."

Olivia's lower lip trembled like a child. Damn that Benz. "I don't know. I just don't know."

"Why don't we call Josh? Okay? I think he would want to help. One phone call, okay? That's it. We only have to start there."

Olivia didn't respond for a while; finally, she nodded. Michaela took her over to the couch and sat down with her. "This will be good. You'll see. You're strong." She shook her head. "I can't understand your mother. Where did she go, and why?"

"I don't know. I really don't."

"Do you know what Benz meant when he said that your mother was taking all of your cash?"

Olivia looked away ashamed. "You were right. I signed that contract for her. Callahan is going to pay me a lot of money to do the photos and Friedman gave my mother some money up front."

Michaela wrapped her arms around Olivia. She couldn't help wonder if Kathleen had taken Olivia's money and skipped town. Maybe Callahan had been right. Kathleen's jealousy took over where Audrey was concerned and she'd killed her. Now she was running. She'd used her daughter and was trying to cover her tracks. Michaela squeezed Olivia tighter. She couldn't avoid the possibility that the girl's mother had not only used and abandoned her, but might also be a murderess.

THIRTY-NINE

The sun finished setting over the Pacific as Olivia paced back and forth on the ocean-front deck of her mother's beach house, chain smoking, while they waited for Josh to show up. She talked nonstop to Michaela, who sat in a lounge chair, continuously waving away the toxic nicotine plume as she listened to the young woman ramble on. Now that Olivia had admitted to her drug use, she was like a well sprung open, and although Michaela had her own set of concerns, she listened to her talk. There was no alternative.

"Funny thing is, you know who got me to even try this shit?" Olivia said. "Bridgette."

"Your stepmother?"

"Oh yeah. My dad thinks she's all better because he hooked her up at Betty Ford, but she was back using a few months later. She does a good job of hiding it from him. But I know all about it. Tons of people do.

Benz gives it to her."

No surprise there.

"Last year at my dad's Christmas party? She gave me some. Told me that she wanted to be friends. That kind of thing. My mom had been driving me crazy. She'd pushed me into these recording sessions where she'd hang out half the time, or make Audrey stay with me for hours. I was wiped out. Bridgette said that the coke would pick me up, and it did."

"Did Audrey know about it?"

Olivia shrugged. "Maybe she suspected something. I don't know. She kept trying to convince my mom that I needed a rest. Audrey said that she wanted to take me to Hawaii or something, just to have a break. I wanted to do that. Last month I was feeling rotten because the drugs keep me up. You know? At first you think they're going to help you get through the day. But they don't. They just make it worse."

"Do you know Audrey's brother, Bob?"

"I met him a few times. He took care of my dad's horses, and also Halliday for my mom. He seemed like a nice guy. He didn't like Bridgette, though. But who does, really?"

"Why do you say that he didn't like her?"

"One time he was over at my dad's and

my dad wasn't there. I was down at the barn. The vet was there — Audrey's brother. And Bridgette was there, which was weird because she doesn't have a lot to do with the horses. She didn't realize I was down there, but she was whispering and I heard her ask him if he'd told anyone."

"Told anyone what?"

"I don't know. That's all I heard her say, because then he turned on her and told her to leave him *effing* alone. She kept trying to ask him stuff, until she saw me there. Then she left. He didn't say anything to me, and I didn't ask. He seemed pretty pissed off though."

Interesting. Maybe Michaela was on the right track where Bridgette was concerned. Maybe she and Bob had had an affair. From everything she'd learned about Bridgette, honoring her vows wasn't high on her priority list. Or maybe she'd shared a secret with him at Betty Ford and she was afraid that he'd tell Hugh what it was. She wanted to believe the latter, as she didn't want to think Bob would mess around with a married woman. This was a piece of information she'd have to mull over a bit.

"Your mom told me that she was bankrupt. So, now she's taken money owed to you from this contract that you signed. Want to fill me in?"

Olivia took a long drag on her cigarette. "My mom is not so great with money. She's great at spending it, but it's my dad who knows how to handle it. Mom has made poor investments, and she spends cash as soon as it's in her hands. She was near declaring bankruptcy when she came to me and begged me to help her. She told me that she knew about me wanting to be a jockey and that if I did this for her just for a few years that she wouldn't ever ask me to do anything else for her again and that she'd let me ride and not bother me about it.

"I agreed."

"Why?"

"She's my mom."

"She has a problem. She's an addict, too. She spends money. Do you think signing away the next few years to Friedman and posing for Callahan with Benz will be the end of it? Come on. You know better than that. I've heard you sing. Your mother is right: You could be a huge star. But if that's not what you want, don't do it so that she can temporarily get out of the hole she's dug herself into and then watch her piss it away again. You'll constantly be supporting her."

"Have you ever said no to your mom or dad?"

Michaela thought about it. She nodded. "You know, I guess I have. My dad is an addict. He's a gambler. And, the last time he wound up doing it, I told him that I couldn't support his habit. I knew that my mom would leave, and I could not stand by and watch him destroy himself. He listened and now he's in a program, which is what you'll have to do. And you'll also have to be tough with your mother. I realize that you love her, but you're not doing either one of you any favors."

"Maybe you're right," Olivia replied and finally stopped pacing. She stood facing the ocean.

Michaela heard the doorbell ring and went inside. It was Josh. "Got here as soon as I could. She okay?" he asked.

"Yes. She's outside, thinking. Might want to give her a few minutes before you go out there."

"Thanks for calling me," he said. "Boy, you have been through it this week, haven't you?"

"We all have, but yes, I will agree that this has not been the best week. I still don't know what to think about who murdered Audrey, and I'm really confused about

Bob's disappearance."

"I saw Hugh earlier and he said that the police are releasing Audrey's body tomorrow. He's started making plans for a funeral service next week."

"Oh. Good. I'll let him know again that if he needs anything, I can help."

"I'm sure he'd appreciate it. You know he was in love with her, don't you?"

Michaela slowly nodded. "Did he tell you that?"

Josh shrugged. "No. Bridgette moved out today. I told you about the yelling and her tearing down the drive the other day?"

"Yes."

"Today, she was back and she had movers picking up her things. I came up to the house to tell Hugh something and she was screaming at him that she knew about Audrey. After Bridgette took off again, he told me that he had loved Audrey and they'd planned to get married."

Michaela didn't know what to say. She already knew this, but she still had doubts that Hugh's love was sincere. But what would be his motive to kill Audrey, who everyone claimed he loved? Even Callahan said that Hugh had been in love with her for two decades.

"Josh?" They both turned to see Olivia

standing in between the French doors that led to the balcony.

"Hey." He walked over and hugged her.

"I'll let you two talk. Would it be okay if I used your mom's computer, Olivia? I need to check my e-mail."

"Sure."

Josh put an arm around Olivia and they walked back outside. Michaela beelined it for Kathleen's office. She had a few things to check before they came back inside.

FORTY

The first thing Michaela did once she sat down at Kathleen's computer was to Google Cara Klein's name. It had been bugging her for a day that she hadn't had the opportunity to look into the woman. Joe also hadn't called her with any new information. She seized opportunities whenever they presented themselves. Now looked as good a time as any.

At first she came across the typical ads for finding someone by that name, but as she scrolled down to the bottom of the page she found an article about a woman named Cara Klein who had been the president of a company called Strong X. The company had filed for Chapter 11 over five years ago, and Cara had stepped down as president and CEO. The company closed its doors within six months after she'd left. The article went on to report that a handful of lawsuits had been filed against Strong X, which was the maker of muscle- and endurance-type supplements for athletes, including runners, gymnasts, and boxers. *Boxers!* Michaela picked up the phone on Kathleen's desk and called Joe.

"You home now?" he asked.

"No."

"What?"

"I don't have a lot of time." She quickly filled him in and he immediately ran with her thoughts.

"Somehow this Cara Klein is linked to Terrell Jardinière. Sorry I hadn't had a chance to follow up on that lead yet with her."

"It's okay," she replied and then told Joe about her encounter with Terrell.

"Oh shit. I follow, Mick. Let me see what I can come up with. Be careful . . . and get your ass home!"

"As soon as I can."

She had a strong gut feeling that she was onto something here. She wasn't sure what it was, but if two and two added up, and this Cara Klein was the same one that Bob had been dating, there was a link of some sort. She knew she couldn't go back to see Terrell; there was no way anyone would let her in. Had Terrell known Cara? Was Cara the missing link to Bob's disappearance and

Audrey's murder?

She went to log off her search and accidentally hit the back menu button. What she saw made her suck in a deep breath of air. There on the screen was a copy of Kathleen's itinerary for today. She was headed to New York City and would be back on Saturday morning. Whirlwind trip. So maybe she wasn't on the run after all. But that wasn't what had taken Michaela's breath away. It was who Kathleen was traveling with — Marshall Friedman. Marshall Friedman's name was on the itinerary. She scowled. In hiding or not, they were up to no good. Had to be.

Her curiosity aroused, she figured it couldn't hurt to do a bit of snooping around Kathleen's office. She first checked to make sure that Josh and Olivia were still out on the deck. They were. Then she rummaged through a few drawers. The photos she'd discovered had been moved. What she was looking for, she didn't know.

But she didn't expect what she did find tucked in with some files inside a leather ottoman that also served as a space saver. She pulled out a file marked "CHARLIE SAMPSON." The Sampson ranch! Charlie Sampson had been Audrey's husband. Michaela opened it up and found an old insurance policy, one that Audrey had taken out on herself with her late husband as beneficiary. An addendum had changed the beneficiaries to Bob Pratt and Kathleen Bowen. The policy's face value was three million dollars. Good grief! With Bob out of the picture, Kathleen stood to inherit a ton of money.

Michaela heard the sliders close, and she quickly put the file back inside the ottoman. As she closed the lid, Josh said, "Looking for something?" He stood in the doorway.

"No. I had seen one of these ottomans in the Pottery Barn catalogue and just wondered how they worked. Great idea. Space saver thing, you know." She yawned. "I am beat. Everything good with Olivia?"

"I think so. She's agreed to go with me and talk to her dad. He'll want to help. It's the right thing to do. Thanks for calling me."

"Not a problem."

"Hey, I know it's getting late, but I think your trailer is ready. Juan mentioned it to me today."

"I need to get back home." The last thing she wanted to do was drive to the Bowen Ranch, even if it meant getting her trailer back and picking up Geyser. "I'll be here Saturday for the Eq Tech Gala."

"Oh good. I'm going."

She nodded. "I'll either pick it up Sunday morning, or I may send my assistant to do it."

"Sure."

Michaela left, sighing as she closed the front door behind her. Josh had eyed her suspiciously a minute ago, and she wasn't sure she trusted him. Hell, she wasn't sure *who* she trusted. She had run the idea of Hugh murdering Audrey over again and again in her head, and it didn't sit right. She couldn't fathom it. But the *boss man* she'd heard Juan and Enrique referring to still had her wondering who that might be. Was it Josh? They all worked at the same place, and Josh held a higher position than either one of the Perez brothers. But now she had all of these other pieces not adding up. Terrell, Cara Klein, Kathleen, and Marshall Friedman. She had a long drive ahead of her. Maybe she'd be able to flesh out her thoughts.

But her thoughts were cut off when she received a call from Ethan. "You'd better come," he said. "It's Rocky."

FORTY-ONE

Michaela barely remembered the drive down to San Diego. She was a mess. Thank God the traffic was moving and a California Highway Patrol guy didn't spot her speeding, because she probably wouldn't have stopped until she made it to the center.

The grounds of the Woodward Center were well lit. She told the guard at the kiosk who she was, and he waved her through. Ethan was waiting for her.

"What is it? What happened?"

Ethan shook his head and placed a hand on her shoulder. "I don't know. We've got him stable now. He's comfortable. I've sedated him some, and we're going through the paces again with the labs. His pressure went up after he ate, along with his cortisol and other hormone levels. He had a seizure, Mick."

"Oh no." Her stomach sank as a wave of horror made her feel dizzy.

"We're testing him for Cushing's disease, which typically doesn't occur in a horse as young as he is, but we need to rule it out. He doesn't look like he has it. He doesn't have the potbelly, or lethargy and a thick crusty neck. Those are symptoms we would likely see with that disease. So, I'm also looking into hypothyroidism, which is pretty rare. It's hard to differentiate between the two though, because with either illness we're going to see the rise in cortisol levels and other hormones. Now his glucose levels aren't way off, and he does not seem excessively thirsty, so I don't think we're looking at diabetes. There are a handful of other possibilities I'm checking into. He could have a tumor on his pituitary gland, either benign or malignant. I just don't know yet. What I need you to do is detail his history for me. Obviously I know what his environment is like, but I want you to write out his daily schedule: workouts, feedings, all of it. I have his medical history. And, we have to look at his entire system: cardiac, respiratory, everything. The thing is, seizures are fairly uncommon in horses. They can be difficult to diagnose. I've ruled out liver or renal disease. I've also been able to rule out hyperkalemia, which is a muscle disorder found in certain lines of quarter horses that can be confused with seizure activity. I've had a CT scan and MRI done on him and neither shows any type of cerebral edema. And, I'm running an EEG. He's been started on Diazepam to control any recurrence of a seizure tonight."

Michaela held up her hand. She'd had enough vet talk. "Can I see him?"

"Of course. We have him in a padded stall, and we've considered putting a padded helmet on him, just in case he goes down again. Right now though, his levels have started dropping and the Diazepam appears to be doing the job. I'm sorry, Mick. We'll find out what's wrong, and take care of him."

She followed Ethan through large steel double doors, where the mixture of antiseptic and familiar horse smells wafted through the air. They passed a surgical suite and walked through another set of doors. Once past them, Michaela spotted Rocky and tears sprung to her eyes. He was inside a stall with his head hung low.

She slid through the stall door and wrapped her arms around Rocky's neck, stroking him underneath his mane. "Hey guy. I'm sorry. I'm so sorry. They're going to make you better, okay? I promise. Then, I'm going to take you home and spoil you

359

with carrots and molasses and a handful of mares." She smiled through her tears, knowing that if he could really understand her, he would've liked the sound of all that. He was such a great animal. She hated seeing him like this. It tore at her heart, her core. God, she loved him. She stayed in his stall for over an hour like that, talking to him and stroking him, while Ethan left them alone. Rocky did seem to perk up, knowing that she was there.

When Ethan came back it was past eleven and her body and mind felt exhausted. "Listen," he said, "I know you won't want to check into a hotel; we have beds here. They aren't great, but you can get some sleep, and that way we can be close by and check on him through the night."

"I don't want to leave him."

"You won't be. We'll be right through those doors, and you can come in anytime and see how he is. He looks pretty happy right now. Once he knew you were here, I noticed he relaxed even more. Come on, I've made you some tea."

She sighed and squeezed Rocky's neck. "I'll be back. Okay. I suppose I could use something to drink."

"And eat? I had a pizza delivered."

"I don't know if I can eat much."

"Give it a try. You won't be doing him any good by starving yourself. Now come on."

She followed Ethan into a break room, where he had the pizza set out. She'd noticed a few other techs and vets in and out since she'd been there, but as the night wore on it grew quiet, which was good. She didn't feel like talking to anyone she didn't know.

They sat down and started in on their late dinner, eating in peace for a few minutes. She decided maybe it was time to lighten the mood. "Won't be long until you'll be a dad."

He smiled. "Yeah, I know. Cool. Some day, it'll be you. You'll be a mom."

"Maybe."

"I'm worried about you, Mick. You look tired to me. Exhausted, actually."

"Well, you look like you're having sympathy for your pregnant wife, or are you trying to match her on the weight gain?" she chided.

"Hey!"

"You told me that I looked exhausted. I can't jab you back a little?"

"It's only a few pounds. Maybe five."

"Or ten."

"You're a pain in the ass."

"So are you. You really ready to be a dad?"

"You know what? I am. I can't wait for this kid to be here. We are going to do everything together."

"I bet you will."

"Summer and I may have had a rough start, but things have calmed down a lot, and I know she isn't the perfect wife, or . . . Wait, let me rephrase that: She actually *is* the perfect wife; she just may not always be my perfect fit. She's a bit too perfect. Hell, who am I kidding? I know I should be home with her right now, but she's just so moody, almost angry all the time." Michaela listened and decided not to put in her two cents. "But she loves me, and I do love her. I really do." Michaela wondered who he was trying to convince of that — her or himself. "I know in my gut that we'll make great parents together. And, I can't wait to be a dad."

"I think that's wonderful."

"It is. Hey, while you're here, do you want to take a look at Halliday?"

"Yeah." She followed him through two large steel doors that led into the intensive care area. It was as sterile as any human hospital. Classical music played softly over the speakers.

"Over here is the hydrotherapy pool." They walked into a separate room with a large pool and a sling off to the side with a lift and pulley setup. Ethan said, "Halliday has spent quite a bit of time in this already, and throughout his rehab he'll spend more time. We get him into the sling and pull him into the water, where he is able to move freely, to help keep his muscles from deteriorating. And also to keep his spirits up. Horses want to move, so the hard part for these guys when they break a leg is making sure they don't lose it mentally. It's a shame that he has to go through this. Come on, he's over here."

They walked through another set of double doors. The new area wasn't quite as antiseptic smelling, but there still was that faint scent of alcohol. Michaela took in more of the normal horse-related smells that she was used to — straw, hay, manure, and horse. There were four stalls in the area. Two were occupied, one with Halliday.

"That's Rosa in there. Came in here for colic surgery yesterday. She's doing much better. Here he is."

Halliday looked up from his feeder. He was in a sling, which held his feet slightly off the ground, but he nickered as they said hello to him. "Poor guy," Michaela said.

"No doubt, but see how bright his eyes are? He's going to make it, Mick, I feel it.

And when he does, I'm sure he'll command quite a stud fee."

"Doesn't bode well for the racing industry, does it?"

"What do you mean? Halliday injuring himself?"

"No, what I'm talking about is all that goes into the racehorse and then when he's injured, possibly even a fatal injury, human greed takes over. What do you think of racing in general?"

"You know, people have been racing horses for centuries, and tons of different breeds. Yes, you see some greed out there. You'll see track owners get their dirt padding down to next to nothing hoping to increase speed and get a record time on their track. It happens, and there are a lot of owners who are against those types of practices. Many of them will pull their horses out of those races. Many won't because of the fines that are put into place by doing so, and by the bureaucratic crap that goes along with it. A lot of owners don't want to make waves. They love their animals, but this can be a money-making business and there is a lot of power and control that goes into it. That said, am I against racing horses? Not really. These animals are built to do this. It's what they're bred for.

Now, get Halliday out into a pasture and he'll be a happy retired animal. But, there will still be that thread inside of him that pushes him to want to run, and get him on a track when all of this is said and done, and he'll feel compelled to break out. What I don't like about racing — or any type of event for that matter when it comes to animals — is exploitation of animals of any kind. Racing tends to have gotten that bad rap over the years, because in many cases it fits."

They gave Halliday some attention and then headed to where the cots were set up. Ethan gave her a pair of sweats and a clean T-shirt from his bag. "I know they'll be huge on you, but at least they're clean."

"Thanks."

"Well, I'll let you get some rest."

"Ethan?"

"Yes?"

"Will you stay me with me? I don't want to be alone."

He studied her for a few seconds. "Yeah. I'll stay."

FORTY-TWO

Michaela and Ethan talked into the wee hours and took turns checking on Rocky, who remained stable throughout the night. It felt like old times between them. They talked about horses, his unborn son, a bit more about Summer. Ethan brought up Jude, but Michaela quickly changed the subject. She also let him in on what she'd been up to over the past week concerning Audrey and Francisco's murders and Bob's disappearance.

"Mick, I've got to agree with your detective boyfriend on this one. Don't mess with it," Ethan said.

"First off, I don't have a boyfriend and second, I feel like I'm close to figuring this out. I'm pretty certain that I have all of the pieces. I'm just not sure how they fit together. Like this thing with Kathleen and Halliday. I know how she can cover his expenses now."

"Oh, yeah. How?"

Michaela explained to Ethan about Olivia and the contract she'd signed with Friedman and Callahan, as well as the old insurance policy.

"She sure sounds like a suspect," Ethan said.

"I know. But so does everyone else."

Ethan agreed with that assessment after she'd finished detailing the week's dramas. "Hey, Ethan?"

"Hmmm?" he asked, sounding like sleep was ready to take over.

"Thank you."

He propped himself up onto his elbow. A night-light that he'd turned on so she'd know how to maneuver if she needed to get up in the middle of the night cast shadows across his face. "For what?"

"For taking care of Rocky, and for listening to me. I've missed you."

"I've missed you, too, Mick." He lay back down.

Michaela rolled over onto her side and surprisingly, fell asleep after a few moments. Even though it had been a late night, she woke up before seven the next morning, as the center came to life. Ethan showed her where she could shower.

"I put your clothes in the wash last night,

while you changed into my sweats. By the way, they look good on you, even if they're a size too big."

"A size? Try a few sizes."

He winked at her. "I got up early and put them in the dryer. There they are." He pointed to a desk in the room where they'd slept. He'd even folded them for her.

"Thanks. I think I will take that shower, after I check my horse."

Rocky appeared to be fine. Ethan had changed up his diet, so he was being fed in smaller increments and more than twice a day. He checked all of his levels after each feeding.

After getting dressed, Michaela poured herself a cup of coffee in the break room, and waited around for the rest of Rocky's test results. She checked her messages. Joe called and told her it was important to call him back.

"I got an address for Cara Klein. And she *is* the same woman who was dating Bob Pratt, and she did work for both Strong X and Eq Tech, but she was in their marketing departments."

"I thought that she owned Strong X."

"Don't know about that."

"Where is she?"

"She's in a hospice facility in San Diego.

She has cancer." Michaela did remember Josh telling her that the woman Bob had been seeing was sick. Cancer? He gave her the address. "That is all we can get on her. Other than that, she was clean. That's all I know. But I did learn something else: There is a connection between Strong X and Terrell Jardinière."

"What's that?"

"Terrell was a spokesman for the company. Rumor has it that the supplements he was taking from them were what caused his stroke. Kind of similar to that company that gave Barry Bonds those supplements that supposedly don't have no connection with steroids." Joe snorted.

"Oh my God. I've got to go, Joe. I'll call you later." Michaela went searching for Ethan.

"What is it?" he asked. One look at her face must have told him that something was wrong.

"That file that I gave you from Bob. The one Audrey had . . ."

"Yeah?"

"Have you looked at it yet?"

"No. I meant to, but then Rocky took that turn and —"

"You need to. When I looked at it, it looked to me like a grouping of horses, not

369

just one case. You need to look at which of those horses were on Eq Tech supplements. I think that something in those supplements could be hurting the horses. It's what's making them sick."

"What?"

"Can you break down the chemical components in the supplements?"

"Someone here can."

"Do it. I've got to see someone. I'll be back."

"Mick, where are you going?

"Just trust me. It's in the supplements."

She left to speak with Cara Klein, who she knew would provide the missing link.

FORTY-THREE

Michaela drove to an area called Mission Valley, northeast of downtown San Diego. The hospice sat high up on a hill overlooking the valley and the many freeways that crisscrossed the area.

Entering, Michaela felt a bit nervous not knowing what she would learn, if anything, that might help find Audrey's killer. A nurse greeted her. "May I help you?"

"I'm here to see Cara Klein. I'm Michaela Bancroft." This woman was way friendlier than the nurse at the home that Terrell was in.

She checked a roster. "I'm sorry, but I don't see you on the list of visitors. I can ask if she'd like to see you."

Michaela nodded. "Tell her that it's about Bob Pratt."

The nurse looked at her oddly, but nodded and walked down the hall. She returned a minute later and told Michaela that Cara was in room 219 and would see her. She walked to the room, where she found a tiny woman lying in bed. She couldn't have been over thirty-five; she had no hair, her face was pulled taut, and her hazel eyes seemed glossed over. She smiled weakly at Michaela and said, "Hi."

"Hello." Michaela closed the door and walked over to the bed. "I'm Michaela Bancroft."

"The nurse told me." Cara slurred her words a little, likely from the pain medications. "You know Bob?"

"Yes." Michaela wasn't sure how to start this conversation. It would be awkward, to say the least. "I was a friend of Audrey, Bob's sister. I don't know if you're aware, but Audrey was murdered a week ago and Bob has disappeared. I was hoping you could help me piece some missing links together."

Cara frowned; her eyes widened. "I'm sorry. I don't think . . . I can help you."

Michaela could hear a tremor in the woman's voice, and she wasn't very convincing. "Please." Dammit. She felt that Cara Klein might actually have some answers. Why did the woman sound scared?

"Cara," she continued, "there are horses being hurt, maybe even dying. I think you know why and I think that whatever is going on with these animals might have something to do with Bob's disappearance and Audrey's murder."

"Yes," she whispered.

"So you do know about this?"

Tears came to Cara's eyes. She sighed. "I do."

Michaela sat down and scooted the chair close to Cara's bed in order to better hear her. "Last weekend at the races was where Audrey was killed. We'd gone together to see Olivia Bowen perform and were watching the races from Kathleen Bowen's box."

"I know them."

"You do?"

Cara nodded and started coughing. The horrid barklike cough lasted a while. Cara placed an oxygen mask over her face for a minute. "Sorry," she said, once the coughing was under control.

"You don't need to apologize."

"I know the Bowens and that entire circle."

Michaela wasn't sure what she meant by that. "Entire circle?"

"The racing scene."

"Do you mean Frederick Callahan, Marshall Friedman?" Michaela knew that each of them owned racehorses. They also knew the Bowens.

"I'd say they're . . . part of that group."
She started coughing again. Michaela saw a
bottle of water on the table next to her and
reached across to give it to her.

Cara shook her head and put the oxygen
back on. After another minute and some
deep breaths, she closed her eyes. Michaela's stomach sank. "Cara?"

The woman opened her eyes. Thank God.
"You'll have to . . . bear with me. It might
take some time, but there are some things
I . . . need to tell you."

FORTY-FOUR

Michaela had been right: Cara Klein had answers. At first there were parts to her story that she doubted. But the woman had been very convincing, and the more she thought about it, and allowed the information to settle in, the more she realized that what Cara told her had been the truth. She now knew what had happened to Bob, and had a good idea as to what went down with Audrey. And she was ready to catch a killer, but she would need some help.

She called Joe and told him what she'd learned. They devised a plan on how she'd trap the killer.

"It's good, Michaela . . . but why not just bring in the cops?" Joe asked.

"The woman who gave me this information made me promise not to go to the police."

"Why?"

"She's afraid. She's been burned a few

times and doesn't trust many people."

"She trusted you."

"I'll fill you in when I see you. Now, can I count on you?"

"When have you not been able to count on me?" She laughed. "I'm in," he said.

Michaela spent Friday night at the Woodward Center again, and to everyone's relief Rocky was doing great. Trusting her instincts, the vets had altered his course of treatment and he was perking up nicely. The chemicals in the supplements were still being broken down. The vets had to send them out to a separate group of chemists, who would be able to better determine what compounds made up the product. They wouldn't have results for a couple of days, but Michaela felt that she was right. And now that Rocky looked better, she also felt better. Ethan did not stay the night again as Summer called, full of complaints. Guilt-ridden for leaving her alone for a few days, he went home.

Saturday morning, Michaela gave Rocky a hug. "You'll be coming home in a couple of days, bud. You're going to get better now." She left her horse behind again, only this time certain that he would make a full recovery.

She got to Los Angeles late in the afternoon and found the Eq Tech apartment. She called Joe one more time. "We're on it," he reassured her.

"Good."

She called Hudson Drake to let him know that she'd made it. "Hey, do you still want that date for tonight?"

"You know it. I take it you're on your way now."

"I just pulled into the parking garage, so I'll see you soon. I'm looking forward to it."

He laughed. "We're going to have a great time. Did you get a gown?"

"I have one." She'd stopped at one of the million malls along Interstate 5, quickly deciding on a simple long silk lavender gown, one of the classic types. Nothing fancy in the least, but she figured it would be appropriate.

"I have a surprise waiting for you inside the apartment," he said.

"You do? What is it?"

"I can't tell you, or it wouldn't be a surprise. I'll pick you up at six."

Michaela unlocked the door to the apartment and was stunned by its opulence. She knew walking through the front courtyard with its water fountains and immaculate garden that it would be nice, but this surpassed *nice.* Her nerves were buzzing. A decorator had done the apartment up beautifully. It was about 1,500 square feet of amazing views of Century City from all angles. The living room area was done in metallic colors of gold, bronze, and olive, with the sofa done in a gold-and-bronze damask pattern. Two matching leather chairs faced a fireplace in front of ceiling-high windows. A vase with a dozen red roses stood on the long mahogany dining room table with a card attached that had her name on it. The flowers were beautiful.

She opened the card. It was from Drake, saying that there would be many surprises tonight.

Michaela headed to the bedroom. She walked with trepidation; what she found sitting on the gold sateen bedspread of a four-poster bed was an amazing gown, its color a perfect shade of pink rose, with a long *V* down the back outlined with small beads and sequins. The front was a scoop neck with folds of silk that looked as though they would lie delicately across a woman's chest. Michaela picked it up. It was the right size — a six. On the bed next to the dress was a pair of shoes the same color of the dress with thin straps and high heels. Looked like Hudson Drake was out to romance her.

Michaela showered, and then slipped the

gorgeous gown over her head, smiling as the fabric fell gracefully along the still-youthful curves of her body. After stepping into the heels and adjusting the straps, she arranged her hair into a sleek chignon at the nape of her neck, and applied more makeup than usual, going dramatic on the eyes and trying hard not to mess up. She was looking at herself in the mirror, applying the last touches of her makeup, adding the simple gold earrings she'd brought with her, when the doorbell rang. Her hands shook.

She opened it to see Hudson standing there. "Amazing," he said. "I knew it would be, though."

"Thank you . . . for all of it. You didn't have to buy a dress for me or the shoes, or even the roses. You've been way too kind."

"All for a beautiful woman. I have one more gift."

"Oh no. I couldn't accept anything else."

He smiled as he brought a small bag out from behind his back and handed it to her. "Open it," he said.

She took out a small handbag, silver with pink roses appliquéd onto it. "This is beautiful. It matches perfectly."

"That was the plan. Now, put whatever you need in it and let's get going. The limo is waiting and I have a bottle of champagne chilling."

The event was held at the Beverly Hills Hotel, the utmost in old Hollywood prestige and money. The red carpet was laid out for all attending. Once inside they saw about three hundred guests milling around, drinking champagne and chatting each other up, all in their diamonds and pearls.

Michaela spotted Olivia walk in, Hugh on one side of her and Josh on the other. She looked sober. She approached them as Hudson was busy speaking with some business associates. Hugh smiled at her. "I heard about what you did for my daughter."

Michaela didn't know what to say.

"I told my dad. Josh convinced me that it was a good idea."

"We're here for you." Josh rubbed Olivia's arm. "I want to thank you, too," he told Michaela.

"I'm going to rehab next week," Olivia said.

"That's good to hear. How about your riding?"

"One day at a time," Hugh said. "But I want her to pursue her dreams. Audrey wanted that for her, too."

Michaela nodded. "She did."

"I've arranged for her service to be next

380

Wednesday. It'll be in Indio."

"Thank you. I wish you would've leaned on me for some help," Michaela said.

"I think it would be appropriate for you to speak."

"I'd love to do that. Oh, about my trailer and Geyser: I told Josh that I would have my assistant, Dwayne, take care of it."

"Of course."

"Well, I should probably get back to my date," she said.

Hugh kissed her on the cheek. "Thank you again," he whispered in her ear.

Michaela smiled and started to return to Hudson, when she spotted none less than the spectacle of Bridgette Bowen sauntering up to the bar flanked by Frederick Callahan, who wore a second ornament on his other arm — a striking, tall blonde. Michaela shook her head. *Some people never learn.* She buzzed by the spectacle, saying, "Bridgette, how are you? I heard about your split from Hugh. It's terrible. So sorry."

Bridgette scooted in tighter next to Callahan. "Some moves are strategic. Some just smart. You think I didn't plan my most recent maneuver?"

Callahan rolled his eyes and grinned.

"I think that you plan everything out very carefully," Michaela said. "Nice to see you,

Freddie. How's your heart?"

She left knowing that her slight would make Bridgette's blood boil.

Steve Benz was setting up on the stage. Michaela walked up to him. "Hey Steve, how's it going?"

Benz glared at her. "Great. The psycho-bitch is here."

"Right. Takes one to know one." She smiled, knowing it was a childish remark, but wanting to continue getting under his skin, which she obviously did. He was such an ass. She really hoped that Smith had sold those photos of Benz and Bridgette to a rag magazine.

Oh yes, all the usual suspects were here, including Kathleen Bowen, who sat next to Marshall Friedman, lots of bling around her neck. Hmmm. Michaela sat down next to them. "How was New York? Nice shopping spree?"

"What? I don't know what you're talking about," Kathleen said aghast.

"Really?"

"What kind of question is that? You know this wacko?" Friedman asked Kathleen.

"I'd rather be a wacko than a jackass," she told him and got up from the table.

"Well, I never," she heard Kathleen say as she walked to her own table.

Sitting down, she heard someone behind her say, "Champagne?" She turned around and smiled.

"Don't mind if I do."

Joe smiled and winked at her. "Told you we had your back," he said in a low voice. "This place is crawling with cousins."

As the evening wore on and patrons went through the scrumptious buffet line, Michaela grew nervous. She knew that the time was fast approaching when their plan would go down. Could she really do it? Maybe she should have another glass of champagne. No, she needed to think clearly.

"Are you all right?" Hudson asked. "You've gotten kind of quiet in the last half hour."

"I'm fine. Tired. That's all." She looked around the table. Hugh, Olivia, and Josh sat at their table along with another couple that Michaela didn't know but who apparently owned a slew of racehorses. Mr. and Mrs. Black — older, sophisticated, and obviously quite wealthy.

Michaela turned to Mr. Black. "Do you use Eq Tech supplements on your racehorses?"

"Of course," he said. "It's a great product. I'm thinking of investing some money in the company." He smiled at Hudson.

"I'm looking forward to it," Hudson said. "I think we can grow this company tenfold and really make a difference around the world in the performance of athletic equines."

The waitstaff was walking around, changing out the cutlery in preparations for the filet mignon about to be served.

"Here, here," Mr. Black said, raising his glass to toast.

Everyone around the table raised their glasses in response. Michaela was slow on the uptake. When they finished, Hudson stood. "I better get up to the microphone and get this auction rolling."

Michaela grabbed his arm. "Wait. I'm sorry, but could I say something? Can I make an announcement?"

Hudson sat back down. "What is it?"

"I think I told you that I'm planning to open up a therapeutic riding center for autistic kids."

"Yes."

"Well," she lowered her voice as the others at the table began talking amongst themselves, "there are a lot of wealthy people here who might be interested in contributing to the center for autism. It's a worthy charity. But I don't want to steal your thunder."

"Oh no, not at all. Please, make your announcement." Hudson stood up with Michaela and escorted her to the stage.

Her hands trembled when she took the microphone. "Good evening, ladies and gentlemen. I'm Michaela Bancroft and I'm here to make a very important announcement." She paused. The crowd's eyes were on her, and once again she didn't know if she could go through with this, until she spotted Joe in the corner. "You see, I lost a very dear friend this week to the hands of a killer."

She spotted Hudson, who had been walking back to their table, stop and turn around, a smile still on his face, but looking at her oddly.

"And the killer is here, in this room."

"She's a nut," Marshall Friedman shouted. "Get her off the stage."

"Michaela? What's this about?" Hugh said, standing.

"Trust me, Hugh; you will want to hear what I have to say. I couldn't figure out why anyone would kill my friend Audrey Pratt. She was one of the sweetest people that I've ever known. The tragedy about the way she lost her life is that she probably had no idea why she was being murdered when it happened. She was killed because someone wanted to hide something. Something he thought that she knew about. But she didn't."

"What are you doing, Michaela?" Hudson asked,

"Good question. I've had an interesting conversation with the Blacks this evening about how highly they value Eq Tech supplements." She eyed the Blacks. "I'm sure many of you here use the product and think it's wonderful. But what would you say if I told you that those supplements can kill your horses?"

The room, which had grown silent now, made a collective gasping sound.

"I told you that she was crazy," Friedman said.

"Psycho-bitch!" Benz yelled out.

"Michaela, maybe you need to have a seat." Callahan stood and started walking toward her. She spotted Joe moving.

"I guess I didn't realize that my date was also the entertainment for the evening. She's had too much to drink. Michaela, come down from there," Hudson said.

She pointed at him. "You orchestrated Bob Pratt's disappearance because he knew the chemicals in your supplements could be deadly. He reported his findings to you and told you that if you didn't take the product off the market, he'd reveal what you were doing." Her words came out in rapid fire now.

"This is insane." Hudson moved closer to the stage.

"No. *You're* insane. When you hired Enrique and Juan Perez to kidnap Bob and take him to Mexico to kill him, you had already learned that Bob had sent a file to his sister that you didn't want anyone to see. A file that proved his findings about the supplements. You stalked her at the races and murdered her when the opportunity was there. You murdered her hired hand Francisco, too, when you surprised him at her ranch while searching for the file. The thing is, what you didn't know is that I ultimately wound up with the file."

"Get down from there! This is all bullshit." Hudson's face was turning red.

Joe made his way to the front of the room. He set a tray down on one of the tables.

"She's telling the truth." The crowd turned to see a man hobbling in, his right eye heavily bandaged. He'd been badly beat up.

"Bob!" Bridgette Bowen exclaimed.

"Oh my God," Hugh said.

A murmur floated through the banquet room. With all eyes on Bob Pratt, Michaela and the rest of the crowd failed to see Hudson grab a steak knife from one of the server's trays. Moving quickly, he lunged at her. She felt the knife strike her leg as she stumbled. Joe and the cousins hadn't been able to move fast enough and Michaela found herself being dragged down off the stage by Hudson, the knife to her throat, blood seeping from her leg.

"You blew it," Hudson said into her ear. "You're coming with me."

She watched Joe and a half dozen other men approaching them.

"Get the fuck back!" Hudson yelled. "I will kill her. I will! Let us walk out of here and she might have a chance to live. Anyone else comes any closer and she dies. Her blood will be on all of your hands."

The men froze as Hudson, his arm still around her neck, backed out of the banquet room. Blood rushed through Michaela's insides, turning them ice cold as she realized these were likely her last moments alive.

Forty-Five

Hudson dragged Michaela up onto the hotel roof. The knife had sliced through her skin on her throat, and she noticed a trickle of blood falling onto her bare arm. He'd manhandled her up the stairs and she'd torn the dress. When she'd spoken with him earlier, then seen the dress and all of the gifts he'd left for her in the apartment, it had taken everything she had to muster up the courage to play out the role of his happy date. The last thing she wanted to do was alert him that she knew Bob Pratt was alive, and that the truth about everything was about to come out.

"I'm telling you, if you want something done right, you have to do it yourself," he hissed. "Those morons, Juan and Enrique, if they'd done the job right, Bob would be dead, and you and I would be on our way to my bedroom."

"I would *never* go to bed with you!" Michaela spat.

He tightened his grip. "You would have. I saw it in your eyes the day that we met. You wanted me. And we could've had a great time together. What a waste. I can't believe Pratt is alive."

It had been Bob who'd made the call to her the other day claiming to be Terrell Jardinière, too afraid to alert anyone other than Cara that he was alive. But he'd heard through Audrey that it had been Michaela who was ultimately responsible for discovering who had murdered her uncle Lou the previous year, and he'd hoped that she would do the same thing for Audrey. And she had.

"You've been doing this for years. Didn't you think that you would eventually get caught? You're a chemist. You know that these supplements that you've been producing, first with Strong X and now Eq Tech, can hurt the user. Why not make a product that doesn't?" She hoped to bide time. Keep him talking and maybe someone would save her. She prayed that a SWAT team was surrounding the area now. She had no other idea how she was going to get out of this alive. Even though it was chilly outside on the roof, she felt perspiration trickling down her back. How could she get this maniac to let her go? He had an ego. Keep him talking. That was all she could think to do until a better plan hopefully worked its way inside her head.

"Are you kidding? My products have proven successful. They make people and horses stronger, faster, and sharper minded. It's proven."

"It's also proven that they do harm. Look at Terrell Jardinière."

"Some people had reactions," he growled.

"He is completely incapacitated."

"It can't be proven that Strong X caused it."

"What about the horses? That *can* be proven."

"You should have minded your own business."

"You shouldn't have murdered my friend. And I know you not only killed Audrey, but Francisco, too. How did you do it anyway? How did you lure Audrey onto the back forty and kill her?"

"I saw it as opportunity. I'd tapped Bob's phone, knew he'd had dinner with her and that he planned to tell her something. I was afraid he told her what he'd found out. So, when I spotted her heading to the track, I called her over. Told her that they wouldn't let her out onto the track. That I'd tried.

Then I told her that Bob was missing. I suggested we take a walk and discuss the options. At that point I didn't realize she was clueless, but I couldn't take the chance."

"You killed an innocent woman! You're really sick, Hudson. What about Francisco? Why did you kill him?"

"I didn't. That was something Juan Perez took care of for me. I sent him out to Audrey's ranch to locate that file and lo and behold he ran into Francisco. Casualty of circumstance, so to speak."

Michaela felt her throat tighten. "Why do you want all this blood on your hands? Don't you care at all? Is money and power all that you want? I also know all about Cara's husband, Shawn Klein."

"Oh please. Cara Klein is an idiot and Shawn was a loser. If you ask me, I did her a favor." He grabbed her arm tightly and dragged her to the side of the building. She looked down. It was a long way. Lights from the hotel gardens reflected off the hotel pool. She doubted she could survive a fall.

Michaela flashed back to her conversation with Cara as Hudson pulled her closer to the edge. "Hudson Drake killed my husband, Shawn," Cara told her. "Supposedly Shawn died in a boating accident, but I know that it was Hudson who killed him.

My husband was a sailor. He'd been on the seas since he was a kid. It was a clear day, and all he was doing was sailing out to the end of Point Loma, which isn't far."

"Why did he do it?" Michaela had asked her.

"We were both working for Strong X. I was in the marketing department and Shawn was the head chemist. Drake asked Shawn to add a drug called diazepethicone to the recipe, saying that some of the athletes they'd been in discussions with had heard of the drug and how it made athletes in Russia stronger, more vital. The problem is, it's a steroid derivative and as you know, steroid use in most sports is completely banned. Hudson's request of Shawn was to find a way to hide the drug within the supplement so that when athletes were tested it would not show up."

"Did your husband do it, put that drug into the Strong X supplements?"

"He did, and he paid the ultimate price for it. Shawn had a bad feeling that what the supplement was comprised of could cause serious damage to athletes, to people in general, but he did what he did because we needed the money and were desperate at the time. I know that sounds horrible, and I won't bore you with the details, but

393

we went through with it. Shawn tucked his ethics way down and became one of Drake's henchmen. Then, Terrell collapsed, and so did a track runner. A kid really, only nineteen, up and coming. His family didn't pursue anything because they didn't put it all together. But Terrell Jardinière's aunt had her suspicions and she started asking questions. Drake agreed to pay her a lot of money to keep her quiet, as well as pay for his medical expenses.

"When Terrell had the stroke, Shawn became scared. He had a bad feeling that eventually it would all blow up in their faces and he'd be the fall guy because he was the head chemist. He decided to deal with it before that happened. He began taking files and copying them, keeping them in a safe-deposit box. He wanted to collect all the evidence he could before he went to the authorities."

"Were you aware of this?"

"No. Not until after he was killed. He made me a video. On it he told me everything that he suspected and what he'd been up to. He also told me where the safe-deposit key was and how to get into it. When I went to the bank, the box was empty. I don't know if he emptied it before he died for some reason, or if they did.

Maybe Drake and his crew learned about it and found the key. My guess is someone got on that boat that day with my husband and tortured him or threatened him until he told them where he was keeping the files he'd copied. Shawn was afraid that our phones were tapped and that they were watching him."

"You continued working for them, though, for Hudson Drake."

"I felt I had to. I was too scared that if I stopped working for him that he would become more suspicious of me and kill me. I thought that maybe I could continue putting a case against him together. That was my hope."

"What happened?"

"After Shawn, they started to phase out Strong X and that part of their human line. They began to go into the equine division claiming they wanted to diversify, and after doing a lot of research they also said the equine market could produce millions of dollars, which it's doing. I also think that they figured they were taking less of a risk by dealing with equine athletes like race-horses."

"How did you meet Bob?"

"Once Drake started to phase out Strong X and change direction, Bob was brought on as the research vet. I met him and thought he was a nice man. We had lunches together. He confided in me about his alcoholism. I got sick last year and was diagnosed with stage IV cancer. I only worked another two months before I had to leave."

Cara continued. "Bob came to me, actually. He said that he didn't like the way some of the test results were turning out with some of the horses he'd been giving the supplements to and that it bothered him. He said that when he went to Drake, he was told that the studies looked great, and for him not to be troubled and just keep doing his work. Bob got scared. He said that Drake used a threatening tone with him when they discussed this. That was only a few weeks ago, before I entered hospice care. I became really worried about Bob. We were still seeing each other on occasion. I even went up to Los Angeles a couple of times in the last few months. He knew that I was concerned and I told him what I thought they'd done to Shawn. He then told me that he was also trying to collect evidence against Eq Tech. I begged him to stop, but I don't think he did. That was the last time I heard from him. Until now. Just yesterday."

Michaela had left the hospital knowing that she had some work ahead of her to get Hudson to confess. She thought that if she accused him in front of a roomful of guests and presented the evidence she'd discovered, he'd crack. Oh, he'd cracked all right. Being taken hostage had not been part of the plan.

"Why don't you just let me go?" Michaela pleaded. "You can get away and no one will find you. I'm sure you've got money in offshore accounts. Do you really want another murder on your hands?"

"I've got plenty of money . . . and as far as killing you? It won't bother me a bit, sweetheart." Still standing behind her, knife at her throat, he kissed her on the cheek. "You've got your choice though: I can either push you off or slice your throat."

"Great options."

"You should have minded your own business."

Michaela knew she didn't have much more than a few seconds. As her brain scrambled for a way out, she heard a loud bang. Hudson's arm fell from her neck and he grabbed at his leg, the knife falling to the ground. "Fuck!" he screamed. Realizing that he'd let her go, he lunged for her, his leg seeping blood.

Michaela, stunned, didn't think, just re-acted, picking up the knife. "Get away, Hudson! Stay away from me!"

He kept stumbling forward. "You're not going to kill me."

Tears stung her eyes. "Get away! I *will* kill you!"

"No you won't —"

Another shot rang out as he again lunged for her. An anguished scream rose from Hudson as he fell against Michaela, the knife piercing his stomach. He stumbled backward, trying to pull the knife out. He stared at her, shocked. Then his body swayed as he took one too many steps backward and, leaning to the side, his body fell off the roof. She backed away and felt arms wrap tightly around her. She turned and cried on Joe's chest.

"I'm sorry, Mick. Sorry we couldn't get to you in time."

"It's okay. I'm okay," she sobbed. "Did you shoot him?"

"No." Dennis Smith, dressed in a tuxedo, came forward.

"Smith? You were here?" She pulled away from Joe to see a smiling Smith standing there, gun in hand.

"Yep. Had to keep tabs on Benz and the rest of the shysters. Made myself a nice deal with one of the tabloids. Looks like I'll get my Tahitian vacation after all. And this tops it off."

She couldn't help but smile. Although her leg hurt, she was thankful Smith had been there. "You saved my life. I can't believe that I didn't spot you in there."

He shrugged. "I'm a private investigator. You weren't supposed to see me."

She thanked him and Joe, happy to be alive.

FORTY-SIX

Sunday, the day after Hudson Drake's death, Michaela was back at home with her animals. Ethan had called and found a link between the chemicals and the damage it was causing to the horses; along with Bob they reported their findings to the *Los Angeles Times.* The story would be a huge one by the following day.

Bob was back at home with Cara; he wanted to care for her during her last days. He'd explained how he'd reached Cara the day before Michaela came to see her, but he'd asked her not to tell anyone that he was still alive, afraid that Drake would find out and finish him off before he could discover a way to put him behind bars. Cara had contacted him after Michaela left, and told him about her visit. They had then contacted Michaela, who with Joe and Bob's help devised what they thought was a foolproof plan to catch Hudson Drake.

What they had not expected was the actual turn of events. However, it had all paid off in the end, as Hudson Drake suffered his own horrible death, thanks to Dennis Smith — a memory Michaela would not soon forget.

After the chaos that had taken place at the hotel, Bob further explained about his connection with Bridgette Bowen — indeed, she had a secret to keep and did not want Bob to expose her. When they were at Betty Ford together, Bridgette had come to Bob's room and tried to seduce him, but he'd wanted no part of it, and she hadn't forgotten the incident. Michaela was sure that Bridgette would recover just fine from her divorce and bounce right back, be it with Callahan or some other rich old geezer.

When the Perez brothers learned what had happened to Drake, they'd made a run for the border, only to be caught by the police and placed in jail.

Olivia was apparently on her way to rehab, and Hugh was shocked and dismayed but relieved that the lies had been exposed.

Kathleen and Marshall Friedman were indeed an item. She would get her half of Audrey's insurance policy. Michaela hoped she would use the money wisely, but doubted it.

Hugh had done his best to put the fear of God into Friedman and Callahan to let his daughter out of the contracts with them. Callahan graciously agreed and Friedman threatened suit, but Hugh was confident he'd back down. He wanted his daughter to pursue her dream of becoming a jockey.

Joe was back with his wife and kids preparing for a Sunday feast and had invited Michaela to join them, but she asked for a rain check, needing a day of rest. She did, however, call the woman from the autism center at home and told her that she would take the job. Dwayne was on his way to get her trailer back and bring Geyser home. She planned to head down to the Humane Society first thing Monday morning and claim Audrey's animals.

And with her brother now home, Audrey could truly rest in peace. Although Michaela was still saddened by her tragic death, she knew that Audrey had not died in vain. No more people — or animals — would suffer at the hands of Hudson Drake ever again, and she knew that Audrey would be proud of that.

As for Camden, Michaela located her in the kitchen preparing dinner. When Camden spotted her, she gave her a hug. "You are one crazy bitch, you know that?"

That morning, Joe had come over and they replayed everything for Camden and Dwayne. "I know."

"You have got to stop tracking down killers. It's not healthy for you."

Michaela laughed. "I guess not."

"Jude has been calling here all day. All week in fact. He knows about what happened and he's worried. The guy really cares about you. You need to call him."

Michaela nodded. She supposed that she would have to do that, but not now.

The doorbell rang and Michaela looked at Camden. "I have no clue," her friend said.

Michaela opened the door; Ethan stood on the other side. "Hey, what's up?"

He beamed. "I was on my way here to tell you some great news, but I have to rush, because I just got more great news."

"What's going on?"

"Real quick. First of all, Halliday looks to be out of the woods. It'll be some time yet before you can bring him home."

"What do you mean, before I can bring him home?"

"He's yours. Kathleen Bowen called the center and said that she was giving the horse to you. That you should have him. Gratis. She said that she felt she had a lot to make amends for. I didn't ask."

"No kidding? What about his expenses?"

"No kidding. Yeah that part, well she did say that she'd cover half, if you would pay the other half."

Michaela laughed. "Of course she did. I'll take the horse." Maybe Kathleen would make wiser decisions when it came to money after all.

"And guess what else?" Ethan said.

"What?"

"I just got a call from Summer. She's been out shopping and she started contractions. Our baby is going to be born today!" he practically yelped. "I'm on my way to the hospital."

"That's great, Ethan. Really great."

"I can't wait."

"Well, what are you doing waiting around here then? You better get going."

"Right." He gave her a quick hug. "I'll call you later."

"You better," she yelled after him.

Camden came up beside Michaela and put an arm around her as she watched Ethan drive away, tears in her eyes. "Let him go, honey. Let him go. It's time." Michaela nodded.

The phone rang. "Will you get that?" she said.

A few seconds later, as Michaela still stood

in the doorway; dust from Ethan's truck settling back down onto the ground, Camden reappeared and handed the phone to her. "For you."

She brought it up to her ear. "Please don't hang up." It was Jude. "Look, I'm not calling to lecture or anything like that. I'm calling to apologize. I know what Garcia told you. After your message canceling our date, I started investigating. I knew Garcia was up to no good. She's tried to get me to go out with her since she started here, even accused me of sexual harassment when I told her no thank you. She found another way to get at me, though: through you. That's it. That's all. I swear."

Michaela didn't respond.

"Michaela?"

"Yes."

"You have to believe me."

She sighed and leaned against the doorway. "You know what, I do believe you."

"Good, so can we have dinner together?"

She paused. "Yes." She remembered what Joe had told her about living half-assed and decided that he was right.

"Yes? Thank you. I am sorry . . ." Michaela heard him talking to someone else. "She said yes." Michaela heard Katie whoop in the background. "Sorry, but my daughter has missed you, too."

Michaela couldn't help but smile as she heard the joy in Jude's voice, recalled his kiss, and listened to Katie's laughter. Her bittersweet tears dried on her face.

The employees of Thorndike Press hope you have enjoyed this Large Print book. All our Thorndike and Wheeler Large Print titles are designed for easy reading, and all our books are made to last. Other Thorndike Press Large Print books are available at your library, through selected bookstores, or directly from us.

For information about titles, please call:
  (800) 223-1244

or visit our Web site at:
  www.gale.com/thorndike
  www.gale.com/wheeler

To share your comments, please write:
  Publisher
  Thorndike Press
  295 Kennedy Memorial Drive
  Waterville, ME 04901